WRECKED for YOU

An Exposed Hearts Novel

KRISTIN MAYER

Wrecked for You
An Exposed Hearts Novel
Copyright © 2018 by K. Mayer Enterprises, Inc.
Published by K. Mayer Enterprises, INC.
Cover Design: Sommer Stein with Perfect Pear Creations
Interior Designer: JT Formatting
Editor: Jen Matera at Write Divas

All rights reserved. Without limiting the rights under copyright reserved above, no part of this publication may be reproduced, stored in or introduced into a retrieval system, or transmitted, in any form, or by any means (electronic, mechanical, photocopying, recording, or otherwise) without the prior written permission of the above copyright owner of this book.

This is a work of fiction. Names, characters, places, brands, media, and incidents are either the product of the author's imagination or are used fictitiously. The author acknowledges the trademarked status and trademark owners of various products referenced in this work of fiction, which have been used without permission. The publication/use of these trademarks is not authorized, associated with, or sponsored by the trademark owners.

Wrecked for You (An Exposed Hearts Novel) / Kristin Mayer – 1st ed.
Library of Congress Cataloging-in-Publication Data
ISBN-13: 978-1-942910-32-9

:
VISIT MY WEBSITE AT
http://www.authorkristinmayer.com

Kelly Elliott,
because she is simply amazing and the bestest friend EVER!
I'm also pretty sure she came up with this kick-ass title.

Note to the Reader

Wrecked for You is written as a stand-alone. However, for the full reading experience I would suggest starting with Drake and Alexa's story in *Intoxicated by You.*

CHAPTER One

Hayden

The lightning startled me as I sat in the car, watching the house glow white from the light. It was a large house in a pretty upscale neighborhood, and for the tenth time, I questioned my presence there.

Should I be here?

For what seemed like forever, I looked at the house, wondering if I'd made the right choice. Another streak of light raced across the sky. *Is she home?* For the last twenty minutes, I'd wrestled with the idea of cranking the car around and heading back home. I reached for the key but froze when the light in the front of the house flipped on. A shadow moved in front of the window.

My heart beat faster, and I gripped the door handle before reminding myself to stay in the car.

Kory.

I knew it was her. Every molecule in my body came to attention as I watched the shadow move across the window.

Should I be here?

It was a tough question. But as I watched her stop in front of the window, I knew the answer.

Yes, I should.

There was no way I could walk away knowing she was so close. I wanted what my brother had—pure fucking happiness. And Kory was the only woman who'd ever had me wanting more.

Last night, while having dinner with our family, my brother Drake had announced his engagement to his girlfriend, Alexa. And for some reason, the advice he had given me about not waiting until it was too late clicked. If I never tried to figure out what had happened with Kory, I would spend the rest of my life regretting it.

Drake's world began and ended with Alexa. I envied that with every ounce of my being.

I want what he has.

The blonde beauty I'd met this summer in Ketchikan had been on my mind nearly every second of every day since she ended things between us.

I shook my head, trying to figure out what I should do. I knew what I *wanted* to do, but I also feared being rejected. I'd never put myself out there like this before. *What if she doesn't want to give us a try?* I had no answer for this.

Stalling, I pulled out my phone and texted my brother. He was the only person I'd told about my plans to come to Washington.

Me: *I'm here.*

Drake: *What did she say?*

Me: *I'm still in the car.*

Drake: *Dude, stop stalling. It's worth the risk, Hayden. I know I sound like a sap, but when you find the person you think could be the one, don't let her go.*

Me: *Thanks.*

Drake's words helped. Either way, I would know where we stood. *Five minutes.* I just needed five minutes, and then I would force myself to get out of the car. First, I had to get my thoughts straightened out before I rang the doorbell. My palms were sweating, so I rubbed them against my jeans. I had never done anything like this before in my life.

But everything changed the last time we made love—something… happened. We'd connected in a way I never thought possible. The intensity had been off the charts.

And it had scared me shitless.

It must have scared her, too. After that night, when I'd flown home to Skagway, communication between us had been minimal at best.

Falling for each other had never been part of the plan. When we started seeing each other, it had been clear from both sides it was just for fun—no strings, no attachments. But that hadn't happened. At all. No, the exact opposite had happened, and I started to care.

And then she'd left.

Her only message? A three-word text.

Heading home. Good-bye.

I hadn't seen the text from Kory for nearly a full day. I'd been in the woods with my other brother, Kane, and there had been exactly zero cell phone service. When I'd tried to call back, the number had been disconnected. A little lost and a lot confused, I'd sat on my ass for nearly three weeks, deciding what to do.

I huffed out a breath that fogged up the lower part of the driver's side window.

Getting her forwarding address from the little restaurant where Kory had worked in Ketchikan had been a miracle. If it hadn't been for the fact that Maggie, the owner, knew me, I wouldn't have known where to find her. But Maggie had taken pity on me, leaving the room to "help a customer" with Kory's forwarding address on top of her desk.

I blew out another long breath, which fogged up the window all over again. The rain was coming down harder. There were no other lights on or shadows appearing in the window. It looked like Kory was home alone.

Hell, I hoped she was.

If another man answered the door, I wasn't sure what I'd do. At times, I'd sensed something weighed heavily on Kory's mind, but then she'd smile and return to her normal, happy self. The last time we'd been together, I felt like we'd seen the depths of each other's souls. Hell, I sounded like a pussy. If Kane knew, he'd give me hell about it like he had Drake.

One minute to go.

If Kory had another man in her life, would I have sensed it? I'd like to think I would have. But I hadn't. So why had she left?

A sense of calmness came over me. In my gut, I knew I had to see her tonight. I couldn't explain it. I'd flown my twin-engine plane here after dinner. It was the only plane out of the three I owned that could fly the distance from Alaska to Washington. Due to the weather, I almost had to cancel the trip. But the storm had held off just long enough to get the all clear to take off.

Is she okay?
What happened?
What made her leave so abruptly?

Originally, Kory hadn't planned to leave Alaska until today. Instead, she'd left nearly a month early. All I had were questions with no answers.

My head hurt as I tried to piece it all together. I wasn't used to these feelings, and quite frankly, they bothered me. The desire to actually *want* a relationship felt foreign. But the thought of never seeing her again was more terrifying.

Now I understood how Drake felt when Alexa abruptly broke up with him two years ago. *Two years.* I wasn't sure how he'd kept it together. After a month, I was a mess.

Another streak of lightning flashed across the sky. The storm was getting worse. There was no way I'd be able to fly home tonight. Air traffic control would never clear us with the stalled front coming in.

Now or never.

I opened the car door and walked up the pathway that led straight to the front door. The heavy rain quickly soaked through my jeans. I'd found a raincoat on the plane, but it did little to keep me dry. The wind was whipping the water around every which way. Once I got to the door, the covered porch helped shelter me some.

I took a deep breath and then knocked three times.

Stay calm. Whatever happens, at least you'll know.

The door opened, and warm light spilled out into the darkness. *My word, she's beautiful.* There she stood in her jeans and light pink T-shirt with her blonde hair pulled up into a bun on the top of her head. It was hard not to pull her to me and kiss the life out of her.

Her startled eyes met mine. She'd been crying. Seeing her red, blotchy eyes and tear-streaked cheeks slayed me. My fists clenched, and I reminded myself not to rush this. Kory's lip quivered. Only a couple of feet separated us, but they felt like the width of a canyon.

I began to speak, but she beat me to it, her voice sounding sadder than I remembered. "Hayden, what are you doing here?"

Shit. Thunder roared through the skies and my heart plummeted. That wasn't the reaction I was hoping for.

Unsure how to respond, I blurted out the first thing that came to mind. "Why did you leave?"

There were a million other things I wanted to ask, like why she was upset, but her question threw me. If things were over, I wasn't going to put myself out there even more.

She looked around outside before pulling me in the house. I stumbled at the sudden movement but caught myself. The door slammed shut, and in the next moment, Kory threw her arms around me, holding me as if her life depended on it. Without another thought, I wound my arms around her, inhaling her sweet vanilla scent. This was the greeting I had hoped for.

This felt right. So fucking right.

Kory let out a sniffle before saying, "You came for me. You actually came. When I needed you the most, you came."

I held her tighter. "I'm sorry it took so long. The way things happened with us and how you left did a number on my head."

She pulled back, and fresh tears filled her eyes. "You have to go back to Alaska and forget you ever met me. You can't be here."

What. The. Fuck.

My hands dropped, and she took a few steps back, shaking her head. "You have to go. You can't be here. They'll be here any minute. I can't involve you like this. It isn't fair to you."

They?

The entire situation didn't sit right with me. Something else was going on. Kory was normally a self-confident woman—unless she had been pretending the entire time. I swallowed hard and asked about the only thing I could think of that might keep us apart. "Are you married?"

Her mouth dropped open in shock. "No. No. Of course not. I would never cheat. It's not that at all. It's… complicated." Taking another step back, she wrapped her arms around herself. "Forget you ever met me. Forget what we were. Please. I don't want you caught up in this mess."

What the fuck is going on? There was one thing for certain. Forgetting Kory Reynolds wasn't going to happen.

CHAPTER Two

Hayden

"Kory, what's going on?"

She repeated on a sob, "You have to leave. You have to go. This isn't part of the plan. You aren't part of the plan."

Without thinking, I went to her and pulled her close. Clutching my wet shirt, she dug her nails to my chest, and I started to panic. This wasn't like Kory at all. "Did someone hurt you?"

She shook her head.

Ding. Dong.

The melodic chiming of the doorbell startled us. Kory took a step back, whispering as she pulled me further into the foyer, "Hayden, you have to hide. Please. They can't know about you. It'll complicate everything."

The look I'd thought was panic before was nothing compared to this. "What's going on, Kory?" If someone thought they were going to hurt her, they had another think coming.

"I'll tell you everything. Just please don't come out of this closet until I open the door. Please. I'm begging you. If you do, I won't be able to tell you anything."

I didn't respond.

"Hayden, if you ever cared for me, *please* trust me. I'm begging you."

The doorbell chimed again. I cupped her face, making sure I could see into her deep blue eyes. "After this we're talking. No bullshit."

"Promise."

She opened the door to the coat closet and pushed me in before slamming it shut again.

I heard rustling, then the door opened, and a blanket was thrown at me. A wet blanket. *What the fuck?* I dropped it on the ground.

The doorbell rang again. Before the chimes were finished, I heard the door open.

"Mother. Father. What are you doing here?" Kory sounded slightly out of breath.

"Did you not get my email? I said your father and I would come by to welcome you home at eight o'clock. Why are your eyes puffy?"

"I was upstairs watching *Steel Magnolias*."

Today? She'd been home longer than today. And I knew she hadn't been upstairs watching a movie because I'd been watching the house for damn well over thirty minutes.

I strained against the door to hear the conversation, but they walked away. *She's hiding me from her parents?* I reached for the doorknob but stopped myself. She'd trusted me to give her the chance to explain. I had to give her that chance.

And if I walked out there, she'd never tell me what was going on. Remaining stock-still, I tried to slow my breathing and keep the irritation at bay.

I hated games.

Which was why I refused to get seriously involved with anyone before.

And now I felt like some sort of pawn.

Give her time to explain.

When she first grabbed me, I'd felt how much she missed me. But then she hid me in a closet. It was confusing as fuck.

Back in Alaska, when we would meet up in Ketchikan, we'd agreed to not share too many personal details—her idea, not mine. And as time passed, I shared more about my family. Kory only mentioned her parents casually, but never gave me much detail.

Footsteps came closer. I quieted my breathing. "Kory, do you have the itinerary?" The feminine voice was clipped.

"Yes, Mother." Kory sounded robotic.

Her mother sighed. "I hope this isn't how you greet Landon tomorrow."

Silence.

Who the hell is Landon? I ground my teeth and reached for the doorknob again. *Another man.* A slow fury began to burn within me. I almost twisted the knob, but I stopped when her mother spoke again. "Don't forget to study the binder. Your clothes are color coded for the different events. There are pictures with the matching accessory pieces you will wear. Are there any questions?"

"No, Mother. I reviewed it earlier."

There was another long pause before her mother said, "Kory, we're doing this for the survival of our family and our future. Your father and I love you dearly. Now get with the program. I spoke to Landon last night. He's ready to move forward and excited to marry you."

Marry? Did she lie to me? If she had, I was leaving and never looking back. Hiding in this closet, I was quickly running out of patience.

"Bye, sweetheart. We're so glad you're back in town. I'll see you tomorrow at the bistro. All the details are in the folder. Kiss. Kiss. We love you."

"Bye, Mother. Father."

Thank fuck, I thought as the front door opened.

"We love you dearly. But please stop watching movies that make you cry. And use the firming moisturizer. We do not need you looking miserable for your first meeting in preparation for your engagement. Your father and I are counting on you."

"Yes, Mother. Good-bye, Father."

"Good-bye, Kory. I'm glad you're home," her father said. His words lacked any sort of emotion.

Preparation for your engagement?

The door shut, and I stood stiffly in the closet, waiting for her to open the door. My muscles were tense, and my head swam with possibilities.

Kory had about two seconds to explain if she did, in fact, have someone else in her life. I heard Kory sigh, and the sound of her footsteps grew louder. The door opened, and I blinked against the light.

Without waiting for Kory to say anything, I stepped out into the foyer. "Who the *hell* is Landon? I need to know what the fuck is going on."

"Come sit down and I'll tell you everything."

CHAPTER Three

Kory

He's here.
In my house.

Throughout this nightmare, I'd convinced myself that my feelings for Hayden couldn't be real, they had been a figment of my imagination. And when I'd needed him the most, he'd come.

I'd been changed by my time in Ketchikan. This was what I'd needed to make the decision that had plagued me since returning home. I could not follow my parents' plan for my future. I wouldn't.

"Let me get you a towel to dry off."

"Thanks."

I ducked into the hall bathroom to grab a white towel. Everything in the house was a shade of white. I hated it. I wanted some color, but it wasn't my decision to make. My parents owned the house. And in my world, that eliminated any decision-making power I might have had.

I handed the towel to Hayden and pulled my cardigan tighter around me. Right before I'd answered the door, I'd put it on to cover my shirt, which had gotten wet when I hugged Hayden earlier.

If my parents had seen the wet spot, they would have had questions I couldn't answer. Thank goodness I'd thought to wipe up the floors with the blanket.

Their finding out about Hayden would end any time I might have left with him. But I knew I had to take control of my life. I just had to summon up the courage to do so. Having Hayden near me fueled that courage I had been too scared to take a hold of.

Hayden ran the towel over his hair a few times. As we made it to the informal sitting room, his shoes squeaked on the white marble floors. The room had no windows, so in case my parents were still watching the house, they wouldn't see the lights on. I paused, worried. "Where did you park?"

"Across the street."

Maribelle and Sam, my neighbors, had people over all the time. It wouldn't raise any suspicions if there was a car parked in front of their house. I tried to calm down. Being high-strung while trying to explain this to Hayden wouldn't help.

I was an emotional mess and bone-tired. Since I'd been home, I'd barely slept. And to top it off, tonight had been a close call with my parents. At least I think they bought the movie story. I always cried buckets when Shelby died in *Steel Magnolias*. The movie defined true and unconditional love on so many levels. It was why I never tired of watching it. That was the type of life I wanted.

I kept staring at Hayden. I couldn't believe he was here. It was like a dream come true. In my wildest dreams, I imagined him swooping in and saving me from this nightmare. I sat on the cream sofa and looked to where Hayden stood in the doorway. My heart beat faster at the sight of him. His blond hair was a little longer, and he had more than a five-o'clock shadow, but he looked amazing to me.

He still affected me in more ways than I could remember. These last few weeks without him had been the worst kind of torment. And after what I had to tell him, I might never see him again. I took a few extra seconds so his image was ingrained in my mind.

His hands flexed impatiently.

I remembered the feeling of being in his arms. For the first time in my life, I'd felt safe. Then tonight, when I saw him on my doorstep, I'd had that same feeling. He'd come to save me from my life. But I feared if I let him stay, it would only hurt him.

Our eyes never left each other's as we tried to read each other's thoughts. I held up my finger to let him know I needed a moment. This was harder than I'd imagined. Hayden gave a stiff nod. He was pissed. And I was terrified he'd leave before I had a chance to explain everything.

Throughout the summer, I'd tried to keep it casual, but I fell for Hayden. Hard. The last night we were together, I'd told him I loved him as I was falling asleep. I pretended to stay asleep and heard him whisper the words, *I love you, too.* It scared me so much. It was the most honest moment in my life. That had been how I dreamed of falling in love as a little girl.

The summer wasn't supposed to entail love. No, it was supposed to have been a good-bye to my freedom. Since I left Ketchikan, I felt like part of me had died. Fate had somehow stepped in to remind me that this was my life. I'd come home and hidden away from the world. How my parents hadn't known I was home was beyond me. But when they'd called, I'd pretended to still be in Alaska. It worked.

Hayden remained rigid as he waited for me to begin. This was such a clusterfuck. The truth of the situation was almost unbelievable. I took a deep breath. "I'm not married or engaged. I want you to know that."

"Then what did I just hear?" His face had grown more remote, his tone colder, and I hated it. Never, in the short time we'd known each other, had he looked at me like this.

I couldn't bear to meet his eyes, so I glanced down at my fingers, hoping the words to explain this hell I called my life would come. "What you heard was my parents reminding me of my perfectly planned-out life. There's an itinerary detailed down to the minute, in some cases, of what I should do and how I should act."

There had been times when I'd been able to convince my parents to make a specific choice by planting seeds—such as going to college and moving out of their house. All the small freedoms I enjoyed came about by careful calculation.

"Come again?"

At least this time he took a few steps into the room and sat in the chair to the right of me. *How do I explain this?* Even to my own ears, it sounded fictitious. "Let me get something. It'll help explain what I'm talking about. I'll be back."

I went to the front formal living room, where I had been before Hayden arrived, and retrieved the white notebook that detailed what my life would be like for the next eighteen months—a total nightmare.

The book felt like it weighed a hundred pounds, and I returned to the more informal sitting room with it. Hayden needed to know everything. I should have told him in Alaska. Leaving the way I did shattered so much between us. Things between us might be beyond repair, which terrified me. If only he could give me a little time to get out of this mess.

I had to make certain that Hayden knew there was no one else. I couldn't allow the memories of us together to be tainted like that. If he never wanted anything else to do with me after this, that was his decision, but I never wanted him to think I'd cheated on him.

When I entered the room, I handed him the notebook. Where our fingers touched, I felt the familiar zap of energy. I knew Hayden felt it, too, because he pulled his fingers back and his eyes met mine. Those gorgeous blue eyes were like a stormy sea.

By the grim set of his jaw, I knew he was still aggravated. "Look at this, and I'll answer your questions."

I waited while he opened the notebook and scanned the first page. His eyes shot to mine. "Who the hell is Landon?"

The cover page had our names on it. I sat back on the couch and tried to keep from crying. "My soon-to-be fiancé, whom I've never dated."

His grip on the notebook tightened, and his knuckles turned white. "I'm trying really hard not to blow a gasket, but this makes no fucking sense. No fucking sense at all."

"Keep reading. You need to see it all for my explanation to make sense."

Hayden's eyes scanned the page, then he flipped to the next. He kept doing this for a few minutes. I knew what the pages said. Tomorrow I was to meet my parents at a local bistro. During that time, we would "accidentally" run into Landon and his family.

He turned to the next page, which would be the day Landon and I would meet for brunch to catch up after the previous day. To show our budding relationship after not seeing each other for quite some time. Due to the size and wealth of our parents' companies, we had to show our relationship progressing naturally. Photographers would be stationed outside the restaurant to capture our first date.

My clothes, shoes, and accessories were laid out each day. Topics of discussions were scripted. It was indicated just how many times I should laugh. I was certain Landon had a similar script.

Hayden turned another page. At least the vein in his neck wasn't protruding quite so much, but his eyebrows scrunched more. More pages flipped. His face shut down as he skimmed, becoming colder with each page. After a few minutes, Hayden looked up. "This is quite the detailed... log, I guess, of how you and Landon are supposed to interact. You're going to receive a proposal in five months?"

"Yes. And I'll be married in fifteen months. All the wedding details are at the end of the binder. My life for the first three months of our marriage is also in there." The thought alone made me nauseous. Landon was a nice guy, but I wasn't in love with him. I suspected he wasn't in love with me, either.

Hayden flipped to the back and shook his head. "So, this is an arranged marriage?"

At least he was getting it. I sighed. "I'm looking at it as more of a business transaction. It's easier for me to process it that way."

"And you want this?"

At that point, I cracked, and my throat tightened. What I wanted didn't matter. "It's not a matter of *want*. It's a matter of duty. I'm not—"

"The fuck it is." The anger in his voice had me stiffening. He stood abruptly, so I did, too, unsure what to make of his reaction. "Do you love him?"

"No." There was no hesitation in my response. "I can't go through with it. I know that. I just haven't figured out how to escape the nightmare. I wanted to be free of this before I came to apologize for how I left."

The admission was out before I could stop it, and I covered my mouth in shock. I hadn't meant to be so forward when I had no idea how Hayden felt.

After a few seconds, Hayden took a step toward me. "That last night in Ketchikan, you said you loved me. Did you mean it?"

Hayden wasn't one to beat around the bush, but I didn't think he would bring up that night so soon. Tears welled in my eyes. If I put myself out there only to be rejected, I wasn't sure I could take it. I glanced down at my knotted fingers. "Hayden, please."

He stepped so close that I could feel the heat of his body. With a thumb under my chin, he lifted my face up to look him in the eye. "I need you to look at me, sweetheart. Please."

Please. Hayden's soft request touched me deep inside and lowered my barriers. I raised my eyes to his. Again, I felt my body pull toward his. If only we could go back to this summer, I would tell Hayden everything. He took another step toward me, bringing our bodies closer, and I could smell his woodsy, outdoors scent. It made me feel safe. All I wanted to do was run my hands through his thick blond hair and ask him to make love to me. When we were together, the rest of the world fell away.

He searched my eyes, so many emotions racing across his features.

"Kory, did you mean it? I need you to be honest with me right now."

I felt my tear run down my cheek. In the last month, I'd cried a lifetime's worth. He deserved to know the truth. If our roles were reversed, I would want to know. "I meant every word. Which is why I had to leave early—before my heart was too far gone and I wasn't able to leave at all."

"Where is Landon?"

I shrugged. "I'm sure he's here in Washington. Or on his way back. He's supposed to be at the luncheon tomorrow. When I got our initial relationship itinerary, I asked Landon what he thought about approaching our parents with the idea of having one last summer to go off and do our own thing. He's a nice guy, just not the guy I want to spend the rest of my life with. We've been acquaintances our entire lives. I don't even think I'm his type."

And there were *clauses* in the agreement. Clauses that made my stomach turn.

"What are you thinking about?" Hayden touched my upper arms.

I sniffled. "This whole situation. I'll be a slave in this relationship."

The pressure of Hayden's hands increased as he squeezed my shoulders. "So then why are you doing this? For your parents? For the company?"

That was the question I had been asking myself since I got back. "I... I thought I knew. But it's so jumbled now." I tried to think about the right words to explain this. "Since I was a little girl, duty and responsibility have been drilled into my head. My parents decided anything and everything I've ever done. If there was something I wanted to do, I had to figure out a way to manipulate the situation so it looked like they'd come up with the idea. I couldn't believe they agreed to give me this summer. It was the best summer of my life. When I got back, I felt like a stranger in my home, my whole life. Everything I want is back in Alaska." I struggled to hold back a sob. "I have been wracking my brain to figure out a way to leave here and go back to you without my parents finding me."

CHAPTER Four

Hayden

What the actual fuck?

I needed a second to process this. Sitting on the couch, I cradled my head. In a million years, I would never have guessed Kory had left Alaska for some crazy situation like this. Having Kory near me felt right, but there were so many fucked-up pieces to this story. Which somehow tainted our story, as well.

She'd never had the right to choose.

There was a lot of doubt in my mind. *Given the choice of any man, would she still choose me?* I hoped to hell she would, but a seed of doubt took root in my mind. I didn't want her to jump from this situation right into my bed. Kory deserved the best, but so did I, and I never wanted to be a regret.

Her hand reached out to touch mine. I knew she was hurting and hated it. I focused back on Kory, who was standing next to me looking vulnerable with her wide eyes and T-shirt slipping off her shoulder. *Is this real?* In every possible scenario in my head, nothing came close to the reality of this one. Needing contact, I reached for her hand, which she quickly gave me. She was so small, but her hand fit perfectly within mine. It was like she was made to be part of me. A surge of possessive protectiveness came over me. Kory was mine. *Mine.*

I had two options: walk away or see if we had a chance. And put that way, there really was no choice. I knew what I wanted to do. But Kory had to choose for herself. "If it was entirely up to you, would you go back to Alaska or stay here to start your life with Landon?"

"Alaska."

There was no hesitation in her response, which felt un-fucking-believably good. "Then choose. Choose Alaska to see where this takes us. That book doesn't control you. You're in charge of your own life."

She looked down. "How would I disappear?"

"Disappear?"

"My parents are adamant that I follow through with this. They aren't going to let me walk away from this. This merger is worth millions to them. Millions to both families. It will tie my parents' e-commerce business with their distribution service."

Shit. "Did you ever mention me?"

She shook her head. "No. They knew where I worked in Ketchikan, but I never mentioned you."

That would make things easier. At some point, we would need to make sure Maggie didn't mention me if Kory's parents came to ask. I imagined Ketchikan would be the first place they'd go. No one else really knew about us. "I have my plane here, so you won't need to buy a plane ticket. If you don't open any accounts until you're ready, that should buy you some time."

She pulled her hand back and, for a moment, appeared lost in thought. "We need to start over. I don't want you to feel forced to stay with me."

It hurt like a son of a bitch, but I agreed. Back in Ketchikan, we'd been fuck buddies, ignoring what was actually happening between us. Hell, there were times I'd flown up there just to see her, but I'd convinced myself it was just to fuck. My body craved her; she'd become my addiction. But what would starting over look like? "How do you want to start over?"

"I don't know yet. I know my feelings for you have only strengthened, but they're more complicated at the same time. Does that make sense?"

"It does." I paused. "Let me ask you a question. Do the fancy-ass car, the designer clothes, this house… does all this matter to you?"

She shook her head. "No, not at all. Anything with strings attached isn't worth having when the strings take away your freedom. I just want to live *my* life. Make *my* choices. And hopefully find *our* way together."

It made sense to me. This wealth came with a prison sentence. Not that I was doing badly for myself. However, I imagined in a business merger worth millions, Kory probably had a lot of money at her disposal. I squeezed her hand. "We'll figure this out."

"And if it doesn't end with us together?" Her brows creased as if the thought of not being together bothered her.

Good, because I feel the same way.

"These last few weeks, I've been in knots about us. About you. The way things ended. My brother told me... he said it's worth it. We don't want to spend our lives wondering *what if.*"

She let out a breath. "I want it, too. Hayden, I haven't been able to stop thinking about you... us... what we had. But I don't want to be kept. I want to be able to survive on my own."

"Then you will. I'll help however I can, however you want."

For the first time, I saw hope in her eyes. The sparkle that I loved. Kory chewed on her lip as she thought about things. I was nervous and wanted nothing more than to give our relationship a shot. But starting it under these crazy circumstances was going to come with its own set of problems.

She stood with a determined look. "I'm ready to start living my life."

I nodded. "Good. We can stay at the motel by the airport. With this weather, there's no way we can fly out tonight. We can spend that time figuring out some things and talking."

"Let me get my stuff."

I stood. Kory leaned in and pressed her lips against my cheek. It was hard not to turn my head. Mere inches separated our lips. She took a step back, locked her eyes with mine, and whispered, "Thank you for saving me."

"Maybe, in different ways, we're saving each other."

"I hope so." Her beautiful blue eyes sparkled. "Did you mean what you said to me that night after I said I loved you?"

It was my turn to answer honestly. "Yes, I did."

Even with all this shit stacked on us, I wanted to be by Kory's side—not to fight her battles, but to be there as she conquered them.

She tucked a loose strand of hair behind her ear. "It won't take me long. I'm only going to pack the stuff I bought with the money I earned while I worked in Ketchikan. There's a suitcase in the hall closet. Would you mind bringing it upstairs. I'm going to write my parents a letter so maybe they won't try to search for me. Can you give me about twenty minutes before you come up?"

"Of course."

When Kory went upstairs, I slowly sat on the couch. If Kory marrying Landon resulted in millions of dollars, I doubted either family would let her go that easily. The book I read was some fucked-up shit. People who went to those extremes weren't going to walk away without some sort of fight.

I pulled out my phone and called the only person I knew I could get solid advice from right now.

"Hello?" Drake answered.

"I need your help."

CHAPTER Five

Kory

My stomach was in knots as the plane approached Skagway. The entire night, I'd tossed and turned after going to bed. Everything felt upside down. But, at the same time, I felt liberated. It was odd. Hayden and I had stayed up talking about our lives—with no restrictions—until one o'clock. Before, we'd kept the details about ourselves to a minimum. Then like a gentleman, he'd gone to his own room. That alone had me ready to say *screw it* and ask him to stay with me.

I missed being in his arms.

It was hard not having him in my bed, but I think we needed to find our way back to each other emotionally before we slept together. Things were too fresh. And I wanted to make sure we had something more than sex between us. I smiled thinking about the conversation last night.

We'd been sitting on the couch in the two-bedroom suite,

munching on popcorn Hayden had purchased at the front desk.

"This is nice," I'd said, feeling almost happy for the first time in weeks.

"It is."

For a while, the sound of crunching popcorn was the only sound in the room. We hadn't figured out what we were going to do when we got to Skagway. I had about five thousand dollars to my name. Over the summer, I'd worked two jobs—waitressing at Maggie's diner and helping her with the books. Maggie had been amazing to me. She'd let me live in her one-room apartment above the diner for a ridiculously low rent. I'd answered her ad on a whim while I was still in Washington and had been thrilled to get the job. Finding that job had been like fate stepping in.

While we'd been munching, Hayden's phone had vibrated with a text message. "That was Drake. When I talked to him earlier, I asked if he knew of anyone renting a place."

On the way to the motel, Hayden had mentioned that he'd brought his brother up to speed with the situation, which I understood. In the morning, he'd be showing up with a stranger. His family, with the exception of Drake, had never heard of me before.

I was still anxious to see how things unfolded but excited to carve the way for my future. "What did he say?"

"His fiancée, Alexa, has a place she wants to show you."

"Wow, I'd love to look at it."

Hayden had cocked his head to the side and watched me for a second. "You said earlier that your parents would come if they could find you."

"Yes, I think they would."

I had never disobeyed my parents. What they would do... well, I wasn't sure.

"I want to propose something."

Cautiously, I'd said, "Okay."

"Wherever you decide to live, I think I should live with you. My place is about thirty minutes from Alexa's. It'll be safer. We don't have to jump into bed together. We can be... roommates."

The word had sounded odd to me, too, and I'd giggled. "Roomies?"

"Yeah, and hopefully that leads to *benefits*."

He'd given me a glimpse of that cocky attitude I loved. I'd winked. "I bet it will."

Hayden had given me his full megawatt grin. "Good to know." Then his expression had sobered. "I want you safe. I get wanting independence, and I want that for you, too. But, I want to make sure you're safe."

His presence would definitely make me feel better. "Why not stay at your place, then? I could pay rent."

"It's small. It's a one-room cabin with a loft bedroom and one bathroom."

A loft bedroom meant we'd be in the same bed together unless one of us took the couch. That sounded miserable. "Why don't we see what Alexa has in mind and the cost. Then we can decide which place."

"Perfect."

I'd leaned closer and put my head on Hayden's shoulder. "Thank you for agreeing to start over with me."

He'd put his arm around me to draw me closer. "It'll be that much better when we decide to go there again."

I'd shivered at the promise behind his words. "Yes, it will."

A bit of turbulence brought me out of my thoughts. I stared up at the cockpit where Hayden expertly flew the plane with his copilot and employee, Anthony. For a second, Hayden turned my way and winked. It made me all tingly inside.

Through all this, Hayden had been amazing. This morning, he'd held me while I cried. Leaving was harder than I'd imagined. All my life, in some way, I'd known what my future held. Now it was a blank slate. The thought was freeing and terrifying at the same time.

After thinking about it most of the night, I decided to call my parents before we boarded the plane this morning. I'd blocked the number before I called, just in case. I wanted them to know I was okay and dissuade them from looking for me. Part of me had hoped they wouldn't pick up, and part wanted to hear their voices. Which was odd considering what they'd done… but maybe not so odd, after all.

In a matter of hours, I'd left everything I had ever known for a chance at a real life, freedom, and… true love. And if I had to make the choice again, I would give it all up for the chance at happiness. I wanted them to know this and understand my point of view.

My parents hadn't picked up.

I left a voicemail telling them I would reach out at some point. When that would be, exactly, I wasn't sure. It wouldn't be until I had a grasp on my new life. Hopefully. So much still hung in the balance. I just hoped Hayden and I were strong enough.

CHAPTER Six

Kory

Hayden came over the headphones to speak since we were in uncontrolled airspace. I'd flown with him frequently over the summer and learned more than I ever thought I could about flying.

"Skagway traffic, King Air November 740 Alpha Whiskey ten miles south, inbound to land runway two zero. Skagway." Hayden's voice was strong, commanding. There was something insanely attractive about hearing him over the headset speaking pilot talk. Once before, we'd fucked in the back of the float plane after he'd landed in a lake surrounded by mountains. Thinking about it sent tingles along my skin.

There was no response, which would be the case if no other pilots were airborne or in the area. Throughout the flight, I remained quiet while listening to Hayden and his copilot, Anthony. I had a lot of mental sorting out to do.

There was so much to do. No matter what, I had a place to

stay. Sooner rather than later, I would need to find a car, cell phone, winter gear, and other essentials. The five thousand wasn't going to last long. I would have to plan out a budget. Living arrangements would have a huge effect on what else I could afford. Hayden had insisted that if we rented Alexa's place, we would split the rent.

Maybe I could get a waitressing job to help kick-start the inflow of money. I had done well with tips at Maggie's. Waitressing wasn't what I wanted to do with the rest of my life, but it was a source of income. As of five months ago, I had a bachelor's degree, but had never had the opportunity to put it to use. Working while I was in college hadn't been an option. Hell, I was lucky I'd gotten the chance to get a degree. When I'd brought up getting my master's, my parents had put a stop to it.

Again, Hayden's voice came over the headphones. "Skagway traffic, King Air November 740 Alpha Whiskey, five mile final two zero. Skagway."

The landing gear came down, signifying that we were close. There would only be one more call before we landed. My family had a private jet, but I'd never been able to sit in the cockpit. The precision it took to fly a plane was mind-boggling. And typically, I'd spent flights with my family going over details of some mind-numbing, overly orchestrated event.

"Skagway traffic, King Air November 740 Alpha Whiskey, short final two zero. Skagway."

The small town of Skagway became more visible. During the summer, cruise ships typically used it as the first stop. Skagway was a historic town. During the Klondike gold rush, people landed in Skagway in hopes of becoming rich. They'd stock up on supplies before heading up the treacherous Yukon

Trail. From the air, it looked similar to Ketchikan, like one of those picturesque old towns written about in history books. I was already in love with the place.

Home.

This was my new home. My fresh start. And I couldn't wait.

The wheels touched down. It was a smooth landing with only a minor screeching protest from the wheels as they touched the pavement. We taxied up to the hangar, where the guys did the post-flight checks and shut down the engines.

Hayden had three planes: a seaplane, this twin-engine, and a smaller Cessna. Most of his income came from booking excursions for passengers on the cruise ships. Hunters also hired him to fly them to remote parts of the state that could only be reached by plane. The size of the excursion and the location determined which plane he used. Prior to today, I had flown in both the seaplane and the Cessna. Today had been the first day in the twin-engine. It had been a smooth flight.

The door to the plane opened and Hayden came back. "You ready, sweetheart?"

"Yes." This was an adventure I couldn't wait to start.

I only had two suitcases. The first held some mementos from my childhood—things I held most dear, like the stuffed teddy bear I got from my grandparents when I was sick with pneumonia at two and the water globe I got after seeing *The Nutcracker* for the first time. Seeing the ballet had been like a dream. Those had been the good days. After I turned five, I'd lost those grandparents to a freak car accident. I remembered being so sad when my parents told me I would never see them again. I never knew my other set of grandparents.

In my other suitcase, I had some clothes, makeup, and a

limited selection of shoes. These were all the things I'd purchased while I'd been in Alaska. By taking only what I'd bought myself, my parents couldn't use the tactic that I somehow owed them something when I saw them next. I wanted nothing from them.

As we walked down the stairs, the briskness of the fall day hit me.

Alaska.

The leaves were already changing, and soon, the trees and landscape would be covered in snow.

Oh, how I loved this state. There was something about the clean, crisp air that awakened my soul. I took another deep breath. *I can't believe I'm here.* When I'd hurriedly left Ketchikan, I never imagined I would be back.

The last night we were together, before telling me he loved me, Hayden had casually mentioned meeting his family. It had wrecked me. I'd known I had to leave before I got in too deep.

Hayden put the suitcases in the back of his truck, and I climbed into the beast. It was strange to think I'd never been in this enormous vehicle before even though I'd been on multiple dates with Hayden. While gigantic, it was clean and smelled of pine. It occurred to me that there were so many things we didn't know about each other. Before he put the truck in drive, he looked at me. "Alexa texted me. Are you ready to see the place? Or would you like to get something to eat first."

If Skagway was anything like Ketchikan, my arrival would most likely not go unnoticed. The tourist season was over, and I would stick out like a sore thumb in a small group of local people. I wasn't ready for that kind of attention today.

Finding a place to live would be nice. "Let's look at the

house. I don't know if I'm up for people right now."

"I understand. I'll text her now."

Nervous butterflies swarmed my stomach as I thought about meeting someone from Hayden's family or soon to be in his family. They must've thought I was crazy. "What does your family think about me?"

"My family doesn't judge. And Alexa is one of the sweetest people I know. She came from a shitty family. Beyond shitty. They tried to ruin her life. So she understands that sometimes family can be tough."

"She sounds amazing." I looked forward to meeting Alexa. Hopefully we could become friends. I'd never really had a girlfriend that I could be myself with. I'd always been too nervous for anyone to find out the truth about my home life. I had few friends over while I was growing up, never had a birthday party with school friends or a slumber party as a teen.

As we drove, Hayden told me a little bit about the town of Skagway. It was small—only about eight hundred people lived there. At a stoplight, I noticed two older women in gold-digging uniforms staring intently at us. They each carried a notepad and a pencil.

Strange.

"That's Sylvia and Elvira, the Twiner sisters. They have a newsletter I'm sure you'll be signed up for as soon as you give them your email. They are the town's gossips, so to speak. You'll grow to love them." He winked.

Oh my. They waved our way as we passed them, and my hand went up automatically. They definitely put a new spin on paparazzi.

"They seem harmless enough," I commented.

He chuckled. "Don't let looks deceive you. Hell, those women have a knack for being at the best place at the worst possible time. They do have good hearts, but man almighty, it sucks to be the center of their attention."

Hopefully, I'd be able to stay out of their crosshairs. That brought up a good point. "What do I say to everyone when they ask me any personal questions?"

"What do you want to tell them? Whatever you decide, I'll relay it to my family and they'll keep that as the story."

It needed to be as close to the truth as possible. "Let me think about it. Maybe that I came up to Ketchikan to try something different. We met, and I decided to move to Skagway. If they ask about my family…" I paused, reality setting in. "I don't have any."

That was easier than creating a family that existed but didn't. And I wasn't the type who wanted everyone to know what happened.

"That works."

Chapter Seven

Kory

Fifteen minutes later, we pulled up to the most adorable blue, two-story house. The white wraparound porch was to die for. I imagined rocking on the front porch, drinking hot cocoa. The leaves on the surrounding trees were at peak color in vivid reds, oranges, and yellows. I wanted to pinch myself. The rent was going to be steep, but since we'd be splitting it, hopefully we could make it work.

It was perfect.

Hayden put his hand on mine. "What do you think?"

"I love it. Wow. I never imagined... just... I have no words. And she wants to rent this place?"

"That's what Drake said. Want to hear what she has to say?"

I smiled and hopped out of the truck. "Yes!"

An older red Chevy truck that appeared to be in good condition was parked off to the side of the house. The large tree in front would be perfect to have a picnic under during the summer.

A blond woman, who was about my size and wearing scrubs, walked out onto the porch. She shielded her eyes from the sun as we approached the front steps. "Hey, guys."

"I thought Drake was coming," Hayden said.

"He's hoping to stop by in a bit. Inspector came by the Red Onion, so he couldn't leave."

Hayden put his hand on my waist, and I loved the warmth of his touch. "Alexa, this is Kory. Kory, Alexa."

I extended my hand for an introductory shake but instead was engulfed in a hug. "It's wonderful to meet you, Kory. Welcome to Skagway."

I immediately felt at ease with her. The unexpected hug was nice, and the nerves that had been building at the thought of meeting Hayden's family ebbed ever so slightly. I waited for the questions or the judgment, but they never came.

Alexa gestured toward the house. "So, this place was my childhood home. It used to be a B and B until my mother changed it." She paused, and I sensed the sadness in her voice. She gave a little shake of her head followed by a sweet smile. "Anyway, that's a long story to share sometime over drinks. Let me give you a tour and see what you think."

"Sounds good." I was anxious to see the place.

As I climbed the stairs, my heart sank a little; I'd never be able to afford it. Even half the rent would most likely be too expensive. But this place felt perfect. A new start for a new adventure. The house looked practically brand new on the inside. Light gray paint with white baseboards gave it a perfect feel. There wasn't any white furniture. That was a welcome sight. But it was still neutral enough that any color could be added to give it the pop it needed.

The counter tops were top-of-the-line black quartz. "This place is beautiful. Was this recently remodeled?"

Again, I saw the sadness in Alexa's eyes. "Yes. It used to have more of a country feel, and I guess it's now more traditional or contemporary. I'm not sure. I still feel like a stranger here." She took a deep breath. "My mom made all these drastic changes while I was away at college in New York. And I wasn't prepared. I'm still… adjusting."

I scolded myself for pressing something that obviously made Alexa feel uncomfortable. Hayden and Alexa were talking about things happening around the town. Something about a man named Ol' Man Rooster.

I was a little lost but didn't want to intrude.

The house was completely furnished with black leather furniture in the living room. The dining room had a mirrored dining room table. It was so different from what I was used to living in. And I loved it.

The three downstairs bedrooms were empty. There were two bathrooms downstairs, one in the hall and the other in the largest of the bedrooms. It was a great layout for a B&B. We climbed the stairs where a door separated it from the lower level.

Alexa said, "When there were guests, we'd lock this door to keep our living space separate."

There were three additional bedrooms upstairs. Two of the three were fully furnished with similar modern furniture. The master bedroom looked over a small pond at the back of the house. It was magnificent. I wanted this place.

Alexa excused herself to take a phone call, and I took the moment to savor the space. Hayden put his hand on my lower back ,and I leaned my head on his shoulder. "Thank you for bringing me to Skagway."

"I wouldn't want you to be anywhere else."

We simply shared the moment with no additional words.

Alexa came back into the room. "Sorry about that. Drake's not going to make it. Crete went home sick, so he's got to stay and cover."

I turned to her. "Oh, no. Is there anything I can do to help?"

"That's sweet to ask. But it should be a slow day. I may head over there to help after I get done at the clinic if it's needed." She held out her hands. "So... what do you think?"

"It's beautiful. This view is my favorite."

Alexa gave me a smile. "This is my favorite view in the house, too. I used to sit on my parents' bed and stare out at the pond. The winters are breathtaking. The frozen water glistens like it has a thousand diamonds on it. My dad taught me how to ice skate and fish there. It's a good place to make memories."

From her forlorn look, it seemed like her parents might have passed away. I would ask Hayden later. "What a blessing to grow up in such a place."

"I think so, too. Take all the time you want to look around. I'll be downstairs."

My childhood seemed dreary compared to this. Out of habit, my mind froze, as if I'd forgotten my script for this situation. I searched for what I was supposed to say, but I had no lines to follow. *Where does this leave me?* Panic rose within me. When I turned, I caught Hayden's eyes but quickly averted my own.

He grabbed my hand and mouthed, *"Are you okay?"*

I nodded and mouthed back, *"I will be."*

I can do this. I want to do this.

The door to downstairs closed, leaving us alone. Hayden wrapped his arms around me. "You sure you're okay?"

"Yes, it's just different. For a second, my mind searched for what I should be saying. When I first started working in Ketchikan, that happened a lot. Then, as time went on, it stopped."

Instead of saying anything else, Hayden held me, which was exactly what I needed. A few minutes later, I asked, "Do you want to see what the rent is?"

"That's entirely up to you."

I turned in his arms. "Let's see what she has to say. If it's too much or more than you want to spend, let me know."

"Okay."

Hand in hand, we went downstairs. Alexa was standing in front of the fireplace, typing on her phone. She looked up and gave me another warm smile.

"I love the place. What is the rent?"

She gave me a wink. "I don't want anything for the rent. If someone doesn't live here, especially through the winter, it'll be harder on the place and cause damage. You're doing me a favor. In exchange for rent and utilities, keep the place up. Then when you get on your feet, you can take over the utilities."

"I—I—I…" I looked at Hayden, who seemed at a loss for words, too. He obviously hadn't expected this offer. Alexa hardly knew me. And I didn't want to take advantage of anyone.

Hayden said, "I'll be living here, too. We can't take this place for free."

"Sure, you can."

This was crazy. *Free.* This had to be out of obligation. "Alexa, I don't want—"

Alexa touched my shoulder. "This isn't a handout. And you guys don't have to feel obligated to say yes. I could honestly use the help. I've talked with Drake about it, and he agrees. Between the Red Onion, the clinic Hollis and I just opened, getting married, and trying to move forward with my incredibly difficult sister and mother, this would be a lot of work for us to take on. We have our place, the cabin, and Drake's apartment at the Red Onion. We're already overwhelmed. It's fate. I got this house, and it was waiting for you to come live here. It needs happiness within its walls. My dad would have loved for this place to be the stepping stone for someone to get back on their feet."

Fate. There was the word again. The one that had initially brought me to Alaska.

The way she spoke about her father led me to believe he had passed away, but it sounded like her mother might not be in the picture. I wasn't sure, but there was hurt in the depths of her eyes. Hurt that I understood.

Alexa continued, "Kory, if you love this place, I want you to live here. If it hadn't been for the support of Drake and his family when I came back, I don't know where I would be."

Tears welled in my eyes, and I squeezed Hayden's hand. "I honestly don't know what to say. Thank you."

"Thank you," Hayden echoed.

Alexa looked at Hayden. "I have some boxes in the back of my truck. Would you mind getting them? Drake had to load them for me. They're pretty heavy."

When Hayden glanced my way, I nodded, and he said, "Sure thing."

CHAPTER Eight

Kory

The screen door shut, leaving us together. I liked Alexa. She had a kind spirit unlike anyone I had ever met.

"Kory, if you need a girl to talk to, I'm here. I know we don't know each other very well—well… at all—but I'm hoping we can change that. Drake told me about your situation, and I just want you to know you're not alone."

Hayden had mentioned he'd given his family a quick overview of what had happened. I was relieved to feel only kindness and acceptance from Alexa. I'd never had a friend who'd been there for me without an ulterior motive. All of the friendships throughout my life had been cultivated for my parents' financial gain. There was something innocent and honest about what she was offering. "I would love that."

She leaned in and gave me a hug. "I'm so glad you're here. I never thought I'd see the day when Hayden Foster would move heaven and earth for a woman."

Move heaven and earth. He'd come for me. It was still hard to believe. "He's wonderful."

"Yes, he is. Drake is excited to meet you, too."

I was nervous to meet his family—especially his brothers. I kept the nerves at bay by rubbing my thumb and index finger together. Somehow, the motion helped me stay focused. "There's Kane, as well, right?"

"Oh yes. He's a little crass and grumpy, but he's loyal to the core."

Hayden came in with the first load. "What the hell are in these?"

"Stuff for Kory."

My eyes widened. Alexa opened the first box. "Last night, I asked Hayden what size you wear. Being the typical guy, he had no idea and said we were about the same size. So I went through all my stuff. I have winter gear, winter clothes, and all sorts of shoes. Accessories, too."

Oh my gosh. I stared at the enormous box with my mouth open. "I can't take your clothes."

Alexa swiped some stray blond hairs that had fallen from her ponytail out of her face. "Trust me, you're doing me a favor. Drake and I are consolidating things, and I needed to clear out the storage units. As I keep going through boxes, I'll bring over more stuff for you to go through. And it won't hurt my feelings if you don't like it."

Not like it? How could I not like it? There were no strings attached to the offering. None. In Ketchikan, I'd experienced the same kindness from people. One time, I had been shopping in a clothing store when it began to pour. The clerk had recognized me from Maggie's and offered to lend her umbrella since I'd forgotten mine. At times, I forgot how Alaska was also a rain forest. It rained over ninety percent of the time.

"This is amazing. I can't believe it. It's just... I have no words to express my gratitude."

Alexa gave me another hug. "I'm glad you like it. The other boxes in the truck have some pots and pans and other kitchen things that were in the storage unit. I think there's one or two sets of sheets upstairs in the linen closet. If not, I—"

I cut her off. "You honestly don't have to do any more."

"Well, if there's something you need, I'm a phone call away." She turned to Hayden. "Can you give Kory my cell phone number?"

"Of course." He nodded. "I'll give her everyone's."

She smiled. "Perfect. Oh, and your mom asked me if there was a date you guys could come over for dinner." Alexa turned back to me. "Amie is dying to meet you. She's the most amazing person I have ever known."

Meeting his parents was a serious step. Before I could stop myself, I blurted out, "Will you be there?"

"If you want us to be, Drake and I can come, for sure."

It would be easier with a familiar face. "If you don't mind."

"Not at all. Are there any dates we should avoid? I'll work on getting a date together."

Hayden rubbed the back of his neck. "I need to check my flight schedule. I know we have a couple of excursions this week. Can I text you later?"

"That works." Alexa paused and blew out a breath. "Elvira and Sylvia already called me to see if I knew who the pretty little blond in your truck was."

Oh dear. The Twiner sisters. Hayden's words from earlier regarding the sisters made me stiffen. I wasn't ready to be in a gossip column. He ran his hands through his hair. "Fuck. I don't want them meddling."

"I know. I had to think fast on my feet." She grimaced. "I didn't think you guys wanted all your personal details splattered in the *Twiner Tellings* newsletter." Looking at me, she sighed, "That'll be another night of drinks. When I came back a little over a month ago, I found my way into several newsletters. And a couple of red-hot editions. It's fine when it's someone else. But I hate being the center of it all."

"Oh, dear." This was worse than I thought. I dreaded the thought of my past being used as fodder for this newsletter. I still hadn't processed what had happened.

Hayden asked, "What did you tell them?"

"That you met Kory while you were away this summer. Things progressed, and she decided to move here since she doesn't have any family."

No family. It was close enough to the truth, I imagined.

When neither of us responded, Alexa twisted her fingers. "Listen, I'm really sorry about the lie. I didn't know how you wanted to handle your parents. I thought it would be easier if you had a more boring past until you decided what you wanted to say. Then, any 'misunderstanding' can be blamed on me."

Without even meeting me, Alexa had looked out for my best interests simply because of Hayden. I rushed to her and grabbed her hand. "Thank you. I'm just really overwhelmed. I appreciate the story you gave them. That's what I want to stick with for the time being."

Alexa smiled at me. "I get it. More than you probably understand. And it'll make it easier without having people meddle in your business while you try to sort it out. You'll most likely make the 'New to Town' section of the *Twiner Tellings*."

Her phone rang, and she stepped back. "Let me get this. One second." She connected the call. "Hey. Okay, I'll be right there. Hollis, she doesn't bite. Stop being melodramatic. I don't know... maybe give her a tour of the clinic. Make her a fancy schmancy coffee. You're smart; figure it out. I swear if you get grumpy I'm going to throw another book at you."

What in the world?

Alexa hung up the phone and rolled her eyes. "My best friend from college came back to Skagway with me. He's a doctor and a bit over the top at times. Sometimes I have to throw books at him to make him see sense."

A firecracker. I liked it.

"I remember Hayden telling me about your clinic. What an amazing accomplishment—and so important for the town. Congrats."

"Thank you." Her phone vibrated, and she sighed. "I have to get back to the clinic before Hollis scares off our new receptionist." At my confused look, she just shook her head. "It's a long story." She pulled a set of keys out of her pocket. "Anyway, here's the keys to the place. Think it over with Hayden. And if you decide you don't want to stay here, I swear it's fine. Oh, and the furniture comes with the house. Hollis ordered an entire houseful before we even got here. Now that he's decided to be 'Alaskan,' he doesn't need this furniture." She rolled her eyes. "Men. Anyway, Ike's making him *manly* furniture." She giggled. "I'm making him sound ridiculous. You'll have to swing by the clinic to fully understand."

"I'd like that. I will never forget your kindness. Thank you."

She smiled. "Anytime. We women dating the Foster men have to stick together. There's so much testosterone with those men it can be a little overwhelming."

"Hey, we aren't that bad," Hayden protested.

Slapping Hayden on the back, she laughed. "Whatever makes you feel better." Then she mouthed to me, *"You'll see."*

And for the first time in my life, I looked forward to what tomorrow would bring—without any sort of schedule or deadline to bring an end to my happiness.

CHAPTER Nine

Hayden

Alexa left, and I sat there, rendered speechless by what she had done. *Rent free.* Keeping up any building could be a lot of work, but people still paid rent. Alexa broke the mold when it came to kindness and compassion. For as long as I'd known her, she wanted to save the world and help anyone she could.

We were silent as we stared at the door. I grabbed Kory's hand, and she squeezed mine in return. She turned my way, bewildered. "Is this a dream?"

I reached out to touch her face. Her skin felt like satin. *I have her in my life.* At least now we had a fighting chance to figure things out without the additional stress of worrying about money. But neither of us had experienced a real relationship before.

"You're not dreaming, sweetheart."

She threw her arms around me, and I held her close, savoring her sweet vanilla scent. This woman was going to be my everything.

"We're going to figure this out, Kory."

"One day at a time, right?"

"Right."

She put a little space between us and looked up into my face. I wanted to kiss her senseless. I was about to lean down when a thought crossed my mind. Kory needed to be romanced, courted, or whatever the fuck Drake had done for Alexa.

I had little doubt she would open up to me if I kissed her. Instead, I brushed my thumb against her lower lip. "The next time I kiss you, there won't be any doubt about where we stand."

She smiled, and I knew I'd made the right decision. "So, we're going out on a date?"

"Yes."

She winked. "I'm going to make you work for it. Here's to starting from the very beginning."

Her words held an underlying implication of no sex, which I figured. My dick screamed at me to argue against it, but like I'd told her in the truck, I wanted her to know I was sure of us. I wanted us to have a real relationship.

"From the beginning."

I looked into her eyes, and the air thickened around us. My body was on fire having her in my arms again. It had been way too long. I would just have to be patient. Kory took another step back, which helped... marginally. Her smile lit up the room. "It's like I blinked, and now there are endless possibilities. I don't know what tomorrow is going to bring."

I held out my hands and she came to me. We moved to sit on the couch. It felt so fucking good to have her in my arms. "And how do you feel about that?"

Chewing on her lip, she stopped to give that some thought. "Excited and terrified at the same time."

"I think that's normal, considering the shit you've gone through."

She curled into my chest. "I like this. When do you have to work next?"

"I've got a couple of day flights with Kane this week. I was going to see if Anthony could take them."

Leaning back, she looked into my eyes. "Don't rearrange for me. I want you to keep your schedule."

"I want to be here for you."

"And you will be. Yes, I have a lot to deal with, but I'm doing good. This summer, I'd already begun processing more than I realized."

Kory's eyes shifted from mine, she stared into the distance. During the summer, something had changed within Kory; she'd become lighter at times. It still couldn't be easy. Maybe a distraction would help. "What do you think about running by the airport with me. I need to do some paperwork and work on some flight plans. And maybe if we have time, we could run by the clinic."

That seemed to do the trick, and Kory came back to me. "I'd love that. Is there a place I can get a phone?"

"For now, I have an extra phone at the office. We'll have to take a trip to Juneau to get you one. I figured we could add a line to my plan. It'll be cheaper and won't leave a paper trail."

She cocked her head. "And I'll pay you for my portion."

This was important to Kory. "That works. It's not necessary, but I know it's something you need to do."

Leaning toward me, she kissed my cheek. "Thank you, Hayden. For everything."

"I'm looking forward to falling in love with you all over again, Kory."

"Me, too."

CHAPTER Ten

Hayden

A couple of hours later, we pulled up to the clinic. Being in my hometown with Kory was better than I'd imagined. At the airport, I'd shown her around the hangar. One thing I loved about Kory was that she was truly interested in what I said. Most girls I'd dated had only been interested on the surface. They'd said they wanted to know, but they actually didn't.

I looked over at her as she took in the clinic. "What an amazing achievement. It's inspiring to see what Alexa has accomplished."

"It is."

Until Alexa had brought Hollis here and opened the clinic, Skagway had been without a doctor. Airlifting to another town for a medical emergency was expensive. Traveling by vehicle or ferry took too long. I loved it here, but we were isolated.

She stared at the front of the clinic. "It must be amazing to feel this sort of accomplishment." She paused for a second before speaking again. "I want to start something from the ground up."

"What is that?"

"I don't know yet, but I'll figure it out. But I want that feeling."

I reached over to touch her hand. "Then you'll find a way to get it."

She looked to where our hands touched before turning to me. "I will. And I can't wait for that day."

We got out of my truck, and I noticed Devney's car was there, too. I'd forgotten that Alexa had mentioned she was going to be the afternoon receptionist. In the morning she was the music teacher at the high school. Due to our town's size, Skagway didn't need a full-time music teacher. To make ends meet, Devney taught piano privately. She was reserved, very quiet. Always had been. From what Alexa had told me, Devney's mom had fallen ill with cancer, and she needed as much money as possible to help pay for treatments.

I hated that for Devney. It had to be hard with her mom living in Washington.

Hollis stepped onto the front porch and ran his fingers through his hair. Something was under his skin. Or I imagined it was someone. *A music teacher named Devney, perhaps?*

I called out, "How's it going?"

"Fantastic. Great. Amazing." The sarcasm dripped from his voice as he ran his hand through his blond hair again and scrubbed his face. He stopped when he noticed Kory and put a smile on his face. "You must be Kory. I'm Hollis Fritz."

"Hey, it's nice to meet you, too. You have a lovely clinic."

"Thanks." Hollis extended his hand. "Welcome to Skagway, where everyone knows what's going on in your life." He chuckled. "I'm originally from New York, so the change has been a little drastic."

Kory smiled. "I get it. I'm from Seattle. When I came to Ketchikan, it was definitely an adjustment. But I think there's something to be said for the change."

I froze at her words. I'd thought we weren't mentioning where Kory was from.

"I would agree."

Then Kory's eyes widened. "Oh! I'm not sure if Alexa told you, but I'd like to focus on the fact that I lived in Ketchikan and not mention anything about Seattle or Washington."

"She filled me in. No worries."

That sent a surge of relief through me, and I saw Kory's shoulders relax. "Thanks."

Hollis looked at me, and the agitation underneath the surface was clear in the grim set of his mouth. For the first time since I'd known Hollis, he seemed stressed. Normally, he was an easygoing person.

Sometimes it helped just to step away. "Hollis, why don't you and I go get the girls some lunch?"

He sighed. "I have a patient in about forty-five minutes. I don't think I have time."

Yeah, things moved a little slower here. It would take us at least an hour to get lunch. Everyone knew everyone here, which caused the Red Onion to be a social stop.

Hell, I couldn't believe I was going to suggest this. "Why

don't we go to, umm... Starbucks. That's fast. Coffees for the ladies."

The people of Skagway rarely went into the Starbucks. Skagway was a regular stop for cruise ships. Tourists frequently visited the local diamond store when they docked, which was where the Starbucks was located.

Kory looked delighted. "There's a Starbucks here? My day just got better."

"Finally! Someone who gets me. I just need to let Alexa know."

We walked into the clinic. The place looked brand new. After Alexa had arrived back into town, Drake had called us to ask if we could help. It had been in bad shape, but we got it fixed up in no time.

Devney sat at the receptionist's desk. Her face lit up when Hollis walked into the room.

Alexa said, "Oh, Kory! You're here. You have to meet Devney. She's the school's music teacher and has agreed to help us at the clinic in the afternoons."

Devney walked over and extended her hand. "It's nice to meet you."

"You, too."

"I thought it would be fun to do a girls' night out," Alexa said.

Devney adjusted her glasses with a smile. "That would be wonderful."

"Ow! Dammit."

We turned. It looked like Hollis had managed to walk into the side table against the wall. I fought back a chuckle, and Alexa gave me a wink. So, this was the drama she'd been dealing with earlier; Hollis obviously had a thing for Devney. And by the looks of it, the feeling was mutual.

"Hollis, are you okay?" Devney asked.

"Uh... yeah. Let me get my phone."

Devney said, "I'm going to check on the lasagna, if that's okay."

Alexa nodded. "Of course."

They left the room, and Alexa bumped Kory's shoulder. "Something is going on between those two. Hollis is denying it, but they are H-O-T for each other." She giggled. "Poor Hollis. He's going to end up black and blue if he can't get it together. He nearly choked himself to death with his stethoscope the other day."

I shook my head, not touching that with a ten-foot pole.

Kory smiled. "I think it's cute."

Time to change the subject. "We were going to take Hollis to get Starbucks. The man looks like he could use it."

"He does. Do you want to stay with us, Kory? We're about to eat lunch. I made a lasagna last night, and Devney brought a salad."

"I'd love that. Let me get my purse from the truck before Hayden leaves."

With a smile, Kory walked out to the truck. She was a natural fit in this town. When the door shut, I lowered my voice. "I wanted to thank you for earlier. Are you sure you want to let us have the place rent-free?"

Alexa gave me a kind smile and put her hand on my shoulder. "If you're with her, that means she's a decent person. Otherwise, you wouldn't have thrown in your forever bachelor card. And it honestly does help me."

I brought her in for a quick hug. "Thanks. If there's ever anything you need, I'm here for you, little sis. Have you guys set a date?"

She sighed. "Not yet. Hopefully soon. I'm not sure if I want a spring wedding or not. Of course, Drake wants a winter wedding. And then, do we keep it small or invite the entire town? Or do we wait longer? I just don't know."

There seemed to be something else brewing in that mind of hers. If it were up to my brother, he'd have married Alexa the day he proposed. With winter upon us, he wanted to be married sooner rather than later. Before I could say anything further, Hollis walked back into the room without Devney.

"Are we ready?" Hollis looked beyond frazzled.

"Yes, what do you girls want?"

Kory came back into the clinic. "I'd love a grande caramel Frappuccino with a shot of espresso and regular whipped cream."

"A what?"

Hollis patted my shoulder. "Don't worry. I got this. Let me teach you the ways, young Starbucker."

Starbucker?

Alexa snapped her fingers as if something had just occurred to her and pointed to several boxes against the wall. "Your mom dropped those by. The quilting circle brought all sort of non-perishable food for you and Kory. I think they wanted to swing by, but I suggested they drop it off here."

This town was damn amazing.

Kory looked at the box, gratitude clear on her face. "Wow, that was so thoughtful and generous. Is there someone I can send a thank-you to?"

"Just the quilting circle. You can give it to Hayden's mom."

"Perfect."

Devney walked back into the room. "It's almost ready."

"Kory is joining us for lunch," Alexa said while she straightened a few files.

"Wonderful. It'll give us a chance to talk. Alexa has spoken so highly of you," Devney said.

It was time for us to go. If Hollis had to be in the room with Devney for long, he might hurt himself again. I walked toward the door. "Let's head out to get the coffee."

CHAPTER Eleven

Hayden

The girls gave us other frou-frou drink orders that sounded like Greek to me. Thankfully, Hollis had it down. We got in the truck, and Hollis leaned back, heaving out a breath that fogged up his window. A chill was setting in the air. November was approaching, and we would have our first frost soon.

Hollis remained silent.

"That rough, huh?" I prompted, putting the truck in gear.

Hollis kept looking out the window. "You have no idea. How are you holding up?"

He must have needed a change of subject or wasn't ready to talk to me. "I guess Alexa filled you in on everything?"

"Yeah, and don't worry, I know the cover story as well. Everyone who's come into the clinic has been talking about it. But Alexa is acting like it's not news to anyone that you were seeing someone. Hopefully, interest is waning. It can't be news when the new doctor in town knows, right?" He chuckled. "This town is something else. It's addicting. I find myself checking my email first thing in the morning for a *Twiners Tellings* newsletter."

"I know the feeling." On a serious note, I added, "Thanks, man, for having my back. I won't ever forget it. And the furniture. If I can buy it from you, let me know."

He put his hand up. "Absolutely not. It's a gift. I want you and Kory to have it."

A gift? That was one hell of a gift. Worth thousands of dollars. "We can't, man."

"Yes, you can. I have no idea what I'm going to do with it. It won't go in the cabin I'm building. Let me do this for you guys. I get what it's like to need a fresh start. And this town saved me in more ways than I think I'd realized. I'd like to return the favor."

Hollis hadn't shared much about his life; I knew his father was dead. He came from a lot of money and had bankrolled the entire clinic against his mother's wishes. "Well, it's appreciated. Thank you. So… is something going on with you and Devney?"

"Why would you ask that?" His shoulders tensed.

Yeah, something is going on.

Pulling up to the stoplight, I held up my hands. "I was just asking."

He let out a deep sigh. The light turned green. I knew what it was like to keep things bottled up. Drake had been there for me. Maybe I could do the same for Hollis. Just be there as someone to listen, too.

"I did something stupid. So fucking stupid."

I waited to see if he was going to say anything else.

Hollis continued as he looked out the window. "Were you at the welcome party at the Red Onion?"

The town loved get-togethers. The quilting circle generally made moose chili when we got together in the fall. There had been a debacle with the Fall Festival this year, so to keep the town from killing the city council, Alexa and Drake had organized a welcome party for Hollis. "Yeah, I stayed in Drake's office with Kane most of the time."

"Right. Well on my way home, I saw Devney walking and I offered to give her a lift. When I pulled up to her house, I opened her door and walked her to the front door. Then... shit, fuck, damn."

I'd never heard Hollis curse this much. It was almost comical to see him so out of sorts.

Maybe he just needed a little prompting. "So, things progressed?"

"Yeah, they progressed. My head is such a mess. And don't you dare tell Alexa. She's been going on and on about the damn lovebug."

Lovebug? This probably isn't the time to ask about that. "I won't say a word."

Hollis threw up his arms; apparently there was more to the story. "Ol' Man Rooster is up my ass to go on a date with his granddaughter, Marlena. The Twiner sisters signed me up for some bachelor auction."

"Okay, so why not just say you're dating Devney?"

He threw his hands up again. "Exactly. But, that's the catch... she doesn't want that. At all. Hell, it's not like I'm proposing to her or asking her to have my child. It's... baffling." He cocked his eyebrow and stared at me.

Sweet, innocent Devney wanted a fuck buddy? I had no

words, so I responded with the only thing I could think of while I processed. "What?"

"Exactly."

"Why?"

This was damn confusing. I was lost.

"She said she's not in the right place for a relationship. But she wants to continue to be fuck buddies. What the hell do I do?"

I nearly choked at hearing my suspicions confirmed. Our sweet little music teacher. Who would have known? I had to think about this for a second. "Do you like her?"

"I'm attracted to her, yes. I have no idea if we have anything in common or if it's just physical. It's been a while since I've dated. College and residency didn't leave me much time. But I had no idea how complicated keeping a relationship uncomplicated would complicate things. Why can't it be simple?"

That was a lot of complicateds.

What a mess.

I was new to this relationship stuff, too. "I don't think it's ever simple when you care about someone. This summer, while Kory and I were denying how we felt, it was complicated. Now that we're trying a conventional relationship, it's complicated. I think the only time it can be simple is when you don't care."

"Not caring isn't possible for me."

Yeah, I got that, too. "Well, you've got two choices; be her fuck buddy or end it. If you end it, then it's over. If you're her fuck buddy, then you can see if things change."

As I turned left, I saw the coffee shop up ahead. A couple of people I didn't recognize crossed the street toward Starbucks. They must have been tourists. Hollis still hadn't responded. "If you're okay with not finding out what *could* happen, then walk away. I've had my share of fuck buddies, and it's not a bad thing. Just remember, don't get too involved if she's not all in. Make some ground rules you're both comfortable with. And use it to blow off steam. If more happens, it does. If it doesn't, then you had a good time."

"That easy?" He sounded doubtful.

"Probably not. Be honest with her and don't make it into a game. And if you feel like you're falling too hard and she's not budging, you might have to walk away."

We parked on the side of the street across from the Starbucks. Hell almighty, I was actually going to go in there. I hoped no one was around to see me. I'd get grief for weeks if it got back to Drake or Kane.

"I must really look frazzled for you to subject yourself to Starbucks," Hollis said. He opened his door. "Come on. This city slicker will show you the way to order Frappuccinos. I know I'm going to need two extra shots of espresso."

CHAPTER Twelve

Kory

I put the final touches on the chicken parmigiana. The tomato sauce and herbs combined with the chicken smelled delicious. I added a little more parsley as a garnish. One requirement of my mother had been to learn how to cook. *A good wife can entertain without hiring it out.* Until this summer, I'd never enjoyed it. Loathed it, actually.

One night over the summer when Hayden had offered to bring dinner, I'd decided I wanted to cook for him instead. The appreciation he showed made me want to cook more. It was my way of showing Hayden how much I cared for him without actually having to show it.

I sprinkled some fresh parmesan on the chicken. "Dinner is almost ready," I called from the kitchen.

"Coming," Hayden answered from the upstairs.

I grinned to myself as I thought about him being upstairs in the shower. It had taken restraint not to join him. My body hummed anytime he was near, and it drove me wild. Hayden had always been a generous lover who put my needs before his own. It wasn't going to take long before we were in the same bed. The sexual tension between us was too high.

If I spent any real time thinking about what it had been like to be with Hayden, my resolve was going to weaken instantly.

Think of something else.

This afternoon spent at Hayden's cabin after the Starbucks run had been charming. I looked forward to a time when we could stay there and wake up snuggled together. We'd packed up a few things for Hayden to bring back. At some point, we'd have to add some personal touches to make this place ours.

The temporary cell phone I was using vibrated on the counter with a reminder.

Noon Flight with Douglas

Until we could get to a bigger city, I was using Hayden's extra phone he had for his business, which was synced with the flight schedule. The alert reminded me that there was still so much to do, like figuring out what to do about a car and a job. It would all come in due time. For now, I was going to enjoy the moment, being able to live in this beautiful home.

How did I let the controlling behavior go on for so long with my parents? The easiest answer was that I'd been scared of upsetting them and terrified I wouldn't be able to survive on my own. In twenty-four hours, my entire world had changed... and Hayden's, too.

I worried what he was really thinking.

Our relationship was new. We loved each other, but at the same time, we were learning about each other, finding our way together.

Strong arms wrapped around my waist from behind me. "This smells delicious. I've missed your cooking."

"I missed it, too. Until you, I never enjoyed it."

"Really?"

I turned in his arms. "Yes, it had always been an expectation of my mother. With you, it wasn't expected but appreciated."

Our eyes connected. Little butterflies danced in my stomach. Yes, we'd slept together multiple times, but in some ways this felt new. My skin tingled where his fingers gripped me tighter. "I can't believe you're here, Kory."

"Me. either."

"What were you thinking about when I walked in?"

I glanced away for a second before meeting his eyes. "Are you okay with everything? I mean me... being here... upsetting your life. I feel like I've wrecked your life."

Not once did he look anywhere but at me. "No, you've brought me to life, Kory."

He leaned closer, and I closed my eyes, letting the anticipation build until his lips touched mine. They were firm and commanding. I melted into his embrace, wrapping my arms around his neck. Once, twice, he swiped his tongue across my lips, and I opened to him. It had been too long since I'd tasted him. He grabbed the back of my neck, deepening the kiss. I let out a moan as his spicy cinnamon flavor engulfed me. He groaned in response and gripped me tighter.

My core tightened, and I leaned closer. His dick pressed against my lower abdomen, and I craved that moment where nothing else mattered.

Hayden slowed the kiss, pulling back ever so slightly. Our

breathing was heavy, and his breath tickled my lips as he said, "I'm all in, Kory. I wanted to wait before I kissed you again. But I need you to feel how much I want this. I can't wait to be with you again. But I'll wait forever if that's what it takes."

I gave him a little kiss. "I feel the same way."

And I knew it wouldn't be long.

"That's good to know." Hayden gave me one of those smiles that made me weak in the knees.

"Are you hungry?"

"Definitely."

Except I knew he wasn't hungry for food. Heat crept up my cheeks. "Why don't we eat? I'll bring dinner in there."

I bit my lip, and Hayden groaned. It had always driven him crazy. "You're making this really fucking hard."

"Am I?" I teased.

Hayden took a step closer, and I backed up into the cabinet. He leaned in, and I felt his breath tickle my neck. "You know what you're doing."

"Maybe."

He pressed his lips against my neck. "Payback, sweetheart," he whispered.

The words sent goose bumps racing down my arm. "I look forward to it."

Paybacks from Hayden normally led to amazing orgasms. I'd always loved getting him wound up.

Slowly, he backed up. "Game on, Kory."

"Game on."

I couldn't stop smiling as I grabbed the dinner plates. The chicken turned out well for not following a recipe. Halfway through our meal, as we were enjoying each other's company, Hayden was about to say something when his phone rang.

"Hey, Eric. Oh, man, I'm so sorry. Yes. Of course. I'll be there in just a few." He hung up the phone with a grim look on his face. "That was Eric Hensley, a longtime friend. His mom has been rushed to the hospital in Anchorage. He asked if I could fly him up there."

"Oh, no. I'm so sorry to hear that."

He looked down. "I don't want to leave you tonight, but…"

No, he had to go. "I'll be fine. I promise. Please take your friend and don't feel bad. Right now, getting Eric to his mom is the most important thing. Why is she in Anchorage?"

"She's in a nursing home up there. It's been tough on Eric and his brother. His mom refused to move in with either of them."

Hayden grabbed his plate.

"I'll get it. Grab your stuff."

"Thanks, sweetheart." His eyebrows were pinched as he turned to leave. "Will you drive me to the airport? I want you to have the truck while I'm gone."

"Of course."

Hayden still looked torn as he left the room. It made me feel warm all over knowing he wanted to be with me as much as I did him. And regardless of what was happening, he kept me at the forefront of his mind.

I knew for certain my heart belonged to Hayden Foster in every way.

CHAPTER
Thirteen

Kory

My heart hurt for Eric. When I'd seen him for those few minutes I'd helped at the hangar to expedite their takeoff, he'd been distraught. Since Anthony had already left, I helped close everything back up before heading home. Hayden was going to call when they landed.

When I got back to the house, I turned off the truck and sat back for a moment. The lights from the living room cast a glow into the yard. This was the most perfect home. I imagined kids running around the yard with laughter filling the air. That had always been a dream of mine: happiness.

One day.

This place was our home with no strings other than taking care of it. The feeling was exhilarating. I relaxed my shoulders and reveled in the moment as the ghosts from my past receded. Maybe I would contact my parents sooner rather than later. I wasn't sure. But I knew I would never go back.

Another set of lights pulled up the driveway. I froze, waiting to see who it was. I wasn't expecting anyone, so the unexpected company put me on edge. I put my hand on the keys, prepared to leave if need be.

The set of lights became a familiar red truck, and Alexa pulled up, waving. The tension eased; I hadn't realized how stressed I was thinking my parents were here to confront me before I'd even mentioned my location.

I savored the clean, crisp air as I got out of the truck. Each day, the hours of sunlight grew fewer and the temperatures dropped a little more. Within the week, we were supposed to get snow. I couldn't wait.

I waved. "Hey, Alexa."

"Hey! Hayden called to let us know he was flying up to Anchorage. I had a thought after we hung up. If you're up to it, we could have a girls' slumber party tonight."

"Really?"

"Yeah, I can call Devney, too. It's up to you; we don't have to do it. I just didn't think you'd want to be alone your first night in Skagway. I know I wouldn't."

That was so thoughtful. I hadn't given it much thought because Hayden needed to be there for his friend. "I'd love that. I have some cold chicken parmigiana in the kitchen we could heat up."

Another set of lights came up the drive, and I stiffened a little.

"That's Drake. He's bringing me some things. I was at the clinic finishing up paperwork with Devney when Hayden called."

I looked back to Alexa. "Oh, I hope Hayden didn't put you up to this."

"Nope. He doesn't even know. He couldn't get ahold of Drake and wanted us to know he was leaving town."

Wow. She had done this just because. It made me giddy. *A slumber party.*

The truck came to a stop, and even though Alexa had assured me it was Drake, my back tensed.

I was a little nervous meeting one of Hayden's brothers without him here. *Remain calm. It'll be fine.* A large, muscular man got out of the truck. In the glow from the porch lights, I could see that Drake had short, dark brown hair. He had the same foreboding presence as Hayden did. From a distance, it was intimidating, and my nerves ratcheted up.

"Hey, baby," Drake greeted his fiancée.

Alexa walked over to him, and he drew her in close. It seemed like such a natural gesture, but it had an intimate feeling, as well. They really appeared to be in love.

Drake tucked Alexa into his side and turned. "Hi, I'm Drake Foster."

"I'm Kory. Kory Reynolds. It's nice to meet you."

"Likewise. If you need anything, give me a call. Lex will give you my number, and you have hers, I'm sure. But I mean it, if you ever need something, call any of us."

Wow. I was momentarily stunned by the offer. "Th-thank you. That means a lot. I know Hayden told you about my… err… um… circumstances. And I know it's not the tradition—"

He held up his hand. "You don't have to explain anything. Past is the past. Just focus on you and Hayden."

That was a good way to look at it. "I will."

He looked at Alexa. "I'm going to stay at the Red Onion tonight, so I'll be close if you need anything."

They probably wanted a little privacy. "I'm going to head inside. If you want to stop by for breakfast in the morning, feel free. I can put on some sort of casserole."

"Thanks. I'll never pass up food."

I walked inside and closed the door. It was hard to contain my excitement. A girls' slumber party. I never had one in high school—or college. It would have been too hard to explain my parents randomly dropping by or the number of rules I had to follow. So I kept to myself.

I reheated the chicken and busied myself with tidying up the place—not that it was messy. But it felt weird standing around waiting for Alexa to come in. I lit the apple pie candle I'd bought when Hayden and I were in town today, and its sweet cinnamon scent filled the air.

Alexa came in carrying her bag. "It's been so long since I've had a slumber party. I'm looking forward to a night of unwinding."

It would definitely be nice to unwind. "Did you want to ask Devney?"

"Sure, I'll text her. After you left today, she said she hoped we could get together soon."

That made me feel good. "Hopefully, she can come. Hayden and I bought a bottle of wine earlier today we can have with dinner."

Alexa pulled out her phone and sent a text. Almost immediately, she got a response. "Devney's in, and she's bringing more wine."

"Good!" I pulled out a couple of plates for dinner and some wine glasses. Alexa followed me into the kitchen. I loved all the state-of-the-art appliances. The gas stove was to die for.

Alexa seemed a little uncomfortable as she looked around

the room. As I opened the wine bottle, I said, "I'm going to be honest. I'm nervous. This is a first for me."

Alexa put her bag down. "Well, it's practically a first for me, too. My other slumber parties in high school normally ended up with Drake coming to get me."

"Why?"

Her brow creased a little. "My best friend in high school was pretty selfish. She ditched me on a regular basis."

That made me feel oddly better, but sad for Alexa at the same time.

Alexa put her hand on my shoulder. "Just be yourself."

"I can do that."

I poured us each a glass of wine while the chicken warmed up. "So, how do you like the house?"

"It's like a dream."

"I'm so glad. After my dad died, my mom gutted the place and sold everything from my childhood. I still feel like a stranger here."

I paused and turned to Alexa. "I'm so sorry about that. Sometimes it's the shittiest hands we're dealt that make us realize how much we have."

"Yes, it is."

Knock.

Knock.

Knock.

"Want me to get that?" Alexa asked.

"Please."

A few moments later, Alexa came in with Devney, who looked super casual in jeans and a sweater. "I brought wine."

Now there were six bottles. Alexa laughed, "Well, instead of a glass, I think I'll just take a bottle."

We laughed, and each grabbed one. "I can definitely use more wine tonight."

Devney grinned. "I wasn't sure what anyone drank so I grabbed a few bottles. I'll take the white wine if no one wants that bottle."

We motioned for her to take it. After uncorking our bottles, we held them up. Alexa said, "A toast: to new friendships."

New friendships, indeed.

CHAPTER Fourteen

Kory

We poured more wine as we sat in the living room. Now I understood why girls had sleepovers so often growing up.

We were all a little tipsy. Devney had resorted to using a straw in her bottle. She'd found some gigantic ones in her bag. As she struggled to get the straw in her mouth, Alexa and I giggled. Devney was slowly coming out of her shell. She'd taken off her shoes and put her glasses aside.

Alexa held up her glass. "A toast: to …"

We waited for her to finish and then laughed when nothing else came out. For the last couple of hours, we'd been toasting anything and everything; the blue sky, penises, orgasms, and carrots. Quite the combination.

My phone rang. I picked it up with a lot of enthusiasm when I saw the name. "How-dy! Hunny! Boo Boo Bear!"

Hayden paused. "Howdy? Boo Boo Bear?"

"Aww, you like your new name?"

The girls snickered, and I couldn't help but join in. I had no idea where that name had come from. So I took another sip.

Hayden chuckled. "Have you been drinking?"

I looked at the girls. "Psst... Hayden wants to know if we've been drinking?"

They shook their heads. "Don't tell him!"

"Sober as a gober."

"Gober?" he asked.

Gober? Where the hell did that come from? "Well, it rhymes with sober. Kind of. If you mispronounce it. Just go with it. What should we toast to?"

"Toast to?"

"We need a toast. We've done big penises, amazing orgasms, orange carrots, juicy pineapples, furry puppies."

There was silence for a second.

"Hayden."

"Orange carrots are important."

I whispered, "He thinks orange carrots are important, too."

Alexa fist pumped. "I knew that was a good one."

"I'm glad you're having fun. Call me when you wake up." He paused for a second. "Toast to happy endings, sweetheart."

That made my insides go mushy. "Aww... this is why I love you."

"Love you, too."

I ended the call and lay back in my chair. "I think he bought us being sober as a gober." That drew more laughter from the girls. "Oh, and we're supposed to toast to happy endings."

We all sighed and toasted.

"Hear, hear."

Devney leaned in to Alexa and me. "I have a secret."

"Oh, a secret!" I said. So far, I'd decided not to tell her about my situation. Maybe I would eventually. With my fuzzy brain, it was hard to focus on not saying anything.

Devney leaned in further and waited for us to join her. This was going to be good. I loved juicy secrets. Alexa and I were perched on the black leather chairs, anticipating.

Devney lowered her voice and picked up her glasses. "These are fake. Completely fake."

We fell out of our seats in hysterics.

"What?" Devney asked. "They make me look smart."

"I—I—I thought you were going to tell…" Alexa could hardly get the words out.

I finished her sentence for her. "We thought you were going to bring up Hollis."

"I think my secret about my glasses is so much better than my attraction to Hollis."

Again, for the hundredth time that night, we couldn't contain the giggles. This was the best night of my life.

Light streamed in, and I winced against the sunlight. Oh man, we'd had a lot to drink last night. I could smell the wine as if it was oozing from my pores. Or maybe it was the empty wine bottles on the coffee table. Throughout the night, I think we'd drunk everything Devney brought. From the pounding in my head, I knew I'd overdone it. I'd only gotten drunk alone a few times in college because I couldn't trust myself not to say something that would alert others to how controlling my parents were.

When I stretched, my feet brushed against something. I withdrew them quickly when I felt Devney. We'd slept on our respective sides of the couch. I cracked my eyes open a little more and saw Alexa in the chair, her arm covering her face. We were going to be in rough shape this morning.

The hammer in my head increased, and I closed my eyes against the pain. When we'd decided to call it a night, heading upstairs had seemed like an impossible feat. So we decided to stay downstairs. Now I wished we'd crawled up the stairs. At least there I could draw the curtains and go back to sleep.

Knock.

Knock.

Knock.

Someone was at the door. *Why, cruel world, why?* I didn't want to move. The other two girls groaned.

"I'll get it," I whispered.

I opened the door to Drake, who stood there, fresh as a daisy. Me, on the other hand? Well, I felt like I'd been run over and pitched into a ditch. I croaked out, "What time is it?"

He checked his watch. "A little after nine. That was the time for breakfast, right?"

"Oh, shit." I slapped my hand to my forehead and then groaned loudly from the pain. "I completely forgot."

He chuckled and came into the house with a box. Alexa walked up to Drake, saving me from my embarrassment. She yawned, "Morning... I hope. My head is pounding."

From his pocket, Drake brought out a bottle of aspirin. "I also have some Gatorade and donuts in the box. Should help with those hangovers. Well, not so much the donuts, but I figured you probably wouldn't feel up to cooking this morning."

"You are amazing. This is why I'm marrying you."

Alexa and I took some Gatorade and aspirin. Devney hadn't moved yet. The cool, refreshing liquid helped. At that moment, I'd have done anything to dull the throbbing pain behind my eyes.

Casually, Drake leaned against the counter, a mischievous smirk on his face. "Did you guys happen to drunk text anyone else?"

I gasped.

"Drunk text?" Alexa's nose scrunched up.

Did we? So much from last night was still a little foggy. The humor in his eyes led me to believe there had been quite the drunk text marathon. "You girls may want to check your phones."

What did we do? Alexa and I scrambled toward our phones.

Devney was sitting up and rubbing her eyes. "Who's here this early? My head hurts. What are you guys doing?"

Devney sounded as rough as I'd felt when I first woke up. As soon as we found our phones, she'd need to get aspirin and Gatorade.

"Drake. He said we need to check our phones. Something about drunk texting."

I threw the blanket on the floor.

"What?" Devney asked, joining the search.

Eureka! My phone had been wedged between the cushions. I opened my text messages and saw the last text was from a group chat. It had me, Alexa, Devney, Hollis, Hayden, and Drake on it.

Oh no. It all started coming back to me when I opened the

texts. And judging by the groans from the other girls, they were remembering, as well.

Alexa: *Helloooooz to you!*

Drake: *Hey, baby. You headed to bed?*

Alexa: *Noo way. The night be young. We gonna keep toasting like it's hot.*

Drake: *You drunk?*

Hayden: *Keep it clean, bro. They've got us all on here.*

Hollis: *I second that. Some things can't be unseen.*

Drake: *Who the fuck is on this?*

Alexa: *Girlz and boyz.*

Me: *I a girl.*

Devney: *Me girl, too.*

Hollis: *I'll play along. I'm a boy.*

Hayden: *Hell, I'll play, too. I'm a boy.*

Drake: *I'm not a boy. I'm a man.*

Hollis: *Changing mine to Alaskan man.*

Hayden: *Alaskan pilot man.*

Drake: *I'm sticking with man. It stands all alone. No need to fancy that shit up.*

Hollis: *Man.*

Hayden: *Man.*

Drake: *You girls still there?*

Alexa: *We paused. Wine. I spokes gurl for group. We have secrets to tell.*

Drake: *Oh, hell.*

Hayden: *Maybe we should put the phones away.*

Hollis: *Intervention needed, stat.*

Alexa: *Nooooo... truths set you free. Beee free!*

Devney: *FREE!*

Me: *Let freedom ring!*

Alexa: *What they said. Wanna hear our psssttt secrets?*

Drake: *This is going to be good.*

Hollis: *Or terrible.*

Alexa: *Hollis equal spoil sport. Drake first.*

Hollis: *I am not.*

Alexa: *Are so.*

Hollis: *Am not.*

Hayden: *Am I going to have to send you two to time out?*

Alexa: *He start it.*

Hollis: *Actually, if you scroll up, you'll see you started it.*

Drake: *Go ahead, baby. Tell me your secret.*

Alexa: *I love you.*

Drake: *I love you, too.*

Alexa: *That's it.*

Drake: *Perfect. Next person.*

Hayden: *What the fuck? That wasn't a secret.*

Hollis: *This is like watching a train wreck and unable to do anything.*

Alexa: *Hayden, next.*

Me: *It's my Boo Boo Bear!*

Hayden: *Kory loves me. I love her, too. That's so sweet. Next person.*

Alexa: *Haha! Yes, but that not all.*

Hayden: *Oh, shit.*

Drake: *Wait, let's back up to Boo Boo bear.*

Me: *That's my name for Hayden. He luuurves it.*

Drake: *Oh, really. That is good to know.*

Hayden: *Fuck a duck.*

Drake: *I'm texting Kane now.*

Hayden: *Asshole.*

Alexa: *Focus! This is not about duck fucking. This is about the pssst secrets.*

Drake: *Go ahead, baby. Continue. Boo Boo Bear is ready for his next secret.*

Hayden: *Double asshole.*

Alexa: *Kory wants more. #wink face#*

Hayden: *Consider it done.*

Hollis: *I'm going to get some disinfectant for my poor phone and bleach for my eyes. That wasn't very code-like, Alexa. And I just don't have anything for Boo Boo Bear. It's not very... Alaskan. Or I hope it's not.*

Alexa: *Let's got a woot woot!*

Me: *Woot! Woot!*

Devney: *Woot! Woot!*

Alexa: *Hollis, your turn.*

Hollis: *Let's pass and say I did.*

Alexa: *Spoil sport. Or maybe it the lovebug?*

Hollis: *Like I've said before. It's impossible for the love bug to bite me. The farthest north you'll find it is in Florida.*

Alexa: *...*

Hollis: *What's ...?*

Alexa: *You putting us to sleep. BAHAHA!*

Hollis: *You're so funny. Well cheerio. Let's call it an evening.*

Alexa: *You funny, Hollis. We have more psst se-cretsssss!*

Hollis: *Why don't you call Drake and tell him your psst secrets?*

Alexa: *Hold pleaze. I'm ignoring spoil sportz messages. We're discussing our pssst secrets.*

Hollis: *There's more than one?*

Alexa: *Duh to the muh! It's gurlz night.*

Drake: *This is getting interesting.*

Hollis: *Or totally boring.*

Hayden: *I'm popping popcorn.*

Drake: *Does Boo Boo Bear share?*

Hayden: *Not with assholes.*

Alexa: *I make deal, Hollis.*

Hollis: *Lay out the terms.*

Alexa: *Extra week off for my wedding.*

Hollis: *Deal.*

Alexa: *The tribe has spoken. No more psst secrets. Night, men.*

Devney: *Night, men.*

Me: *Night, men.*

Devney: *I can't believe he fell for it.*

Me: *Me either.*

Alexa: *Me, too! Best plan ever.*

Devney: *Why are we texting? We're in same room.*

Me: *Cuz we're soooo drunk.*

Alexa: *True dat.*

Drake: *Sweetheart, you're still on the group text.*

Hollis: *Well played, my friend. Well played.*

Alexa: *Haha! Oops! I still get it!*

Hollis: *Of course.*

Alexa: *Oh, and Devney wants everyone to know ... her glasses be fake.*

Hollis: *Fake?*

Alexa: *They no worky.*

Devney: *But they smart.*

Alexa: *True dat.*

Me: *True dat.*

Alexa: *Night, men.*

Devney: *Night, men.*

Me: *Night, men.*

Drake: *Night, baby. I'll bring by breakfast and some aspirin in the morning.*

Alexa: *Luuuv you.*

Drake: *Love you, too.*

Hollis: *Night to all. And to all a good night.*

Drake: *Let's give a special good night to Boo Boo Bear.*

Hollis: *Night, Boo Boo Bear.*

Alexa: *Night, Boo Boo Bear.*

Devney: *Night, Boo Boo Bear.*

Me: *Hollis: Night, Boo Boo Bear.*

Hayden: *Night, sweetheart. And to the rest, here's my middle finger.*

There had been another text from Hayden to just me.

Hayden: *Sweet dreams, Kory. I miss you and can't wait to have you back in my arms.*

Kory: *Miss you, too. Hurry home.*

Hayden: *I plan to.*

"Oh, my word."

The three of us looked at each other and started laughing all over again.

Devney gasped. "Oh dear. I thought I dreamed about this. Well, it's out there. My glasses are fake."

That brought around another set of giggles. Who cared about the pounding in my head? Drake had a smirk on his face. "I'm glad you girls had fun."

Devney bolted upright, apparently realizing the time. "Oh, dear. I have a music lesson in ninety minutes. I'll see you guys later. Had a lot of fun."

"Wait, take some aspirin and Gatorade," I said.

Devney grabbed both, and in a flash, she was out the door. I waved bye to her from the front porch. I was so glad she'd come. We had connected as friends in a way I never thought possible.

As she drove away, I thought back on our conversation with Devney last night. We'd only had about half a bottle of wine by that point and had still been relatively sober.

We'd moved to the living room after eating dinner. All of us had changed into our pajamas and were enjoying the heat from a low fire burning in the fireplace.

Devney had taken another sip. "Can I get your advice?

And it stays between us?"

"Sure," Alexa and I had replied in unison.

"So... Hollis and I slept together." Alexa had gasped with this information, but Devney continued her story. "Afterward, I got scared and told him I wanted a relationship with no strings. He seemed okay with it, but then today he said he couldn't do it."

Alexa had leaned forward. "So... you just want to be fuck buddies?"

"No, I want that toe-curling love, but I'm scared of what people will think. Hollis has so much money. And I've had to take a third job."

I'd scooted over closer to her. "Devney, what you have or don't have doesn't matter. If you like each other, that's what counts."

"I guess. I think I've just made a mess of everything. Hollis must think I'm crazy."

Alexa had smiled. "No, I think he likes you, too."

She'd looked so sad and utterly defeated. "What do I do?"

"Tell him the truth," I'd said. The truth was always better than the lie. If I hadn't told Hayden the truth about how I felt, we wouldn't be together.

For a second, Alexa had just stared into her wineglass. "I probably should take your advice, too, Kory. I've been putting off setting a wedding date because I'm scared to ask Ike to walk me down the aisle. Drake mentioned asking him to be his best man, which means he'll need him, too."

My heart hurt for Alexa. I hadn't lost my father, but mine had been cold and distant my entire life.

"I'm afraid that I'm going to wake up and this will all be a dream," I commented.

Devney had grabbed my hand and then Alexa's. "Alexa, Drake is amazing and loves you so. Just talk to him. And Kory, Hayden is over the moon for you. I've known the Foster men all my life, and let me tell you… he's smitten as a kitten."

It was hard to believe I'd been in Skagway for only twenty-four hours yet felt more at home than I ever had in my entire life. People I'd barely met were more like my family than my own flesh and blood.

CHAPTER Fifteen

Kory

After showering, I pulled my hair on top of my head in a messy bun before heading downstairs to grab a donut. The hot water had helped to flush out the alcohol lingering in my system. And the smell of wine was finally gone. The thought alone made my stomach turn over. It would probably be a while before I could drink wine again. When I came down the stairs, Drake and Alexa were sitting on the couch. She was curled into his side.

"Can I get you guys anything?" I asked to fill the silence.

I fidgeted with my hands. Drake seemed nice, but I still didn't feel like I knew him well enough to be casual. It was nothing he'd done. I was scared I would mess up and make the wrong impression. *Old habits die hard.* For my entire life, I'd had to watch every move I made, ensuring it was the right one. And now… it was just me living in the moment. I loved it, but it kept me on edge at the same time.

Alexa sat up with a big smile on her face. "We're good. Drake and I have decided to get married around Christmas. I'm going to ask Ike to walk me down the aisle today."

Drake looked like he might burst with excitement at finally having a date set.

That meant their talk had gone well. I sat on the black leather chair opposite them. "That's wonderful. Where are you going to have it?"

She shrugged. "I'm not sure. We're going to keep it family only, but I'd like it to be a place where I feel connected to my dad, too. I want to feel like he's part of it. We could have it at the cabin, but that isn't the feel I'm looking for."

An idea came to me. "Why not have it here? This is an excellent space to entertain. It'll be cold, of course, so outdoors is out of the question, but Ike could walk you down the stairs to the fireplace." I was getting excited, and I started to speak with my hands. "Since it'll be Christmas time, we could decorate the fireplace with heavy greenery and accent it with your colors. Give it a country feel like you initially described as home to me. Depending on the number of people, the dining room could make an excellent reception area for the cake."

Alexa's eyes were delighted. "Oh my! That's perfect. Have you done this before?"

"Well, I helped my mother a lot with parties. But I did graduate this last May with a degree in event planning. I'd love to help if you'd like."

"I would more than like. I would love. We'd pay you." Alexa was nearly dancing in her seat.

I flicked my wrist while shaking my head. "No, no way am I taking anything. Consider this my gift to you guys. Please."

"Yes!" Alexa stood up and we started jumping together. "Thank you. This is going to be exciting."

Things settled, and Drake stood, looking at his watch. "I need to get back to the Red Onion."

Alexa looked at me. "I'm going to go help Drake at the Red Onion. I'm going to help him get caught up with some paperwork. Do you mind if I run back by here later on after Drake and I talk about what we want?"

"Please do. I'm going to unpack, but I'll be here."

"Perfect."

From the look on Drake's face, I imagined he'd agree to anything if Alexa would marry him sooner rather than later. Weddings were such beautiful events. Every time I attended one, I was filled with hope. The day partners said their vows was a day of new beginnings. The couple's future was theirs to seize.

The house was quiet after everyone left. Unlike my house in Seattle, this place had a peaceful quiet about it. My house had been a tomb. I made some hot tea and decided to take a few minutes for myself outside on the porch.

The rocking chair on the back porch creaked as I rocked. It was a bit chilly on this October day, so I drew the blanket around me a little tighter. The sun cast beautiful rays of light on the field in front of me. There was a calmness that captivated me. It was still hard to believe this place was mine.

I allowed myself to get lost in thought. *How was I so lucky to meet a man like Hayden?* Fate had pushed me to go to Ketchikan. I smiled thinking about the first time I met him at Maggie's. We'd stared at each other from across the room for what felt like forever. I hadn't been able to take my eyes off him. A couple of weeks later, he asked me out for coffee. It was there I decided I wanted to experience raw passion with someone, and Hayden was perfect.

He was a bachelor.

He said he never wanted to get married.

He didn't want any strings.

After the first time we made love, I knew I was in trouble. There was so much more to what we had, and neither of us wanted to admit it.

The arrangement had been perfect... until it wasn't.

And now we were committed to each other.

I took another sip of my tea and closed my eyes. Hopefully in the next hour or so, Hayden would be getting home. He'd called to check in this morning before I'd gotten in the shower. As it turned out, Eric's brother, Scott, was on vacation with his family in California. So Hayden wanted to stay until he could get there. That poor family. My heart ached for them.

But I missed Hayden. We needed time together.

Just the thought of seeing him again brought the butterflies to the surface. This morning, Hayden hadn't mentioned anything about the text Alexa had sent. I didn't regret having her send it, even after I'd sobered up. I trusted Hayden to know when it was the right time. Maybe that was what had set me free for the next step. Or maybe I felt settled sooner than I'd expected. *Who knows?* All I knew was that I was okay with it.

Hopefully we were together sooner rather than later. I was ready to be in his arms as he made sweet, passionate love to me. There were no longer any secrets between Hayden and me. I truly wasn't afraid of what my parents would think if they found out. At first, when we met in Ketchikan, I was wary of communicating with Hayden. I never gave him my real number. I worried my parents were tracking my activity. The last thing I needed was them having Hayden's information.

My parents.

I wondered what was going on with them. If I'd stayed, Landon and I would have commenced our fake relationship by now. The thought made me sick. If Hayden hadn't showed up... I'd still be there trying to figure out how to leave. But I wouldn't have married Landon. The thought of going through with it turned my stomach. We only had one life to live, and mine would have been wasted. Completely.

I finished the last sip of my tea; the warmth felt good. It was the perfect balance in the colder temperature. As I set down my cup, my phone vibrated.

> **Hayden:** *I'm headed to pick up Eric's brother from the airport. Then I'll be headed home. Anthony is taking the tour for me this afternoon. I may have to take the one tomorrow. We'll see.*
>
> **Me:** *Is there anything I can do for Eric's family or help Anthony at the hangar? And don't worry about the tours. Do whatever needs to be done. I'm excited to see you.*
>
> **Hayden:** *I'll check with Anthony and keep you posted about Eric. I miss you, Kory. I'm sorry I had to leave right after you got here.*
>
> **Me:** *Hurry home. And please don't worry. It was nice hanging with the girls last night.*
>
> **Hayden:** *I'm glad you had fun.*
>
> **Me:** *I'm so sorry about Boo Boo Bear getting out.*

Hayden: *It's fine, sweetheart. I've got dirt on my brothers, too. I'm confident in my manhood enough to withstand Boo Boo bear.*

Me: *Good! See you soon.*

Hayden: *Can't wait.*

This was where I was supposed to be. There would continue to be a distant, dark cloud looming over me until I settled things with my parents. Maybe someday they'd come to respect my decisions. I wondered if they'd tried to reach out to me via email. I'd mentioned in my voicemail that would be how I'd reach out to them at some point when I was ready to talk with them.

Without meaning to, I drifted inside toward the laptop Hayden had left on the counter. He'd mentioned I could use it any time I needed. I went to the web address and logged into my general mailbox. Taking a deep breath, I waited for it to load.

I had two new messages; one from my mother and one from Landon.

I hadn't thought much about Landon through all this. Maybe I should have. I felt a little guilty having not given much thought to the shitstorm he was probably dealing with at home.

Which do I open first?

I stared at the two messages while I chewed on my lip. Opening the email was harder than I expected. I'm sure one was a reprimand from my parents. But Landon would be kind.

The worst one first.

I opened the one from my mother. The shouty caps in the

subject line irritated me. I hated shouty caps. I took a deep breath before I started to read.

Remember, they are no longer in control. You don't have to respond.

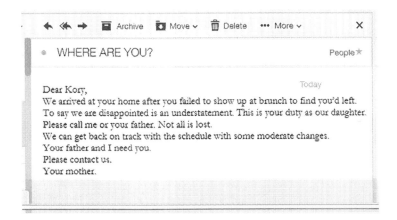

I sighed. The moment I told them where I was, they would be here within forty-eight hours. Guaranteed. And I wasn't ready to deal with the drama until I knew Hayden would be around. Plus, I wanted Hayden and I to have just a little more time together as a couple.

If I was a little more established with a job and a plan, I might feel more confident. If I could show them I could make it on my own, it might help convince them to stop this sham marriage with Landon. Maybe then they would respect my choices, and we could find a way to be an actual family. While doubtful, I remained hopeful.

Next, I opened the email from Landon.

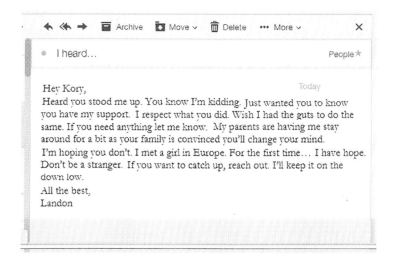

I smiled at Landon's email. He'd always been a nice guy. But that's all he had ever been... a nice guy. There had never been a spark that made my toes curl or the anticipation of when I would see him next. Yes, he was good-looking, some would say extremely good-looking, but he wasn't the one. He never had been or would be the person I wanted to spend the rest of my life with.

At some point I would reach out to him. But if his parents were monitoring his account like my parents were monitoring mine, they'd tell my parents in a second to help bring me back to my former prison of a life.

I would rather die than go back to that life.

Never ever again would I be controlled.

Never.

CHAPTER Sixteen

Hayden

I let out a deep breath as I got into the spare truck we kept at the hangar. Normally, we kept it as a courtesy vehicle for the summer when tourist season was high. But it wasn't something I advertised. Now, I needed it. Until we got Kory's car situation figured out, it would help us get by. Kory had about five thousand dollars to her name, and that wasn't going to get her a safe car for the snow and ice. This truck would be good. It wasn't as big as mine, but it was safe.

Anthony walked out of the hangar. "Hey, man, got a second?"

Shit. I'd meant to talk to him before I left. I was anxious to see Kory.

I shifted the truck back into park. "Sure, what's going on?"

"Well, I was thinking about Kory and her offer to help. Would she be interested in helping us clean up the files? It's a mess in there."

I smiled. "I'll ask, but I'm sure she would."

"Great. Since Sarah went back to school, things have gone to shit."

They had. Sarah had been a nice college student who wanted to spend the summer in Alaska. She'd made some serious improvements in our filing. "I'll check. Do you need anything for the flight this afternoon?"

"No, I don't think so. It should be easy. Just flying up to Misty Fjords National Park to do a lake landing."

I nodded. "If you need anything, let me know."

"Sure thing."

He rapped his knuckles on the hood of the truck before heading back inside. It had been a long couple of days, and I was ready to relax and just be with Kory. Eric and Scott were at the hospital with their mom. Before I'd left, they made the difficult decision about hospice. Her heart was giving out, and she was too weak to survive surgery. Eric's mom had decided she wanted to live out her days as comfortable as possible. She'd be buried in Skagway when she passed.

Life was a bitch at times.

I rolled my neck as I turned left to drive through town. I wanted to pick up some flowers for my girl. Last night, in the group text, Alexa hinted Kory was ready. One, she was drunk. And two, it felt too soon. I wanted it to be special. It might take some planning, but I'd figure it out.

Romance wasn't my thing. But for the first time, I wanted it to be everything Kory wanted. *What do I do? Fuck.* This must be what my mom referred to as courting. Hell, I was out of my league. Before I showed up to the house, I needed a game plan.

Otherwise, my dick would win.

There was one person who knew about this sappy shit. Hell, he'd built Alexa a cabin on the off chance she'd return to Alaska after she'd broken up with him. I dialed my brother.

"Hey, man," Drake answered.

"Hey, you busy?"

"Lex is finishing up lunch here before she goes out to talk to Kory about the wedding. What's up?"

Wedding? The last I'd heard, when Drake and I talked last night after the drunk texts, Alexa hadn't set a date. "So you've set a date?"

"Three days before Christmas."

"Congratulations, man. I knew you were stressing about that."

Drake sighed. "Yeah, thanks. Just a couple more months. What's going on?"

"Can I come by? I need some advice."

"Sure thing. Just come on back to my office. Want anything to eat?"

"Burger. Fries. And probably a beer."

"Sounds good. I'll get it ready."

I tried to focus as I drove to the Red Onion. Drake was so much better at this shit than I was. From the moment he met Alexa, he'd never hidden how much he cared for her. My other brother, Kane, refused to even acknowledge he had feelings. He was a brute, but loyal to the core. And I ended up somewhere in the middle. Feelings scared me, but deep down, I always wanted what Drake had. Up until Kory, I'd refused to admit it to anyone. The forever bachelor was mostly for show. I used sex to block out my real feelings.

A few minutes later, I pulled up in front of the Red Onion. Elvira and Sylvia spotted me and started walking my way. I dragged a hand down my face.

The last thing I wanted was to deal with them, but if I dodged them, they'd be after me like flies on shit. They were in their late sixties, but these women were full of pith and vinegar. At the same time, they were the heart of this community. Even though tourist season was over, they still had on what they deemed authentic gold digger uniforms in case anyone new came through town.

I got out of the truck and casually nodded to the Twiner sisters. "Afternoon, ladies."

"Hey, Hayden, how are you doing?" Sylvia asked with a sweet smile. Oh, she was trying to butter me up.

"Good. About to have lunch with my brother. How are you doing?"

She pulled out her pencil from her satchel and grabbed the notebook that dangled around her neck. "I'm glad I ran into you. You've been mighty hard to get ahold of lately." She paused, waiting for me to say something. I just tipped my head, hoping to get this over with sooner rather than later. "So, word on the street is you're taken now."

Yep, I was going to be in another newsletter. *Shit*. That would make two this week. *Double shit.* Now I knew how Alexa felt after first arriving. She'd made it in a couple of red hot *Twiner Tellings* emails. *Keep it casual.* I leaned against my truck like I had nowhere else to be.

"I've been seeing Kory for a while, but a man has to keep some secrets to himself." I gave them a wink, and they giggled.

"We can't wait to meet Kory. The poor dear. Alexa told us she has no family. We're glad she came to Skagway."

"Me, too."

They made a few notes. "Well, thanks for the interview. We just wanted to make sure we had our facts straight."

That was easier than I'd imagined. I owed Alexa big time for keeping the story uninteresting. I was about to say goodbye when Elvira asked, "Do you have Kory's email? We figure she'd want to be added to the *Twiner Tellings*."

There was no escaping it. I pulled out my phone and gave it to them. If I didn't, they would hunt Kory down.

"Oh, perfect. Thank you, dearie. It's a shame you aren't going to be in the bachelor auction this year. At least we have that yummy doctor." Elvira tucked her pencil into her gray bun.

Oh shit, poor Hollis. Each year, I had to fly out of town to avoid that damn bachelor auction.

"Anytime, Elvira. The ladies are going to have a real treat this year at the auction." I tipped my head. "Have a great day." I glanced across the street and saw Ol' Man Rooster. He'd be the perfect diversion in case they wanted to keep chatting. "Looks like someone may want to speak to you."

They giggled and headed across the street. "Bye, Hayden."

"Bye, ladies."

Ol' Man Rooster was the male version of the Twiner sisters. He knew everything about everyone. And he'd put his sights on Hollis, too. Poor Hollis was now the man Ol' Man Rooster wanted his granddaughter Marlena to marry. And she seemed to like that idea a lot. The *Twiner Tellings* had already matched them together and expected Hollis to go for a pretty penny in the auction. Throw in the Devney issue, and Hollis had quite the drama.

The Twiner sisters sashayed over to Ol' Man Rooster, who appeared happy to see them.

Crisis averted.

Hell, those women were tenacious. No one wanted to see them, much less talk to them, but everyone loved reading the newsletters for whatever antics they uncovered.

CHAPTER Seventeen

Hayden

I nodded to Drake's bartender, Crete, as I walked through the bar toward his office. "You feeling better?"

"Yeah, much better. I asked Drake if I could come in for a couple of hours to work. Doc Fritz said I wasn't contagious. Just some sinus issues." Crete was a good guy. He'd lost his dad in the same logging accident that had taken Alexa's father. Now he helped support his mom and siblings. The guy had a heart of gold.

"Good to hear. Keep feeling better."

"I will, man. Thanks. Drake is in the back."

"Thanks."

When I opened the door, Alexa was grabbing her purse.

She gave me a grin. "Hey, Hayden."

"Hey, Lex." I scooped her up, eliciting a laugh. When I turned to face Drake, he had a scowl on his face. One, he hated anyone else calling her Lex, and two, he was a bit possessive and didn't approve of the over-the-top hugs... which is why I did it as often as possible.

I set Alexa down and draped my arm over her shoulders. "You're engaged to the man, and he still can't stand it."

Alexa laughed. "You're incorrigible."

"Stop being an asshole." Drake pointedly stared at me.

I raised an eyebrow. "I'll stop on one condition."

Drake folded his arms across his chest. "And that is?"

"No more Boo Boo Bear. And make sure Kane stays off my ass about it, too."

Drake said nothing, just sat there with a smirk.

I pulled Alexa in for another hug. "I think I might just start calling you Lex all the time."

Alexa mashed her lips together, and Drake shook his head. "Deal. But you stop all that shit from now on."

"Deal."

That was easier than I'd expected. The nickname was funny coming from Kory... not my brothers, who would give me shit until the day I died.

Alexa patted my shoulder. "I'm going to let you boys have some man time. I have a proposal for Kory and want to talk to her about her wedding ideas. We're doing a Christmas wedding." She pointed at Drake. "Behave yourself."

He walked around the desk. "I'll walk you out. I'll be right back, dickhead."

"Okay, princess."

He flipped me the bird as he walked out the door. Getting under his skin never got old. Never. Taking a seat, I waited for Drake and let Kory know I had stopped to see my brother first. A couple of minutes later, he walked back in with a tray of food. The smells reminded me of how hungry I was. The last time I'd eaten was yesterday at lunch.

Drake set it down in front of me. "You're lucky I didn't spit in it."

"Dude, you make it too easy to aggravate you."

"Yeah, well now that you've got a girl, you'll see how it feels."

"We'll see."

Drake took a seat, nodding in a way that clearly said, *Yeah, we will.* Shit. "So, you'll be a married man in about two months."

"It can't come soon enough. Thank fuck Lex finally told me why she was stalling on picking a date."

I was ravenous. I took a bite of the burger and sighed. *Amazing.* "Why's that?" I asked around a mouthful of food.

"She was nervous about asking Dad to walk her down the aisle since I'd mentioned asking him to be best man. I should have realized it. We asked Dad, and he said he'd be honored. And we're keeping it simple. Kory suggested we get married at Lex's family's house. We love the idea."

"Wow, a lot happened while I was away."

"Yeah. I got to meet Kory last night and saw her again this morning. I like her. Lex adores her."

I had forgotten Drake stopped by to meet her. He was protective of Alexa and probably wanted to check out Kory, which I understood.

"I'm glad you like her. Means a lot to have the support of the family." Before things got too emotional, I changed the subject. "Hell, those text messages last night."

Drake laughed. "Fuck, they were funny."

"Yeah, they were."

He leaned back in his chair. "So, what's going on?"

My brother was never one to beat around the bush. He said what was on his mind and didn't mince words. Drake had been an old soul for as long as I could remember.

I took a swig of beer to wash down the burger. "This thing with Kory has me in knots. I don't know… it's just… I'm a wreck. I've never had a girlfriend—not like a real girlfriend, where it mattered. When she came back here, we started over. After last night, she's giving signals to move forward, which is a hell of a lot faster than I planned. She might think she's ready, but I think we need more time."

"Her parents sound like assholes. How's she coping?"

"They are. Everything about us isn't conventional. Yes, we like each other, love each other. But we're not to marriage proposal stage yet. I don't know. It's just so complicated."

Drake took a drink of his own beer. "Relationships are like that. Lex and I had to deal with her mother and sister, who hated me. Then all the shit when Lex's dad died. Are you afraid about what could happen if things don't work out?"

Maybe that was what scared me. I hadn't thought about it. "Well, yeah… I mean, I love her. She loves me. But we've never been in love before. Hell, I'm not making sense. I want her to see how much I care about her. Make it special. Then I worry she's not going to find what she's looking for here. What is she going to do here in Skagway? I mean… I just don't know what I mean."

For a second, Drake leaned back in his chair and steepled his index fingers under his chin. Finally, he said, "Lex has a proposal she wants Kory to hear. It has potential to be a job—a career."

"What is it?"

"I can tell you, but do you want to know or do you want

to let Kory tell you?"

He had a point. If I already knew about it, she might think I orchestrated it. I'd wait for Kory to talk to me. "I'll wait. So... what do I do about my other issue?"

Drake ran his hands through his hair. "When Lex came back to open the clinic, I had no idea how far I should push. How much help I should offer. When I should take it to the next level. What I did know was that Lex had to know I was there for her to support her dreams any way I could." Drake leaned forward. "You guys will figure it out. And you'll know when it's time to take it to the next level."

"How do you make sure it's not all about the sex?"

He shrugged. "I don't know. That wasn't an issue for Lex and me because we had a history. But maybe... you keep waiting for a bit. Plan something that has to wait until a certain date."

Drake had confirmed what I'd figured I should do.

He added, "If you want to see... take it out of the equation. You'll either get stronger or..."

We'd fall apart.

I let out a long breath before standing to shake my brother's hand. "Thanks, Drake."

"Anytime. Like I've told you before... the risk is worth it."

CHAPTER Eighteen

Kory

"What do you think of my proposal?" Alexa asked after explaining her business proposition.

It was like a dream come true. "I can't believe this is happening." *Someone pinch me.* Alexa's brows drew together, and I realized how I might have sounded. "I can't tell you how thankful I am for this. I never imagined something like this could happen. What made you think of this?"

Inside, I was screaming with excitement, but I tried to remain calm. My heart pounded double time, and my mind raced with the possibilities.

Alexa gave me a gentle smile. Her earlier concern seemed to have vanished. "When we were talking about the wedding plans this morning, I saw the fire in your eyes. It gave me the idea to keep this place running… not to mention the additional income source. Drake agreed as long as you were up for it."

Drake and Alexa had what I wanted in a relationship. They put each other first and cared what the other one thought. From what Alexa had shared last night, they acted as a unit. That was the kind of relationship I wanted.

"This… it's just amazing. It's an incredible opportunity. I promise I won't disappoint you."

Part of me wondered if Hayden had been involved in this idea. I hoped not, but I'd have to ask him to be certain. I didn't want to ask Alexa in case it made me seem ungrateful.

"I know you won't, Kory. So tell me, what do you think?"

My mind was awhirl with the possibilities. I ticked off the first few things that came to mind. I could clarify them later. "We could do bridal showers, baby showers, summer parties, weddings, birthday parties… the possibilities are endless. We could rent the space for photography sessions. The landscape is breathtaking. During the summer months, I can see photographers looking for a space that has beautiful grassy areas, mountains, water. It's magical."

"It is. My dad always told me he wanted his home to be the place that brought immeasurable happiness to his kids."

Kids. Without thinking, I asked, "Do you have any siblings?"

"One, but we're estranged. She's actually leaving the area with her husband and my mother to start over. It's hard to believe I'm related to them. We're like night and day."

My heart hurt for Alexa. She was so kind, but I could see the pain in her eyes. I reached out my hand. "For what it's worth, sometimes the best of family isn't blood related. Those who want to cause us harm don't deserve to be part of our lives."

As I spoke, the words rang true deep within. If my parents

didn't want what was best for me, they didn't deserve to have me in their lives.

Alexa said, "That's true. Thank you. I needed to hear that. It's hard, though, knowing people who are supposed to be engrained to love you don't. The rejection is hard to work through at times. It's… tough not being able to go to the one person you should be able to."

"I know. For me, I wanted to scream and cry out at times. But even if I had, my parents wouldn't have heard me. These hardships make us stronger people. It makes us want more for our kids."

"It does. Thanks, I needed that. Of course, I talk to Drake about it, but his family is fantastic and it's hard to comprehend when you haven't lived it."

I nodded in agreement. Alexa shook her head like she was chasing away the negative thoughts. "I love your ideas. I won't be able to devote much time, if any. This would be your thing all the way."

I scooted to the end of the leather couch. "I'll do everything. The income from the events could cover my rent and bills. I could create standard packages and customers could pick and choose options to add to make their event perfect. Then I'd set it up accordingly." I pointed to the chandelier in the living room and then turned toward the dining room. "This area is perfect for a dance floor or dining room. The three downstairs bedrooms could be used for dressing rooms or staging areas."

Alexa nodded approvingly. "Can you make a list of the things we'd need?"

"Yes, for sure."

Alexa stood. "What do you think about lodging?"

I thought about that as I walked around the room. "I don't think that's necessary, and if we don't go that route, it'll keep the downstairs rooms available depending on the event. I'd need your help with pricing; I have no idea what's reasonable for Skagway. We could offer a discount for locals to show support for our neighbors and work with the cruise lines to offer destination events to their customers."

For bridal events, we could set up the downstairs bedrooms for changing areas and bridal salons. There was a shed in the back of the house where we could store extra furniture. Maybe we could create a job or two for the people of Skagway if the business took off.

"It all sounds good. Right now, we only have the community center or the Red Onion, which isn't necessarily suitable for a wedding reception. I can think of several instances when someone wanted something different, but there wasn't anything available." Alexa's eyes lit up, and she snapped her fingers. "I have a cabin that belonged to my dad and his parents. It's got three bedrooms. We could add lodging there as part of the packages."

I was growing more excited by the moment. We could offer a deal, complete with lodging. If I was going to live here for the foreseeable future, I would rather not have people stay in the house overnight. When I got a place of my own, we could offer rooms upstairs, if need be. "That would be fabulous. We could offer a honeymoon package and have champagne on ice waiting back at the cabin. As part of my hospitality studies, I found that often it was the little things that matter. Customer satisfaction is in the details. It's what drives the five-star business ratings."

"I agree." Alexa stood, tucking her hair behind her ears.

"Put together a budget for me. And regardless, you'll live here rent free."

I gasped, shaking my head. "I can't stay here rent free."

"You'll be taking care of the house and the cabin. I was going to have to pay someone to do that. Or rent it out to some stranger I don't trust. I have faith that you're going to take care of this place like it's your own. Like I said earlier, there is no way Drake and I could take this on. So, it's a trade-off and takes a huge load off our minds."

This might actually work.

"I've talked to Drake. We can front the money to set things up. Once that's repaid from the income, what would you say to a thirty percent for me and seventy for you? We'd have to set up a percentage to retain for incidentals, but we can work that out."

My mouth fell open. *Seventy percent?* "What? That's too much."

"You'll be managing things completely. I'll provide the initial startup cash and the facilities, but after that the business should be able to support anything needed. You'll earn that seventy percent. And it's another source of income for us that we wouldn't have otherwise. What do you think?"

I jumped up and down. "I say yes. This is what I've always wanted to do. I'd like to talk it over with Hayden, too."

"Of course. He dropped by the Red Onion as I was leaving. I told him I had something I wanted to run by you but didn't share any of the details. I figured you'd want to do that."

So Hayden hadn't been involved. This offer had been made based on the abilities I'd exhibited this morning. It was hard to contain the giddiness inside. I never imagined I'd actually get to follow my dream and have my own career.

It was a win-win situation. I'd have a way to earn a living, and this created another income source for Alexa. Plus, it kept her extra homes in use instead of empty to deteriorate. I started making a list of to-do s. "When do you think I could see the cabin? And we probably want to make some time to get anything personal you don't want people touching out of there and figure out where you'd like it to go. Maybe set up an owner's closet for when you do decide to go there."

Alexa said, "Good point. Let's see… tomorrow is Sunday. What if we go out there before lunch? That way you'll be able to work on whatever you need next week. We could also review the initial list of supplies to get started."

"I'll pull some information together."

She reached out to give me a hug. "Great. See you tomorrow."

I was determined to make this successful. With enough blood, sweat, and tears, anything was possible.

I waved good-bye as Alexa pulled away. When I was alone, I danced around on the porch with my hands in the air, letting the pent-up excitement finally break free.

Life was perfect. Absolutely perfect.

CHAPTER Nineteen

Hayden

I pulled up to our new home and turned off the engine. It was hard to believe the woman I loved was behind those doors. As if my thoughts had reached her, Kory stepped out onto the porch. She was breathtaking, waving to me with an angelic smile on her face. How she managed to be so untarnished after the life she'd had was beyond me. I couldn't imagine a world where parents didn't put their kids first.

Kids.

I'd never really thought about having a family, but I realized it was something I wanted. Not right away,of course, but for the first time, I saw my path leading toward a family. Before any of that, though, Kory and I needed time to ourselves to ensure we built a solid foundation.

She took a couple of steps toward me and leaned against the white post of the porch as I got out of the truck. My heart was so fucking full—I never wanted to lose this simple moment. It was beautiful, and I fixed the vision in my brain. When things got tough, I would think about this moment.

I knew things wouldn't remain this simple. Our journey had just started, and life always had a way of throwing a wrench in things. Drake and Alexa were proof of that. But with love, anything was possible.

I grabbed the flowers I'd bought and got out of the truck. Kory's grin grew when she saw them in my hand. I'd found a small flower section in one of the stores in Anchorage. With winter coming, they were hard to find.

Kory was so beautiful. The dark circles had vanished, and the stress that had been visible on her face was gone. She looked so different from when she'd been in Seattle.

"Hey, sweetheart," I said when I was a few feet away. "It's so good to be back. I missed you."

"I missed you, too." Before I made it to the top step, she jumped into my arms. The paper wrapping up the flowers crinkled against her back as I held her. Kory brushed her lips against mine. "It's good to have you home."

Home.

I was home. Moments like these made all the other shit we were dealing with unimportant. I savored her sweet vanilla scent and squeezed her tighter with my free hand. "It's good to be home."

The words should have felt foreign on my tongue, but they didn't. "I brought you something."

I set her down and held out the flowers. Kory's eyes lit up. "These are beautiful. I love them." She tipped her head down to smell them. "This is the first time I've ever gotten flowers just because."

"Consider it the first of many."

She stood on her tiptoes and kissed my cheek. "I hope so. Let me get these in a vase."

As I watched her sashay back to the kitchen, I knew I needed to come up with a plan pretty fucking fast to be with Kory. "How was your day?"

"Fantastic. Alexa came by with a proposal, and now I have a job."

"She mentioned talking to you about something. I've been curious to find out what it is."

Kory beamed and animatedly started telling me about Alexa's business plan and how it came about. Her passion for the idea was clear. It was how I felt about flying. As I listened, I fell more in love with this woman.

After she finished, Kory took a deep breath and waited expectantly for my reaction. She didn't want to confirm with Alexa until she talked to me about it. Though I would never stop her, it felt good… like we were becoming a couple that were partners. "That sounds like a fantastic opportunity. If it's what you want, I say go for it."

She squealed. "It is. I can't describe it, but it's like everything in my entire life was leading to this. I have a purpose. Now, I need to get a car."

And that was the perfect segue to my offer. I knew it was important for Kory to earn her way. She needed this, and I wanted to support her. "I talked to Anthony about your offer to help. He had a suggestion. But don't feel like you have to say yes."

"Of course, I'll always be honest with you. What is it?"

"Our temp, Sarah, left when the tourist season ended a couple of weeks ago. Her position had been temporary, but since she left, we realized we need someone, at least part time.

It's been a madhouse keeping up with the paperwork. The office is a wreck. What would you say to working a few days a week for a couple of hours as your schedule permits? In exchange you can use the truck."

She cocked her head. "I would help you regardless. You don't have to pay me."

I took a deep breath, hoping this came out right. On the way home, I'd thought about the best way to present this without making Kory feel helpless or useless. "That's sweet of you. But I also want you in a safe vehicle with winter on its way. The truck has snow tires and chains and can handle the weather. After you experience a winter here, you'll know better what type of vehicle you want. And Anthony honestly wants out of filing the paperwork. Plus, he sucks at it."

For a second, she watched me and then winked. "Deal. As long as you and Anthony are okay with it."

"We're more than okay with it. Trust me. You'll be doing us a favor. And you can set your own schedule."

She jumped into my arms, wrapping her legs around me again. The happiness was contagious, and I spun her around.

"Thank you." She gave me a kiss. "Thank you." And another kiss. "Thank you." And another kiss.

Our lips stayed connected this time. I swiped my tongue against her lips and was immediately granted access to her mouth. She tasted of berries. Our kiss grew heated, and when she began to grind on me, I nearly lost all self-control. The kiss broke for the briefest of seconds. "Did you mean what was alluded to in the text last night?" I asked.

I wanted to be sure.

"Yes." Kory's eyes blazed with desire. I had my answer.

It took everything in me to pull back. "Then let me make

it special for you. It may take some time, but it will be worth it."

She searched my eyes and said, "I like the sound of that."

I had to figure something out—and fast. I walked us to the couch and sat. She kissed the side of my face and whispered, "Enough about me. How are you? Can I get you anything?"

I squeezed her tighter. Kory was so considerate, not just concerned with herself, but worried about me. All my life, I'd imagined all relationships were selfish after seeing several of my friends screwed over by girls. I thought my parents and Drake were exceptions to the rule.

I'd been wrong.

"This, right here, is all I need, sweetheart."

"Oh my, you are swooning me hard, Mr. Foster."

"I aim to please."

I felt my phone vibrate in my pocket and pulled it out with my free hand.

Mom: *We're going to have dinner tomorrow at the house. Would you and Kory like to come?*

Mom was probably chomping at the bit to meet Kory. I was surprised she'd managed enough restraint to stay away this long. Alexa had mentioned setting up a date for dinner, but I hadn't been able to connect with her about that yet. If it hadn't been so hectic, I would have already introduced them. I put the phone down and asked Kory, "Mom and Dad are having a family dinner tomorrow. Want to go?"

"Yes, I'd love to meet them. Who will be there?"

I liked that she wasn't nervous about meeting them like

she had been before. Instead, she seemed excited. "Probably Alexa, Drake, and maybe Kane. I'm not sure—he may be on a hunt."

"I can't wait. Let me know if I can bring anything."

"I will."

Me: *Sounds good. Kory wants to know if she can bring anything. What time?*

Mom: *How does 6 work? Alexa's bringing some cookies. No pressure for Kory to bring anything.*

"Mom said no pressure to bring anything. Alexa's bringing cookies."

"I'll bake a pie."

I whipped my head up to look at her. "The chocolate one?"

Over the summer, Kory had baked for me a few times. I loved her pie. Damn, her chocolate pie was phenomenal.

"Yeah, I'll make that. I know it's your favorite."

"May want to make two. The Fosters can put away a good amount of pie."

She giggled. "Two it is. Will you let your mom know?"

"Later. Right now, I want to focus on me and you." I gave her a brief kiss before settling into the couch. I was fucking exhausted, but I fought the need to sleep. I enjoyed having her in my arms. It wasn't too long ago I thought I'd never have her in my life again.

Kory turned on the TV, and slowly my eyes closed. I could never imagine my life going back to what it had been before Kory.

CHAPTER Twenty

Kory

We pulled up in front of a log house that looked like something from a movie. The green tin roof was a beautiful complement to the dark wood of the cabin. I bet in the summer it was magical against the green foliage that surrounded it. The colder autumn nights had knocked back most of the vegetation, and it wouldn't take but one or two frosts to completely kill what was left of the summer greenery. The long days of the summer combined with the significant rainfall created a rain forest with cooler temperatures.

In Ketchikan, the flowers were three and four times bigger than they were in Seattle. Mornings before working my shift at Maggie's, I used to take long walks and admire the untouched beauty.

Maggie. I had enjoyed catching up with her on the phone today. I hoped to go visit her at some point, but it most likely wouldn't be until the summer, once I got settled. I would fly up with Hayden on one of his flights.

Off to the side of the log cabin were two other trucks. I recognized Drake's, and I assumed the other one was probably Kane's. Or maybe it was Ike's, but I imagined his truck was parked in the garage or maybe in the shop he used for personal projects. Hayden had showed me the family lumber mill on our way here and told me all about his father's work. It was an impressive family business.

Tonight, I would meet the rest of the family. I tried not to think too much about it.

Everyone was so accomplished. I felt inadequate in comparison and maybe a little undeserving. I knew it was my insecurity talking—Hayden never made me feel anything less than perfect, but old habits were hard to let go.

I squared my shoulders and refused to let my nerves affect my meeting with them. Hayden's parents stepped out onto the front porch. Both had on jeans and a flannel shirt. They were precious in their most likely unplanned coordination. I hoped Hayden and I looked like that one day. It was like they were truly in sync with each other—picture perfect.

As we got out, Hayden took the pies from me. Hayden favored his mother in coloring, but he had his dad's build.

His mother came down the steps to meet us halfway. "You must be Kory. It is so nice to meet you. I'm Amie. This is my husband, Ike."

"It's nice to meet you, Mr. and Mrs. Foster. I've heard so many wonderful things about you." I hoped I sounded confident. I wanted them to like me.

His mother held out her arms to hug me, and I hesitantly stepped into the embrace. "Please, call us Amie and Ike. We're not formal at all. Come on in." Amie put her arm around my shoulder and guided me toward the front door. I looked at Hayden, whose warm, infectious grin brought a smile to my face. Amie stopped us before we entered the house. "I want to apologize on the front side for the boys' behavior. I try. I really do."

Hayden chuckled. "Mom, it's not that bad."

She tsk-tsked. "Alexa and I are so glad our ranks are increasing in numbers."

"I'm glad I can help even the playing field," I added.

Inside, the first thing I noticed was the homey feel I'd expected with the warm colors accenting the dark wood. There were several animals mounted on the walls including deer, moose, and a bear. Off to the left hung a series of beautiful oil paintings of what I assumed were parts of Alaska.

Alexa greeted me with a hug. "Hey there."

"Hey." I returned the hug, and when I drew back, I saw Drake. "Good to see you again, Drake."

"Good to see you, too." He approached me and whispered, "Just go with it. I'm trying to piss off Hayden."

In the next second, he picked me up in a bear hug and twirled me around. I laughed—I couldn't help myself. Hayden had mentioned how he liked to get under Drake's skin by doing the same thing to Alexa. Drake kept twirling me, and Alexa erupted in a fit of giggles.

Drake continued to spin me around.

"Okay, asshole, you've made your point." Hayden sounded grumpy, which made me snicker.

His mom chastised them both. "Language, Hayden. Drake, stop aggravating your brother."

"Sorry, Mom," they said in unison.

I nearly lost it hearing these men apologize. From the

sound of it, they'd done it a thousand times. Somehow, I managed to keep my composure. Alexa had her lips mashed together like she was fighting a smile.

Drake put me down. "Thanks for being a good sport. Hayden has been driving me crazy with that sh—stuff for years. How do you feel about me calling you Kor?"

Hayden smacked Drake on the back of the head. "Stop being a di—meaniehead."

I laughed again. I couldn't help it. This was what I always pictured a real family to be like. And I loved it.

Amie sighed. "Lord, give me strength. Dinner is in five. Boys, please don't scare Kory off, watch your language, and stop aggravating each other."

Ike and Amie left the room, and I relished the feeling of being part of a family for the first time since I was a child.

CHAPTER Twenty-One

Kory

There was only one person in the family I hadn't met yet. He had a husky, who sat beside him. I extended my hand. "Hi, I'm Kory."

"Kane." He gave my hand a quick shake before retracting his own. "Give my brother hell for me."

Hayden let out a huff. "Stop being an ass."

I tried to diffuse the arguing. "Nice to meet you. And who is this sweet dog?"

I kneeled and held my hand out to allow the dog to get used to me.

"Mariah."

"Oh my goodness, you're so pretty."

In two seconds, she was licking my hand. "Oh, sweet puppy kisses. I never had a dog growing up, but I always wanted one."

Kane seemed to soften. There was a harsh ruggedness

about him that Hayden and Drake didn't have. He was definitely a little more distant. I stood, and he nodded, "She's a keeper. I found her abandoned in the woods."

I gasped. "Oh no! I'm glad you saved her."

He nodded. Then he turned to Hayden. "*Meaniehead*? Really?"

Drake put his hand on Kane's shoulder. "Does he get the title of *princess* now? I think we've found someone more deserving of it than me."

Apparently, Drake had slept in one time and Kane gave him the nickname to irritate him. It stuck. These brothers were hysterical.

"Abso-fuckin-lutely," Kane said.

Hayden rolled his eyes and flipped them off. "Real mature, guys. Real mature. I'm not a princess."

Alexa gave me a wink. "This is why we needed more girls around here. At some point we're going to get enough votes for *Pretty Woman* instead of one of those action movies."

"Or *Steel Magnolias*. I love that movie," I said.

Alexa gave me a high five. "Me, too. I feel another girls' night coming."

The guys shook their heads, and Kane muttered, "I'm never watching that pansy-ass shit. Never. I'd rather have my balls in a vice."

I nearly choked at Kane's bluntness. Hayden had warned me about Kane, but it was hard to imagine until you actually met him. He really was an enigma. For the brief seconds we'd talked about Mariah, I'd seen him soften. He had clearly built up many defenses to keep people out. I recognized a wounded soul.

"The Foster men will continue to maintain the vote, guys. Sorry to burst your bubble," Hayden said.

Drake put his arm around Alexa. "Baby, we're going to have boys, and that's just going to put us more in the lead."

Alexa held up her hand. "Umm... medically speaking it's a fifty-fifty shot. We could have girls."

The men had a look of disbelief on their faces. Kane shook his head. "Foster men only have boys. And I'm not getting involved ever," Kane added. "Ever. So I won't be adding to the female population."

He seemed pretty resolute about it, which meant he was probably going to fall the hardest when he met his special someone. Hayden had also been against relationships. It only took the right person crossing your path to alter your world. I would know.

Hayden held up his arms in victory. "Problem solved. Action movies will continue to rule on Foster family movie night."

I saw Alexa's face soften at the mention of babies, and she and Drake stared at each other.

Then Kane hit Drake in the back of the head. "Keep looking like a pussy and you'll get the princess title back."

"Fuck off. The moment you get a girl, you'll have the princess title for life."

Kane looked smug. "Deal. But for now, the lovestruck puppy gets it."

"Agreed," Drake said.

Hayden blew out a breath. "You guys are such asses."

"Takes one to know one," Kane said and then gave me a wink. *Definitely an enigma.* But with that one gesture, I felt like I'd been welcomed into the family, which was important.

Kane didn't come across as a guy who willingly opened his arms to anyone.

These boys were a handful. My oh my, if Alexa and Drake had a bunch of boys, we'd all be in trouble.

Alexa seemed confident as she said, "At some point, we'll win. Just wait. It may not be in numbers, but we'll figure it out."

Amie walked into the room. "Dinner's ready."

In the dining room, there was a huge table with unique carvings around the lip of it. When I got closer, I could see that they were trees with the letter F in block lettering every eight or nine inches along the rim. It was incredible. "Wow, this table is beautiful."

"Thank you, my dear. I made it with the help of my boys," Ike said.

"Wow. Just wow. The craftsmanship is remarkable." Someday, I'd have to order some furniture from Ike.

Seated at the table, I ran my hands along the wood. It was so smooth. Amie brought in the roast, and succulent smells filled the air. I said, "This looks fantastic. Roast is one of my favorites."

"It's Hayden's favorite dish, too. I'll give you the recipe later if you'd like."

"I'd like that very much."

Amie handed the carving knife to Ike while saying, "And I can't wait to taste your chocolate pie. It smells delicious. I'd love the recipe."

"Of course. I made it for Hayden a few times this summer. I think it's his fave."

He gave me a wink. "It's out of this world."

It was enlightening watching this family interact with

each other with no pretenses. Kane added a one-word comment here and there, but he was definitely the quietest one of the group. Not any less part of it, just not as outspoken in everyday conversation.

When dinner came to an end, I helped Alexa and Amie clean up while the boys retired to the back porch with their pieces of pie and the cookies Alexa had made. They'd offered to help, but Amie shooed them out of the way. I believed it was to spend a little more one-on-one time with me. Whatever the reason, I enjoyed it. I put away the last dish while Amie poured hot tea for us to go with our pie.

"Mmm, this is amazing. Definitely want the recipe," Amie said.

The combination of chocolate, meringue, and pie crust was heaven. "I'll bring it by next week if that sounds good."

Amie's smile reached her eyes. "I'd love that. Just let me know what day. Maybe we could do lunch."

"Perfect." I looked at Alexa. The last thing I wanted was for her to feel left out. "If you'd like to join us, I'd love to have you."

"That's so sweet. But weekdays are typically a little crazy with the clinic. We're doing flu shots right now, which is adding to the already hectic schedule. You guys will have fun. Next time, we can do a group thing."

It appeared to be Alexa's way of letting Amie and I get to know each other, I imagined. From what I'd seen among my parents' friends and their families, at times, people became jealous with newcomers. This wasn't the case here.

Drake walked in. "Hey, baby, you ready to go home? We... uh... have an early morning."

There was obviously more to his comment, and I pressed

my lips together to keep from laughing. The Foster men weren't very subtle.

Alexa looked at her watch. "Oh my, look at the time. Night, guys."

It was cute that after dating for so many years, they were still so in love.

"Night," we called as they left.

Their departure left Amie and me alone in the kitchen. I waited for the nerves to come, but they didn't—I felt completely at home here. As the front door closed, I said, "They are amazing people. I've enjoyed getting to know Alexa so much. I've never met someone so kind. I don't think I'll ever be able to repay her."

"She has such a kind spirit and she's perfect for Drake. Each of my boys is so different. Drake, under his tough exterior, has a tender heart and knows what he wants. He's never been afraid of his emotions. Alexa fits him."

She patted my hand. "And it looks like Hayden has met his match. Underneath his tough exterior, he's a little unsure of how to process his emotions. You give him the time and understanding he needs to work through it."

Heat spread through my cheeks. "How can you tell after one night?"

"Mother's intuition. A mother always wants the best for her kids, but they have to find their way. And when they meet the right person, they bloom. Of course, my boys would roll their eyes at what I'm saying. But Hayden now has the same peace about him Drake does. He's beginning to realize that love is a strong and powerful thing. And it doesn't weaken you."

Amie was so insightful. I had to ask, "What about Kane?"

"Well, it's going to take someone as persistent and bullheaded as him to crack that exterior. But if she sticks with it, I imagine he'll be a marshmallow inside."

The thought made me giggle. "They say the toughest ones fall the hardest."

"That they do."

"Well, thank you for welcoming me into your home tonight."

"It's a pleasure. I've been excited to meet you. Alexa had a lot of nice things to say about you. It warms my heart seeing my boys' girls getting along. I'd always hoped that would be the case. I'm sorry I didn't come over sooner. It's so hard being a mother sometimes. I didn't want to smother you, but I also didn't want you to think we didn't care."

I reached out to Amie's hand. "No, I never gave it a second thought. It's been a whirlwind. I should have reached out as well but I was honestly nervous about what you might think. This wasn't the most conventional way to start a relationship."

She put her other hand on top of mine. "All that matters is how you and Hayden feel about each other. The rest will work itself out. Ike and I will never judge someone's past because that's what it is... the past. What counts is what you make of the future. If you ever need to talk or just want to chat, know you can call me. And it'll stay between us."

"Thank you. I appreciate it more than you know."

I took a sip of tea to get my emotions in check. With this family, I realized I was getting more than I ever dreamed I could have.

CHAPTER Twenty-Two

Hayden

A week later, I was at Hollis's apartment, which was upstairs from the clinic, sipping a beer. He'd texted me to see if I wanted to come hang with him before the town meeting tonight. After we shot the shit for about an hour, he said he wanted to show me something and disappeared into his room. I checked my watch. Fifteen minutes had passed. *What the hell is he doing?* We needed to leave in the next few minutes. It had been a hell of a week. Eric's mom had passed away, so Kory and I had attended the funeral. I couldn't imagine losing my parents at such a young age.

My phone vibrated with a text.

> **Kory:** *What time are you getting to the town hall?*
>
> **Me:** *Still waiting on Hollis. Might be a few minutes late.*

Kory: *No worries. We'll save you a seat. We're about to head there.*

"Hollis, hurry up. We're going to be late."
"Almost ready."
Almost ready? What the hell is he doing?
Bored, I began to look around. There was something on his coffee table that caught my eye. I picked up what looked like an invitation.

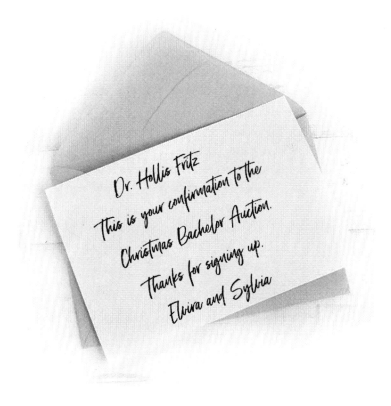

Dr. Hollis Fritz
This is your confirmation to the Christmas Bachelor Auction.
Thanks for signing up.
Elvira and Sylvia

I chuckled and glanced at the magazines scattered on his coffee table. They looked anything but intriguing. Medical journals were probably about as interesting as watching paint dry. Nevertheless, the boredom got to me and I began to skim through one. After one page, I nearly fell asleep. Something about antibodies and bacterial cultures. No thank you. The thought turned my stomach, and I set aside my beer after seeing one of the pictures.

Hollis and I had been hanging out more lately as his schedule permitted. It seemed like the girls enjoyed getting together. And Hollis was generally home reading and studying medicine. Lately, he was doing everything he could to avoid Ol' Man Rooster and his attempts to convince Hollis to wed his granddaughter. From what Kory had told me, Marlena dropped off baked goodies daily, and it was starting to piss Devney off. However, Devney hadn't retracted the fuck buddy statement.

It would be interesting to see how this played out.

Hollis finally came out of his bedroom wearing jeans and a flannel shirt. "I think this works for my first Alaska town meeting. What do you think?"

I cocked my eyebrow.

"Listen, I get it. I do. But Alexa is off with Kory and couldn't swing by to check it out. She's trying to force me to ask someone else to break the ice between us. But she didn't realize I could just ask you."

It sounded like Devney hadn't spoken to Hollis. Kory had hinted that I should get Hollis to talk to Devney, but she hadn't told me why. This week, Hollis hadn't seemed in the mood to talk about it. Maybe tonight he'd be more open.

Smirking, I said, "I'm glad to know I rank so high on your outfit-selector list."

Hollis rolled his eyes. I didn't typically talk outfits with guys, but with Hollis, that was part of who he was. He was obsessed with his clothing and wearing what an "Alaskan" would wear, doing what an "Alaskan" would do. "That'll work. Just don't bring whatever the hell hat you had on the other day."

"My Paul Bunyan hat?"

I cocked my head. "Didn't he wear some sort of beanie? That shit you had on was not a beanie. And he's not Alaskan, dude."

Hell, the fact that I knew Hollis referred to his hat as a Paul Bunyan hat was embarrassing enough.

He looked shocked. "That hat is a classic. Who cares if I have my folklore mixed up? He probably wanted to be Alaskan. And if Paul Bunyan had known about these hats, he would have traded in his beanie." Then he added, "How can you not like the hat?"

"It's a little... um... furry for my liking."

Hollis scoffed. "It's Alaskan. I'll get you one for Christmas."

Oh hell, now we were all probably going to get Paul Bunyan hats for Christmas. *Shit, now I'm calling them Paul Bunyan hats.*

Before I could respond, he added, "When we build my cabin, I'm going to stand on the front porch with red suspenders, my hat, and an ax."

"And hopefully jeans and a shirt. Otherwise, text me a warning so I don't pop by."

Hollis chuckled. "Will do."

"How are things with Devney going?"

He sat, all humor gone. "Man, I'm so confused. She wanted to be fuck buddies. I appreciate your advice, but I couldn't do it. I just couldn't play the games. I watched my mom and dad play those games in their marriage, and it nearly ruined them. That's not what I want. And starting off any type of relationship like that would seem to set the tone for the rest of the relationship."

That made sense. I wasn't sure what else to say, so I changed topics.

"How's your mom doing?" I knew Hollis had some turmoil with his mother about moving to Alaska.

"She's good. I think she's finally accepted that I've chosen this. We've been talking. And I think we're on a path to reconciling."

"That's good. I'm glad. That has to make things easier."

Hollis's phone rang. "Let me get this. I'll be right back."

One night, Hollis opened up completely about what had been going on with his mom and more about his parents' marriage. At first his mom had been against him coming to Alaska. But after they talked, he realized that it was that she didn't want him to leave New York after his dad shot himself. According to Hollis, her "communication method wasn't conveyed in the most productive way." His parents' marriage had been a tumultuous one, full of fighting and affairs. After a lot of thought, he decided that separate, his parents were great, but together, they imploded. That could have been why she played the games with Hollis. It was what she had been conditioned to do. Hopefully, they could work it out.

The more I thought about it, the more it made sense that he wouldn't do casual with Devney.

Hollis came back in the room. "Sorry about that. I got the top breast cancer doctor at the Mayo Clinic to agree to see Devney's mother. Dr. Devorak is going to prescribe a plan for Patricia to follow in Washington. He'll monitor her progress and adjust as needed."

"Wow."

"Don't say anything. I don't want her to feel pressured or that I'm forcing her into a relationship. It's just something I wanted to do for her. Hell, I hate seeing her working three jobs. Her brother's picked up another job, plus he's letting their mother live with him. The insurance their mother has is crap and isn't paying for much. So, I'm taking care of it."

I knew Hollis was a good man, but he just went up several notches in my book. Despite his quirkiness, he had a good heart. Tipping my beer to him, I said, "I won't say a word. That's mighty decent of you, Hollis."

"Let's just hope the prognosis comes back favorable and it's not too advanced."

"I hope so, too. I can't imagine. Let me know if there's anything I can do."

"Will do."

I finished my beer and we left for the town meeting. It would be the last one until our Christmas Jubilee, weather permitting. "So, I saw the confirmation for the bachelor auction on the table."

"Don't remind me. I'm still figuring out how to get out of it." He looked at me, his face blank. "Marlena told me earlier this week she would be sure to win the auction."

I chuckled. "Is there a wedding being planned I don't know about?"

"If there is, the groom has no idea about it, either."

"If you go missing, I'll check the chapel."

Hollis chuckled. "Good plan. I've got four weeks to figure out how to get out of both messes."

An alert on his phone caught Hollis's attention, and he checked his email. "Alexa's going to be thrilled. I was able to get the architect moved up to create the plans for the surgical room. The way it is now, the clinic has too many particulates, which could increase the chance for infection. But in a life-or-death situation, it's better than nothing."

"This town appreciates you being here." Over the years, so many people had died unnecessarily because the town didn't have a doctor.

"The feeling's mutual. I hope to take on an intern in a few years to help spread the word. I know there are other smaller towns in Alaska that need doctors. Maybe that will help encourage doctors to give it a try. We'll see. I need to operate my own practice for a few more years before any credible medical facility will let me be part of their intern program."

"That'll be good."

Hollis was a good man. By bringing attention to Alaska's needs, he was helping future generations get the health care they needed.

CHAPTER Twenty-Three

Hayden

As we pulled up to the parking lot, there were still cars arriving for the meeting, so we weren't too late. There were only a few minutes until the meeting started. Mayor Richards liked to be prompt.

Low murmurs filled the room as people lingered in groups and caught up with each other. Kory waved me over. Man, I loved having her here, watching her fit in. I loved everything about being in a relationship. She never pushed or demanded a definition of where we were headed. We both had an end goal of a family one day but wanted to enjoy the ride.

I sat down next to my girl and gave her a kiss. "Did you have fun?" I asked.

This afternoon Kory, Alexa, and Devney had baked cookies with the quilting circle for the town meeting. The quilting circle usually supplied refreshments for these things.

Kory was beaming. "It was a blast. I think I'm going to

learn how to quilt at the beginning of the year. Alexa and Devney are going to join, too."

"That sounds good. It's a good group of women."

"Yeah, they are. And they welcomed me right in. I can't wait to host their New Year's Eve party."

The ladies of Skagway went above and beyond to make a difference in our town.

Mayor Richards sounded the gavel. At the front of the room, Drake sat on the left side of the table. He'd been part of the city council for the past couple of years because he wanted to make a difference. I searched the room for Kane and found him standing in the back. Mariah sat beside him. The town had accepted Mariah wholeheartedly; it was just expected that Mariah would be there if Kane was.

The room quieted down. Hollis sat beside me straight as a board, eyes forward. From the corner of my eye, I saw Devney leaning forward to get his attention, but he refused to look.

The gavel sounded again. "Thanks for joining us tonight for our last town meeting of the season until our Christmas Jubilee."

The next moment, there was a loud clang as Hollis slipped from his chair. He quickly popped to his feet, his hand in the air. "All good here. No need to worry. Just a bit slippery."

The room erupted in giggles. Every single girl there probably had their eyes on Hollis. Mayor Richards smiled. "Glad to hear the good doctor came out unscathed. Thanks for joining us, Dr. Fritz. I'm going to skip ahead a few items. Would you mind joining me for a second?"

Hollis looked to me, and I shrugged. Alexa got up with her camera and stood against the wall. I had no idea what was going on. Hollis approached the front of the room, and Kory leaned over and whispered, "What on earth is he wearing?"

"His Alaskan gear."

She smirked, shaking her head. I noticed Devney staring at Hollis; there was so much emotion on her face. Leaning over, she asked, "Did he tell you what he did for my mother? My brother just called to tell me. I know it was him."

Her eyes welled up with tears. Hopefully they were tears of happiness. I wasn't sure what to say. "He's a good man."

She nodded, wiping at her eyes.

Mayor Richards put his arm around Hollis. "The town of Skagway appreciates you leaving New York City for an Alaskan adventure."

Hollis said, "It's a pleasure serving this great town I now call home."

One minute the man fell out of his seat, the next minute he was speaking in front of an entire town with poise. Hollis was definitely unlike anyone else I'd ever met.

"There's nothing we could do to repay you for what you're doing for this town. So we thought we'd honor you in another way."

Hollis gave an easy smile. "No repayment is necessary."

"Well, we think otherwise. First, we wanted to give you a key to the city and declare today to be Dr. Hollis Fritz Day."

Hollis accepted the key as the whole town applauded. "What an honor. I will hang this in the clinic and treasure it forever. Thank you."

Hollis looked at the key with pride. This meant more to him than he would ever let on.

The mayor picked up a plaque but kept it facing away from the crowd. "Also, as mayor of this town, I wanted to present you with your very own Alaskan certificate. It certifies you as a true Alaskan."

I don't think I had ever seen Hollis grin so big. He took the plaque and studied it. "I might blow this up and wallpaper the clinic with it."

Everyone in the room laughed.

He held the plaque close to him. "Thank you. Thank you for this. I'm so grateful you're not holding my coffee choices against me."

His easygoing nature only brought on more laugher. The mayor and Hollis posed for pictures. After Hollis sat back down, the mayor stepped up to the podium. "Next up on the agenda, Kory Reynolds has asked for a couple of minutes to speak."

Kory gave me a nervous smile as she got up and headed to the podium. This morning, she'd stressed over choosing her outfit. I thought she looked great in anything she wore, but apparently that wasn't the right answer. Finally, she'd decided on black slacks with a dark orange shirt. With Thanksgiving approaching, she considered it *festive*. She was calm and confident. "Hey everyone. As Mayor Richards mentioned, my name is Kory Reynolds, and I'm new to the area. This town has been so receptive, and I wanted you all to know I appreciate the kindness you've all shown. I'm looking forward to making Skagway my new home."

People applauded, and Kory paused. As it died down, she resumed her speech. "Alexa Owens and I are starting a new business that we wanted you all to be aware of. What used to be the Owens B and B will soon become a venue to host events such as weddings, bridal showers, birthday parties, retirement parties, girls' nights out, fundraisers, and so forth. In addition to the B and B, which is lovely, by the way, we will also offer lodging at the log cabin. If you're interested, please reach out to one of us. If you're a Skagway resident and book in the month of December for an event any time next year, you'll receive twenty percent off. I look forward to getting to know this town. Thank you so much."

Kory took a step away when someone called from the crowd, "Kory, how long before you open?"

"We'll be ready to host in three weeks. We're waiting on some supplies and some furnishings. For the month of December, we're running some great discounts, which would be on top of the twenty percent, while we work out the kinks."

"Great, I'll be in touch." It was Morgan, the loan officer, who had spoken. Maybe she was planning an event for the bank.

"Sounds fantastic. Thank you all."

The townspeople applauded, and I was filled with pride. Kory was in her element, waving as she walked back to her seat next to me.

"I'm so proud of you, sweetheart."

"Thank you."

I gave her a quick kiss while the mayor moved on to the next item of business. "For the new town sign, we're about two thousand dollars short. We'd hoped to place the order for it to be ready for the spring tourist season, but we're going to have to wait."

Elvira raised her hand as she walked to the front of the room. Sylvia wasn't too far behind. Of course, they didn't wait for Mayor Richards to call on them. They would start speaking anyway.

"Yes, Elvira and Sylvia."

Elvira nearly yelled her question. "Well, we want to know if we can do our fundraiser right now? It'll get us closer to the goal. We've got an idea that'll bring in the buckaroos."

The mayor looked to the city council, and each nodded. Drake had a smirk on his face, and he turned to Hollis.

Oh shit. Shit. Shit.

"First up, we'd like to call Kane Foster."

I looked back to where Kane had been standing. The emergency exit door was clicking closed, and he was nowhere to be seen. I chuckled. There was no way that bastard would stand up there for a bachelor auction. It was a good try on the Twiner sisters' part, though. But Kane would never be part of it.

Pulling out my phone, I decided to mess with him.

Me: *Hey, I saved a seat for you. Want to join us?*

Kane: *You're so funny, princess.*

Me: *I thought so. Maybe I should tell the Twiner sisters to go ahead and auction you for a later date.*

The next thing I got was a picture of Kane flipping me off.

I smiled. Then looked up after they called Kane for the third time. Sylvia leaned closer into the mic. "Oh, dear. I think we just missed him. Okay, on to the next one. Hollis Fritz, please come join us at the podium."

I looked to the seat next to me and saw it was empty. Hollis was halfway down the aisle. "Can someone stop the hottie doctor? He's trying to evade us."

Hollis turned around and smiled. "I was just getting some

coffee with my new plaque."

The town laughed, and Hollis turned to walk up to the front of the room. First, he stopped in front of us and leaned in. "Buy me. Whatever it costs, buy me, and I'll pay you back."

I nearly choked with laughter as he walked up to the front of the room. Hollis was a good sport. Elvira walked around him with her hands splayed out like Vanna White while Sylvia spoke. "The good doctor agreed to be part of our auction for the town fundraiser. We had planned to do it at the jubilee, but there's no time like the present. Now come on, ladies, what do you want to bid for a date with our fine doctor? We need to make some money for our new sign."

It figured the Twiner sisters would be so concerned about the sign. They loved tourist season and educating the folks on the history of Skagway.

Elvira leaned closer to the mic. "Who knows, it could lead to wedding bells. I know if I were a lot younger, I'd snatch up this whippersnapper. For the fun of it, I'll bid three hundred dollars."

Hollis's eyes grew round, but otherwise, he was able to school his features. I was about to laugh out loud at the thought of him going on a date with either Elvira or Sylvia. He turned my way, giving me the *you-better-bid-on-me* look.

"Three hundred and fifty dollars," Samone and Jane called out.

Hollis looked a little more nervous. He was moving from the elderly to the town ladies who liked to get around with the different men. I knew they'd been after Hollis, as well.

Marlena stood as her grandfather, Ol' Man Rooster, held up four fingers. She called out, "Four hundred."

"Five hundred," Samone and Jane countered.

"Five fifty," Marlena countered back.

Sylvia leaned in. "We have a 'win this hunk now' option for two thousand dollars."

"Two thousand dollars," a new bidder called out.

The voice came from close by, really close by. Like, two-seats-down close by. *Oh, hell yeah.*

Elvira put her hands up to her eyes, scouring the crowd. "Who said that?"

"I did." Devney stood. "I bid two thousand dollars for the 'win the hunk now' option."

Oh, holy fuck.

Hollis was transfixed as he stared at Devney.

"Sold." The sound of the gavel echoed through the room.

Kory squeezed my leg, and Alexa grabbed Drake. I swore I heard squealing. But we might have a war. I scanned the room to see what the losers had to say.

Marlena, Samone, and Jane were clearly pissed as they watched Devney walk up to the podium with her checkbook.

Ol' Man Rooster stood. "How about a second date auction?"

Elvira was about to say something when Devney leaned into the microphone. "I'm sorry, but Dr. Hollis is officially off the market."

That goofy-ass grin on Hollis's face was almost embarrassing. *Maybe I might be able to give him the princess nickname?*

Mayor Richards came back to the podium. "Well, looks like we have enough funds for our sign. Thank you, Elvira and Sylvia. And a huge thank you to Dr. Hollis for agreeing to help."

Hollis looked at Devney with an adoring smile as she

wrote the check. She adjusted her glasses. It was hard not to smile at the knowledge that they were fake and just for appearances. In some ways, she and Hollis were exactly alike: a little socially awkward with big hearts.

Kory whispered, "That's the beginning of a happily ever after."

"I think you might be right."

CHAPTER Twenty-Four

Hayden

I stood at the window, sipping a cup of coffee. A fresh blanket of snow lay on the ground. Yesterday, when the snow came in, I was concerned I would have to change our plans for tomorrow. If there was any moisture in the air, I couldn't fly due to freezing. I pulled up the weather radar app I used on my phone. For the next three days, we were supposed to have flyable weather. I only needed two—one to get there and one to get back.

The last week had been heaven and hell. Kory was driving me wild with her teasing. Ever since the town meeting, Kory had made it clear she was ready for the next stage. My *I want to make it special* speeches were becoming ineffective. We were two people about to explode from our pent-up sexual energy.

My original plans had fallen through five days ago due to weather. Hopefully, this worked. *The weather better hold out*

or I might lose my mind.
My phone vibrated with a text.

Arthur: *All set the way you requested.*

Me: *Thanks. Weather is doing as predicted. I'll be there around 3 or 4 tomorrow.*

Arthur: *That works. Key is under the mat.*

We were ready for the next stage. Tomorrow was the day. After being here together for over two weeks, it was obvious the relationship wasn't purely about sex. Every moment together was savored. Sex wasn't just about the orgasm, but about being with each other. I now understood what Drake meant when he said he had never been concerned that his and Alexa's relationship might have been based on sex.

We were the real deal.

In the last week, our schedules settled into more of a routine. Flying had been pretty much a no-go due to the weather. Instead, I worked at the hangar to get caught up. Kory came in for a couple of hours in the mornings and then worked feverishly for the rest of the day getting the entertainment planning business off the ground. Alexa's dad's cabin was ready to be rented. There were a couple of different groups looking to rent out the cabin for a week or two during January and February. The supplies had been ordered for the party planning. Things were on track.

And the people of Skagway were excited about the new event-planning part. The bank was going to host their Christmas party there. Then there was Drake and Alexa's wedding. Another couple was flying in to get married in the middle of

March and stay at the cabin for two weeks. Every booking mattered and brought their new company that much closer to operating in the black.

Kory had received an email that the chairs would be in Juneau within the next few days. Drake's delivery guy, Reeser, was going to transport them for us. After a long conversation, Kory and I had decided to front the money for the supplies ourselves. Alexa and Drake had offered, but it wasn't right. They'd done so much. And the percentage they were giving Kory was generous. Beyond generous. It was because of their generosity that Kory was able to jump into a career as opposed to waiting tables or being a receptionist at the hangar.

The money wasn't a big deal to me, but it was important for her to have this all to herself. So she'd only allowed me to help if I agreed that she'd pay me back first from the money she earned. I had so much respect for Kory. She wanted to work and do as much of this as possible on her own.

I heard the sound of feet on the stairs, and I braced myself. More than likely, she would be dressed in something skimpy this morning like she had been yesterday. Luckily, I had an excuse—had to meet Anthony early at the hangar.

"Morning, sweetheart," I called, still looking out the window.

Don't turn around.

"Morning." She put her arms around me, pressing her breasts against my back.

Fuck. Stay facing forward.

"Do you want some breakfast?" she purred.

I swallowed hard. "Umm... I'm good. I'm just going to have some coffee. Maybe go to the hangar."

There were only so many times I was going to be able to

use the hangar as an excuse.

She released me. "Okay, I'm going to make up some pancakes."

Crisis averted.

I heard the cabinet doors opening and closing in the kitchen. "Hey, Hayden?"

"Yeah?"

Please don't ask me to come in there. Please just tell me something that requires a verbal response.

"Could you come help me, please?"

Motherfucker.

"Of course." I set my coffee cup on the coaster and took a deep breath. *Stay strong. Only one more day. You can do this.* I kept this as my mantra as I walked into the kitchen. The refrigerator and freezer doors were opened so I couldn't see Kory.

Get in. Get out. Go take a shower.

"What do you need, sweetheart?"

"Can you get the glass pitcher in the top cabinet above the stove? I don't want to have to get the step stool."

Now I felt bad for not wanting to help. This was getting ridiculous. *Twenty-four hours. Only twenty-four more hours. Why did I decide to do this?* Stupid brother. If it wasn't for Drake and his over-the-top, romantic ideas, I'd be having sex right now.

"Of course. Let me get that for you."

Keeping my eyes facing forward, I opened up the cabinet and got the pitcher. If I kept looking at the floor as I left, I could go take a long shower and jack off for the millionth time in the last two weeks. I turned and nearly dropped the pitcher.

"Holy fuck!"

Kory uncrossed and recrossed her legs, giving me a teasing peek of her thong as she sat on the counter. She had on some purple lacy number that was sexy as fuck. "So, I've been waiting for you, but it seems like I have to take matters into my own hands."

"O-or y-you could wait a li-little lo-longer. I... uh... was..." I was a damn mess, seeing her like this. "I mean... tomorrow... we..."

She hopped off the counter, strode toward me confidently, and stopped just a few inches from me. That teasing grin never left her face, and her nipples were hard against the nearly sheer material.

"I have a question for you, Mr. Foster."

She stared into my eyes as she ran her hands down my chest.

"What is that?" I swallowed hard.

Her fingers traced against the waistband of my pants. My dick was at full mast, causing the little bit of resolve I had left to fade away. *Make it special. Stay strong.* I could see her nipples through the sheer lace. Kory dropped to her knees and pulled my lounge pants down far enough to release my dick. A second later, her mouth came over me, and any coherent thought I might have had about waiting left my brain. "Fuck, sweetheart, that feels good."

She took me in all the way into her mouth. Kory was amazing with her mouth. Her tongue stroked me while her lips moved up and down my shaft. Hell, I was going to come fast if she kept up this speed. I was nearing my orgasm when she pulled away and stood up.

I smirked. *Well played, Ms. Reynolds.*

Kory licked her lips. "So, Mr. Foster, my question is: are you going to finish what I started."

I stalked toward her, and Kory took a step back, a grin playing on her lips. "With pleasure."

In the next second, I scooped her up, and her legs wrapped around my waist. My lips crashed against hers. With my free hand, I yanked away her thong, and she gasped against my lips.

"I'll buy you another one."

She ground her pussy against my dick, and I nearly slipped into her tight heat. I paused midstep. "I don't have on a condom, sweetheart."

"I just want to feel you."

She pushed further down. Hell, she was so warm. I leaned her against the wall and thrust in. It was incredible. I had never been inside a woman without protection, and it was the best damn feeling in the world. I had to focus to not come on the spot.

Kory moaned as I pumped into her. Her inner walls contracted around me as her first orgasm shook her body. I should have primed her more. But Kory kept grinding on me. Next time, I would take it slow. She flexed her hips again. I wasn't done. I moved us to the table and set her down. "Again, sweetheart."

"Yes."

She supported herself with her arm as I moved in and out, watching where our bodies were connected.

"So fucking hot."

"Oh, Hayden, don't stop. I'm going to come again."

We were crazy with the suppressed sexual need. I pushed harder, grunting as Kory screamed out my name. Her body slouched back onto the table. I picked her up, loving the satisfied look in her eyes.

Her eyes widened. "You haven't come yet."

"No, I need to get a condom."

Her lips found mind. "I'm on birth control. I want to feel you come inside me."

That was all it took; I brought us to the floor and pushed inside her. It wasn't going to take me long, but I wanted Kory to come with me again. Sweat beaded on my skin as I thrust into her over and over. Finally, her walls contracted one last time, and I lost it. I gave her everything I had before collapsing and rolling to the side, bringing her with me. "That was un-fucking-believable."

"Took the words right out of my mouth."

I cradled her face. "Well, I was going to take you somewhere special tomorrow. The weather finally cooperated. I'd still like to go if you're up to it."

Kory snuggled into my side. "I'd love to. And I know you were trying to make it special. But this is our kind of special. I don't need fancy and over the top."

"I love you, Kory."

"I love you, too." She gave me a chaste kiss and then sprang up. "I'm going to take a shower." As she walked away, she turned and bit her lip seductively. "Want to join me?"

"Abso-fucking-lutely."

CHAPTER Twenty-Five

Hayden

It was nice having a lazy Saturday. We sat in front of a crackling fire, unconcerned that it was already ten in the morning. Kory was curled against my side with the laptop on her lap. Things were good between us. I popped my neck as I got my flight prepped for tomorrow. I still wanted to take Kory away for a special night.

"So, I've decided to respond back to Landon and my mom."

That took me by surprise. She'd shown me the emails they'd sent. Her mom and dad continued to send similar messages daily. Landon had only sent the one. I knew I was biased since Landon had been meant to marry Kory, but a man who let a woman take a fall for him... well, he wasn't much of a man.

I put my tablet down. "What do you plan to say?"

"I've been thinking about it for the last couple of days. I

feel like now's the right time."

Which meant Kory felt confident in her new life. That was definitely a plus. "I support your decision as long as it's what you *want* to do."

"Do you want to see?" Kory asked, chewing on her lip.

I shifted to give her my full attention. "Yeah, I'd love to."

Kory handed me the laptop, and I adjusted it on my lap. Kory pointed to the screen and said, "I minimized both of them. Just click on the one you want to see."

First up was the letter to her parents.

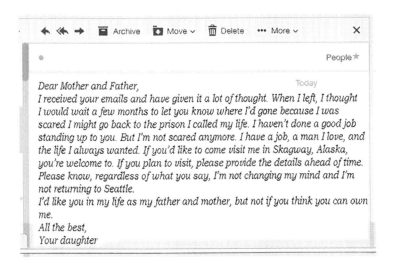

Dear Mother and Father,
I received your emails and have given it a lot of thought. When I left, I thought I would wait a few months to let you know where I'd gone because I was scared I might go back to the prison I called my life. I haven't done a good job standing up to you. But I'm not scared anymore. I have a job, a man I love, and the life I always wanted. If you'd like to come visit me in Skagway, Alaska, you're welcome to. If you plan to visit, please provide the details ahead of time. Please know, regardless of what you say, I'm not changing my mind and I'm not returning to Seattle.
I'd like you in my life as my father and mother, but not if you think you can own me.
All the best,
Your daughter

I was a little stunned. Her confidence surprised me. She'd been so frail when I found her in Washington. I knew she'd gained strength, but I hadn't realized how much. "I think it's good. Incredible, actually."

"You do?"

"Yeah, I do. You've always been strong enough to stand up to them. You just had to believe in yourself."

Kory's smile lit up the room. She leaned over and hit send on the email. Next up, I opened Landon's email.

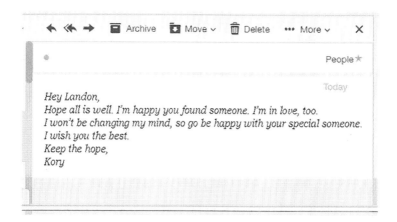

Hey Landon,
Hope all is well. I'm happy you found someone. I'm in love, too.
I won't be changing my mind, so go be happy with your special someone.
I wish you the best.
Keep the hope,
Kory

That was short and to the point, as well. I noticed she hadn't asked him to come visit her. "Looks good to me, too."

She pressed send. "Well, it feels good to have that done. It's felt like unfinished business, and now I feel like I can keep moving forward. I'm sure they'll come at some point."

"When do you think?"

"I don't know. I asked them to let me know first." She shrugged. "They can't make me leave. And if they show up unannounced, I don't have to see them. We'll play that by ear."

I hated that we still had this looming over us. However, Kory seemed ready to face whatever might be coming our way. Hopefully, we were ready as a couple. Sometimes it got complicated when family got involved. I'd seen that with Alexa and Drake.

She put the laptop off to the side and resumed her place next to me. "I feel better now that it's off my plate. I don't feel like I'm hiding anymore."

I trusted Kory, but I dreaded what was to come. I doubted her parents were just going to roll over and accept her decisions. No one went from that controlling to accepting without some kind of explanation.

CHAPTER Twenty-Six

Kory

I stirred, and Hayden's arms tightened around me. "Morning, sweetheart."

"Morning." I opened my eyes to see his beautiful blue ones gazing at me. His lips grazed mine for a small taste. We'd spent the night making love. It had been beautifully intimate, and I couldn't imagine it being any better anywhere else. What happened yesterday was perfect for us. I never needed fancy; I needed his heart. This was what happiness felt like.

"Thank you for a magical night," I whispered.

"I'll give you the world, Kory. Everything I have." He pulled back to put some space between us. The love I saw in his face was everything I needed or wanted. Everything else was just the small details in life that didn't matter at the end of the day. "Do you wish we'd waited until today?"

I giggled. "I practically assaulted you in the kitchen. That should be answer enough."

"It was a good kind of assault. The best kind." He winked. "I'd love to take you away if you still want to go."

Getting away would be nice. Hopefully, business would continue to pick up. If that happened, it would be hard to slip away until I could afford to hire someone to help.

Dream big and strive every day to achieve greatness.

"I'd love to. Where are we going?" I was so excited for the surprise.

"My friend has a cabin on a lake and—"

I had to struggle to keep myself from squealing. "And what?"

"Pretty much the only way to get there is by plane."

I leaned over and kissed him hard. "This is like one of those dates you see in a movie. We'll be flying there by plane. Oh my gosh!" I gave him another kiss. "I'm so excited!"

Hayden had flown me around before, but this was different. We were officially together this time, and he had planned this date. Before, we hadn't labeled anything since we were too afraid to commit.

Hayden reached out and brushed his knuckles along my cheek. "I love you."

His words soothed my soul. "Love you, too."

The warmth I always felt when I was near him blossomed within me. Hayden sat up, listening intently, and the sheet dropped to his waist. I was instantly distracted by the sight of his toned body.

"Was that the door?" he asked.

I sat up, holding the sheet to my chest. "I didn't hear anything." Mentally I ran through my plans for the day, but nothing came to mind.

Straining, I listened closely.

Knock.

Knock.

Knock.

That was definitely the door and definitely an unexpected visitor. Business didn't officially open until December.

Hayden got out of bed. "Shit. I'll be right back. If that's one or both of my brothers, so help me, I'm going to kill them."

If it was anyone in his family, it was Kane. The guy had no concept of time. If something needed to get done, he worked nonstop to get it accomplished. But he was a brilliant businessman. I'd checked out his website and he charged a pretty penny for his hunts. And he was way more tech savvy than he came across.

Hayden pulled on a pair of jeans from the floor. He glanced my way before pulling a shirt over his head. "You're staring awfully hard."

"I like what I see. Hurry back."

Hopefully, it wouldn't take too long to get rid of whoever was at the door. After running his hands through his blond hair, he said, "Be right back. If it's one of my brothers, I'm going to slam the door in his face, come back up here, and then beat the shit out of him later."

I laughed again. "I'll be waiting."

In a brazen move, I dropped the sheet to give him an eyeful. My nipples pebbled under his stare.

"Stay just like that."

He left the room and I fell back with a huge grin. I loved my life. All of it. Things were perfect. Each day with Hayden pushed my past farther away. Who would have thought it had only been a little over two weeks?

And shortly, I would get to feel him inside me again. There was nothing to compare to the intimacy of being with each other.

I heard Hayden hit the stairs on his way back up. A few seconds later, he came in the bedroom with a troubled look on his face. I shot up, immediately concerned. "What's wrong? Did something happen?"

Did one of his brothers come with bad news?

"Your parents are here."

For a second everything stopped. I couldn't have heard him correctly. "My *parents*?"

"Yes, they want to talk to you. They say it's urgent."

I gasped. "My parents. They're here. Did they say why?"

Hayden scrubbed his hand over his beard. "No, they didn't. But they were pretty adamant about speaking with you."

With the sheet wrapped around me, I ran over to the window and peered outside. "How'd they get here?"

"Doug."

He owned a one-man taxi service in town—the only taxi service in town. Sometimes his wife, Darlene, helped out, but their five kids under the age of ten kept her busy. I hurried to the other window and saw Doug's pickup truck waiting. It looked like my parents were paying him to stick around, which meant they probably weren't planning to stay long.

I wasn't sure if I should join them and see what they wanted or if I should stay put. If I hid, they would never see how much I had changed. They would be relentless. Now that they knew where I was, they would find a way to reach out to me.

"Where are they now?"

"Freezing their asses off on the front porch. I wanted you to have the choice, so I shut the door in their faces. If I need to have Sheriff Bolton come out, I will."

I knew my parents would come, but I never imagined it would be today. I'd hoped they would respect my wishes and coordinate a date and time. It was probably best to get this over with so I wouldn't have to live with the dread hanging over my head. And if Sheriff Bolton got involved, he'd know I had a family. To everyone in Skagway, I was parentless.

I got dressed. "Okay, we'll talk to them now."

Hayden picked up his phone from the nightstand. "I want to have my brothers on standby. Just in case."

That seemed a little dramatic. But after what my parents had pulled, I figured it made sense. "Okay. I'll brush my teeth while you call them."

My hands only shook a little as I put the toothpaste on the toothbrush. I sat down for a second to take a few deep breaths and calm down. *I can do this. They have no control over me.* With renewed strength, I brushed my teeth. *I am strong. I can stand up to them. They have no power.* All the same, I was scared. This was new territory to me. Leaving a confident voicemail and sending a strong email were entirely different than standing up to them face-to-face.

I brushed my hair before walking back into the bedroom. Hayden sat on the bed with a pensive look on his face. "Drake and Kane are on their way. They're going to hang back unless we need them. I know it's a bit over the top, but I don't want to take a chance. Your parents blatantly ignored your wishes and just showed up uninvited."

Yeah, they had. I had been naïve yesterday when I sent

the email. "Maybe I shouldn't have contacted them."

"Don't doubt yourself. I'm glad you felt confident enough to reach out to them. They aren't going to start controlling you again. This is your life."

"Our life," I said.

He smiled. "Our life."

That helped, but the worry still lingered. The last time I faced my parents, I was a different person.

Hayden reached over and released my lip. I didn't realized I'd been biting it. "Everything will be okay."

"Do you think they'll try something?"

"They can try. They have no power over you, Kory. Remember that."

Needing the comfort, I reached out and hugged Hayden. Without pause, he pulled me into his lap. "I never want to leave you. I want you to know that."

"That's good to hear, sweetheart." Hayden's phone vibrated. "Drake is here. Kane is still a few minutes out. You ready to see them?"

His phone vibrated again. "Dad's coming, too."

Now Ike was involved. I hated that. "I hope they don't think I'm too much trouble."

It wasn't every day a girl with crazy parents came to town. It wasn't the ideal catch for anyone's son. But I'd seen his parents several times over the last week. Lunch with Amie had been really nice. I was beginning to feel as if I had a place within the Foster family. The last thing I wanted was to be set back.

Hayden's hand cradled my face. "No, not at all. We protect our family."

Protect. Parents were supposed to protect their children.

But in this instance, my parents were the ones I needed protection against.

The fact that Hayden's family treated me as one of their own after such a short amount of time was almost overwhelming. They were a true family who loved each other. And I would give that to my kids one day... unconditional love.

I took a deep breath.

Hayden asked, "You ready?"

This time I was. *I am strong enough to stand up to them.* "Yes."

Hayden stood, and I leaned up on my tiptoes to kiss him. "Thank you."

"I'd do anything for you."

I pressed my lips against his once more. With him by my side, anything was possible. Hand in hand, we walked down the stairs. My heart sped up as we approached the front door. *They can't make me do anything I don't want to do.* Arriving this soon seemed a desperate move on their part. Regardless, I was never going back.

Never.

Hayden reached for the door, but I touched his hand. "Let me."

I needed to be in control of the situation. It was time for me to stand up to them. For my show of strength, I got an approving smile in return, but there was an underlying worry in his features. I touched his face. "Nothing they can say will take me away from you."

"I just don't want you hurt."

Neither did I. But that wasn't something I was able to guarantee, so I remained silent. I took a deep breath and opened the door. My parents stared back at me. For a second, I thought I saw a smile on my mother's face, but it melted away, leaving her face etched in stone. Dad had dark circles underneath his eyes. For a moment, no one said anything. It was like they wanted to speak but held themselves back. It was a familiar feeling; so many times I'd felt this growing up.

"Mother, Father. I'm surprised to see you. What brings you to Skagway?"

Mother shook her head. "Trying to save our daughter."

Trying to save me. That wasn't the answer I'd been expecting.

"What?" I asked.

My father stepped forward. "Can we come in? We need to talk, but this isn't something we can discuss on the front porch."

Something was definitely not right, but I couldn't tell if they were playing a game or not.

Hayden looked at me, and I squared my shoulders. "I'm not leaving. I'm not going back or marrying Landon. My decision is final. Please don't try to talk me into this. The merger can happen without us marrying."

Dad's shoulders sagged; he looked defeated. "We figured as much, which makes it imperative for you to know the truth. You may change your mind."

Change my mind? All eyes were on me as they waited for my decision. "I'll hear you out, but my decision is final. It doesn't matter what you say, I won't go home."

"Just hear us out, please," Mother asked.

I couldn't remember the last time I heard my mother say please. I was taken aback.

The way Mother's face turned grim seemed all wrong to me. *Is this just a different approach to manipulating me?* I turned to face Hayden; his eyebrow was cocked as he watched them. My mind raced with possibilities of what could be wrong, but I came up empty.

I opened the door wider. "Okay. Come in."

Before they had a chance to cross the threshold, Hayden's arm shot across the doorway and halted their entry. "Don't try anything or you'll be asked to leave. Forcibly, if necessary." Hayden's tone was harsh and filled with warning.

"Understood," my father said.

We walked into the living, and I stayed close to Hayden. Having him near helped center me. My parents sat on the couch, and I took the chair across from them. They were the picture of a *Leave It to Beaver* family; Mother in her pearls and cardigan, Father in his custom suit. It was unnerving how perfect they looked yet how broken we were as a family. I didn't believe they understood what the word *casual* meant.

Hayden texted something into his phone while he propped himself on the arm of the chair I was seated in. He was probably communicating with his family. To hide my nerves, I crossed my legs and intertwined my fingers.

My parents are here.

And it hadn't started off well.

As we stared at each other, I wondered where it all went wrong. As a child, I'd had glimpses of happiness, baking with my mother and catching a ball with my father. Something had changed right after my fifth birthday. They'd become cold and unloving. Instead of Mom and Dad, they requested I only called them Mother and Father.

I cleared my throat, my manners taking over. "Mother, Father, this is my boyfriend, Hayden." I looked at Hayden. "This is my mother, Margerie, and my father, Tate."

They gave cursory nods. I imagined they already met earlier. The room fell silent, so I prompted, "You mentioned trying to save me. Can you be a little more specific?"

Father took the lead, which was unusual when communicating with me. "Kory, your mother and I implore you to come back home with us. It's for your safety."

I shook my head. "I hope you really don't expect me to fall for this. I'm not leaving. I meant what I said in my emails, voicemail, and just now while you were on the front porch." I blew out a breath, and Hayden touched my shoulder. *I am strong. I can do this. They cannot make me do anything.* Staring at my parents as if seeing them for the first time, I finally felt the words I had been chanting become reality.

My mother's stone-cold features were harsh. We'd always been similar in looks, but our personalities were exactly the opposite.

How can I be their child? We were worlds apart.

We stared at each other, no one saying a word. It was a tactic my parents had used on me many times to get me to succumb to their demands. And generally, I cracked and conformed to whatever notion they expected of me.

This time was different. And it felt incredible to truly believe in myself.

My mother must have sensed my determination, and she sighed in defeat. Again, I saw something more than the impenetrable force from her. Dad looked at her, and they had a silent conversation right there in front of me. Whatever they communicated, my father agreed with one stiff nod and focused back to me.

Dread began to set in. Whatever they were about to say was going to be terrible. I knew it.

And I had a feeling this next part wasn't about manipulation. Something in my gut told me that my world would be forever changed by their words.

My muscles stiffened.

"Kory, I know things haven't been normal through your childhood since about the time you turned five. There's a reason behind all this."

So they knew. "What's that?"

"We're... it's..." Father adjusted his collar. "There's a reason your entire childhood had been planned, regimented. There's a purpose for you. We had planned to tell you over these next fifteen months as you assumed your role beside Landon."

My role beside Landon? I waited for them to explain further. Father scrubbed a hand down his face and shook his head. But I wanted answers. "Father, what's going on?"

"You've been groomed to take your place by Landon in the Fraternity."

"'Fraternity'? Like for college?"

Father shook his head. "No. We're an order. An organization of sorts."

What. The. Hell.

My mouth opened, but nothing came out.

CHAPTER Twenty-Seven

Hayden

An organization of sorts?

I watched Tate's every move to determine if he was lying. From what I could tell, he appeared to be telling the truth. His eyes never darted left or right, his posture wasn't twitchy, and he had a casual confidence about him that backed up his words. But he'd spent a lifetime pretending not to care about Kory, so I imagined he could put on a good show.

Kory hadn't moved since her dad responded. It was as if time stood still, and she was frozen. I couldn't imagine what was going on in her head. My girl was strong, but this weird shit was rocking her world.

Still, no one said anything. So I took the lead. "What do you mean by 'an organization of sorts'? What does that involve?"

Tate looked at me. "It means everything. We ensure our financial futures—and by doing so, ensure the future of the Fraternity. Everything is carefully planned out. If necessary, we make arrangements that are most suitable for our leaders. Financial arrangements, economic arrangements…marriage arrangements. It's survival of the fittest."

"Are you leaders in this Fraternity? Am I… considered a future leader?" Kory was apparently still stunned and barely able to get out the questions.

Again, her father responded, "No, your mother and I are not. For lack of a better term, we'd be considered board members by comparison. However, Landon will be our next leader. And you are meant to be the future leader's wife."

I gritted my teeth and focused on remaining calm. *She's meant to be my wife, asshole. Wait. What the hell? Wife?* I hadn't meant to go there, but I guess I just did. Later, I would process that thought. *Stay calm and levelheaded just like when you fly.*

The way her father spoke about it without any emotion was beyond me. It was nearly impossible to process this and keep up with what question needed to be asked next.

"W-wife?" Kory's voice shook.

I touched Kory's shoulder, and she looked up at me. I mouthed, *"You and me."*

Kory took a deep breath and visibly relaxed. I kept eye contact for a minute more before I focused back on her parents. There was no chance in hell she was going to marry that asshole. Over my dead body.

"Yes, a lot of money has gone into preparing for this," her father calmly stated.

Who the fuck cares?

Kory gasped, and I ground my teeth together. *Stay on task. Blowing up won't get the answers we need.* I asked, "Does Landon know?"

"Yes," her dad replied. Again, his face was unreadable. "He's been groomed for this role his entire life."

Bastard. His email had been playing Kory, trying to bait her into trusting him with her location. "So, he hasn't fallen in love with a girl in Europe?"

Digging for information from these people was starting to piss me off. *Spit it out and stop playing games.*

Her father adjusted his suit jacket. "No, he doesn't have anyone. Landon just wanted Kory to tell him where she was. He was going to come and bring her back. By force, if necessary."

By force? What kind of dick was he to take a woman against her will? I needed to stay calm. If I reacted with a hot head, it wouldn't help our situation. But it was seriously getting harder to stay in check. "Does Landon know where she is now?"

Without missing a beat, he said, "Not yet. But he will. We'll have to advise him upon our return. I would rather not, but we have no choice."

I stood towering over them. "I'm losing my patience with this bullshit. I suggest you start explaining what's going on. She's your fucking daughter. Why on earth would you tell him?"

Her dad shook his head, appearing calm and collected. "You don't get it. We have no choice." Her dad's voice began to rise. "Do you think I *want* this for my daughter?" His agitation grew, breaking through his calm and cool facade. "Do you think it didn't kill me *every day* to see how miserable she was when that spoiled little shit walked into our house? The moment he saw her swinging in the backyard, he claimed my daughter as his. She was five years old. I had grown my company too big, too fast, and Landon's father wanted a piece of it." He paced back and forth, his desperation finally clear. "I had no choice. Just like her mother and I had no choice to be in the Fraternity. Our parents were part of it, which means we're part of it." He held out his hands. "None of us has a choice. Kory is part of it."

Kory's lip trembled, and her voice broke. "I want a choice. I don't want that life."

Upsetting Kory wasn't my point. The fear in her voice eased my temper some, and it seemed to affect her father, as well, and he sat back down on the couch. I saw something more—was that love?—when he looked at his daughter. Because of that softening of his stance, I slowly lowered myself back down onto the arm of the chair.

Kory cradled her face in her hands and shook her head. "I don't understand."

Her mother touched her father's arm, and he nodded. He and I were too worked up right now to continue. "Kory, honey, Landon wants you to help him lead our people. When you were little, we had his parents over for dinner. They brought Landon, who was about eight at the time. You have to understand—we had no say in the matter. Once he claimed you, we could either agree or die. His parents have been grooming him to be leader since he could talk. After that night, we were told exactly how we had to raise you. Landon and his parents directed everything—even down to the way we treated you. You're expected to produce heirs—future leaders for the Fraternity. Many leaders. That's why the wedding was to take place when it was. Your doctors believed you would be at your peak time to conceive."

What. The. Fuck.

I gripped the chair tight. "Over my fucking dead body."

Kory put a gentle hand on my leg and mouthed my words back to me. Still, I could see the fear in the depths of her beautiful blue eyes. Kory shook her head and looked back at her mother. "My gynecologist was involved?"

"She's part of the Fraternity. Actually, she was brought on to monitor every aspect of your health and make sure you were okay."

For a second Kory's eyes lost focus. "I can't believe it. She shared everything about me."

The lack of denial confirmed it. I balled my right fist off the side of the couch where Kory couldn't see it. The depth of their betrayal was unbelievable. I wasn't a father, but I knew for certain there would never be a price tag attached to my child.

"Landon wanted to make sure you were okay. It's considered a great honor to be chosen."

A great honor? These people were unbelievable. Kory's own mother was justifying his actions.

There was no way in hell Landon was taking Kory from me. No way in hell. And I would fucking kill him if he thought she would be having his children. I squeezed Kory's shoulder in reassurance. "That isn't happening."

Kory looked up at me with those big blue eyes, and I could tell she was scared—even more so than before. I reassured her again. "It's not happening. As long as you want to stay here, you're staying here."

Sniffles from across the couch brought me up short. Her mother dabbed a tear, then arranged her features into some semblance of calm. "I tried to not get attached. I knew this day would come. But I see you so happy, and it's killing me. We were told if we didn't comply, they'd kill us and still take you. I never imagined the Fraternity capable of this. I mean, yes, they've done things, but... I just don't know."

What the ever-loving hell? It was like dealing with Dr. Jekyll and Mr. Hyde. Her parents were upset yet defended Landon and the Fraternity. It was brainwashing at its finest.

"Mother, I'm not going back. I love Hayden, and I'm staying in Alaska." Kory seemed calmer and had regained some of the strength in her voice.

Her mother retrieved another tissue from her purse. "Kory, you have no idea how ruthless these people can be. If we don't go back and tell them we've located you, they'll kill us."

Kory gasped, putting her hand to her mouth. It sounded like they truly didn't want to expose Kory. Well at least part of them didn't, anyway.

This Fraternity having this much power over them was incomprehensible. It was time to cut through the shit. "Are you on your daughter's side or the Fraternity's?"

"Our daughter's. But it is complicated," her father said.

It really wasn't that complicated. I pinched the bridge of my nose—my patience was growing thin. "Then tell us what we need to know. I'm growing tired of the games, so I can only imagine how your daughter feels."

"Landon is going to come to Alaska for Kory. And he's going to do everything he can to tie her to him. And I mean *everything*," her father said.

"What does that mean?" I stood, aggression radiating from me.

Her father stood, too. "It means he'll do whatever is necessary to ensure the survival of the Fraternity. Force her to marry him, carry his child."

Now Kory balled her fists. "I would never marry him."

Her father sighed. "Kory, he's not above forcing you without your consent. That's who he's become. He's ruthless. Your mother and I have tried to find a way to get out of this, to get *you* out of this. But every option ends up with them finding out and taking you anyway. We'd be dead and unable to help you. There is *no* choice."

"Why not find another girl?" I asked. There had to be someone who wanted to be the leader's wife. Some sick fuck wanting to rule a group of people. It still seemed fictitious, but based on how they'd treated their daughter all her life, somehow it made sense.

I still held onto the hope that they wanted what was best for her. Or maybe it was a trick. Hell, I wasn't sure.

Her mother said, "Our people don't leave. How would it look if our leader allowed his future wife to leave? It'll make him look weak. Everyone knows he's chosen Kory. All the elders have known his choice since he made the decision. Everyone is anxious for the next regime to take over."

Not everyone.

I glanced down at Kory and saw tears streaming down her face. "I won't let him take you." I knew I was repeating myself, but every time they reiterated the shit they were spewing, Kory needed to hear that I hadn't changed my mind about being with her.

She looked up at me, her eyes sad. "Don't you see? You wouldn't be in this mess if I had just stayed away." It broke my heart to see her like this.

This wasn't working. I needed to talk to Kory alone. Emotions were all over the place. And if her parents saw her falling apart, they might mistake it for weakness instead of her simply trying to manage a fucked-up situation with the people who were supposed to protect her. What I had to say wasn't anything her parents needed to hear.

I took out my phone and texted the group chat with my brothers and dad.

Me: *Things have gotten complicated. Drake and Kane, can you come in here? Dad, can you stand watch?*

Drake: *On my way.*

Kane: *On my way.*

Dad: *I'm on point. Let me know if you need anything.*

Me: *I will.*

I trusted her parents about as far as I could throw them, so leaving them unattended in our home wasn't an option. "My brothers are coming inside. I'm going to talk to Kory for a minute. Then we'll see where that leaves us."

Wisely, they chose to remain silent.

Kory looked at me with uncertainty in her eyes, and for the first time, I wondered if she would choose to go back home. My heart might actually break if she left. I would fight to keep her with every ounce of love I had. But at the end of the day, I couldn't force her to stay. Or it would make me the same kind of monsters as her parents.

Drake and Kane walked in. They took off their jackets and glanced toward me. The tension in the air was thick. Mariah sat at Kane's side, the hair on the back of her neck standing at attention. Kane motioned for Mariah to sit by the door. They had some sort of sign language no one else knew. It was uncanny how much Kane connected with his husky.

Kory's parents' eyes widened at the sight of the dog. Mariah leaned forward as if she were stalking her prey. Mariah was an anomaly to her breed. Normally, huskies weren't effective guard dogs, but Kane had invested a lot of training in her.

Kory's mother leaned closer into her father when my brothers walked farther into the room. Yeah, Drake and Kane were scary bastards just from their sheer size and the scowls on their faces. Add in a husky who showed her teeth, and I hoped we came off as people not to fuck with.

I gave introductions. "These are my brothers, Drake and Kane. This is Tate and Margerie Reynolds, Kory's parents. Give me a few minutes, guys."

Kane sat on the arm of the chair, staring at Kory's parents in that awkward way that made a person want to squirm. "You got it."

I held out my hand to Kory, and she squeezed my fingers. We walked to the back bedroom. I closed the door before leading her to the walk-in closet and shutting that door as well. I wanted as much privacy as possible.

Kory threw her arms around me. "I can't believe this is happening. All those terrible things they said. Hayden…" She didn't finish before she broke down in sobs.

I held her tighter. Anything she needed, I would give it to her. "I've got you, sweetheart. And I'll never let you go."

She gripped me tighter, her nails digging into my back. "Hayden, what am I going to do?"

This was where I put it all out there and hoped like hell she chose me. "What do you want to do?"

"Hayden, do you realize what all they said? I believe them. Deep down in my gut, I know what they're saying is true. It makes so much sense now. I remember times before I turned five when we were happy. Then I just remember them being cold. It wasn't long after my grandparents died. I thought I had imagined the happy times, made them up because I couldn't bear to not have their love. But it was true. What kind of people force parents to distance themselves from their child? Threaten parents and takes their children? It's like they are part of the mob or something like it."

I had no idea. But I also noticed she hadn't answer my question. I had to know the answer. It would be the foundation for every decision we made and might alter my life forever. This desperation I felt was one of the reasons I never wanted to be involved. But knowing how happy I could be with Kory made it all worth it in the end. I swallowed hard, preparing myself for the rejection. "What do you want to do?"

She pulled back and looked into my eyes. "I don't want to cause you problems."

Again, that wasn't an answer. I needed to know. I had to know. "That's not what I asked. What do *you* want, Kory? If there were no other factors, what would you chose?"

"I would choose you. I don't want to leave Alaska, leave you. But I don't want them to hurt you, either. They said Landon would do whatever was necessary. That might include hurting those I loved."

Thank fuck. I put my forehead to hers. "Then you'll stay here. We'll find a way to get through this."

"I want nothing more than to be with you."

I ran my finger along her cheek. "We're going to get our happy ending."

CHAPTER Twenty-Eight

Hayden

When we walked back into the room, the tension could be cut with a knife. Kory's parents stood, their masks not completely in place. Some of the coldness had evaporated.

Her mother tucked her clutch underneath her arm. "We don't have much time. We need to leave."

Leave? Already?

Beside me Kory tensed. Her parents' erratic behavior was hard to follow. They flew all this way, then before we'd had a chance to grasp what was going on, they were ready to go. This had all the makings of a double cross.

Kory took a step forward, and I made sure to mirror her movement. If they tried anything, I wanted to be ready. "Mother, Father, I have so many questions."

The pleading in her voice broke my heart. If I could take this pain away from her, I would.

"The less you know, the better. If you want a life outside of the Fraternity, we can't say too much."

That made sense. But were they willing to let her go that easily? Her father's shoulders were more stiff now, though, and her parents were exchanging furtive glances back and forth. Something was off... or had changed. "What's really going on? Why the sudden change in when you have to leave?"

"He got a text," Kane said, nodding toward Kory's father. "After that, they exchanged a look. I think their plans changed."

Kane was an expert at reading people. He sensed the smallest of movements and changes in demeanor. And his less-than-friendly appearance made him a little more scary than the average person.

No one said a word. Kory's mother looked down at her feet, and her father adjusted his cuff links. There seemed to be an internal struggle within them.

Kory pleaded. "Mother, Father. Please. You weren't able to stop my childhood from being taken, but we can protect my future."

For a second, I saw real emotion on her mother's face before she hid it away. "I'm sorry, Kory."

Crestfallen, Kory took a step back. I remained where I was and asked, "Your allegiance stays with the Fraternity?"

Her parents were unraveling more. Her father ran his hand down his face and let out a long breath. Her mother mashed her lips together for a second to compose herself. "Yes and no. We have no choice. If we leave, we'll be killed and Kory will be taken." She turned the attention toward her daughter. "You were always our priority. We had no idea you would be picked for such a prominent role. Most members of the Fraternity live long, normal lives. But the future wife of the president is a different story. There isn't a day that goes by that we don't regret having them over for dinner. Our world is cruel at times. And other times, it's amazing. We have connections everywhere. Money is never an issue. But with anything good, there must be bad. It's the price we pay."

What. The. Actual. Fuck.

Part of them wanted to care for their child, yet the other part supported what the Fraternity stood for. They seemed to accept the bad just because it was what they were taught.

Kory closed her eyes for a second. Drake ran his hand through his hair, showing the faintest sign of stress. The only outward sign Kane showed was the widening of his eyes. At least I wasn't the only one affected. This was some messed-up shit. And I wasn't sure what it meant.

"Why was I allowed to go to Alaska this summer?" Kory asked, finding her voice.

She touched my hand, and I grabbed hers. A few seconds later, she pressed herself against my side. There was some kind of silent communication between her parents before her father nodded.

"It was Landon's idea. He arranged it. He'd sensed some unrest in you and wanted to send you off, assuming you'd fail and come home. The weekly reports we received from Maggie never indicated you'd met anyone and generally talked about how miserable you were. On your last day there, she reported you were happy to be heading home. That's why we came to see you that night—to welcome you back and see if you missed your life. But you were the same as before. It didn't make sense until we found out you'd met someone. When did you meet Hayden?"

They had no idea Kory had come home early. None. Maggie had protected her.

"Maggie was involved?" The hurt was apparent in Kory's voice. And I couldn't blame her. Through the summer, she and Maggie had become close. And since arriving in Skagway, Kory had spoken with her a couple of times. But Maggie had also protected Kory. This was so convoluted. But we'd find time to sort through the mess later.

Kory's mother rubbed her temples. "In a limited fashion, from what I understand. We weren't allowed to see any of the communication. I do know Maggie was told you were a troubled person and was given a hefty amount to offer you a job."

Kory looked defeated. "It was all a game. Like my life."

Her parents had no answer. So... Maggie had probably figured out that Kory's parents had lied and that she was a good person, and she had stuck it to them. I knew I liked her for a reason. She was a wily thing, but it didn't completely wipe away her betrayal.

Kory closed her eyes for a second. "Will Maggie be okay?"

"It depends on if she lied."

With a straight face, Kory lied right to them. "No, she didn't. I kept Hayden a secret."

I imagined that after a lifetime of lying to her parents, she was able to pull it off. This was the Kory who'd kept her parents from me this summer. It was unnerving to see her like this again. Now that I knew what it was like to have all of Kory, I never wanted to go back to this half Kory again.

Her mother looked away. "Then she'll be fine. She confirmed as much when Landon questioned her." She sighed.

"We never expected you to meet someone. Landon required us to record our conversations over the summer. We had no idea. He was convinced you were ready to come home. And he was prepared to move forward and make you his wife."

By showering her with affection, which he thought Kory was starved for. *What a complete asshole.* "Why wasn't Kory told about the Fraternity when she was younger?"

Her father said, "Typically, our children begin learning about the Fraternity at ten. However, Landon wanted Kory untouched. He wanted to be in total control of her introduction into the Fraternity. It had been his choice to keep Kory out of the life until it was time. He believed it would make her more malleable." Landon had thought he could play psychological games with Kory.

Landon planned to save her from her home and then mold her into his toy.

I needed time to regroup. There were still too many unknowns for us to determine the best path. First, we needed more answers… information… anything. "So, you go home. See Landon and his family. What happens next?"

Kory's father stepped in. It was like they were tag-teaming. "Most likely, they know we received the email and that we came here. What we tell them, I'm not sure, but I'm open to suggestions."

This seemed to be a small step forward.

Kane stood. "Mariah, stay. No one leaves. Family meeting, guys." The husky gave a low growl. Kane looked at Kory's parents. "I suggest you stay put. You try to leave, it won't be pretty."

Their eyes went wide as saucers. If we hadn't been in the situation we were in, it might have been comical.

Kane nodded to me as he walked by. We fell in line with Drake bringing up the rear. The hallway echoed with our footsteps as we headed to the bedroom Kory and I had gone to earlier.

The door closing behind us made the anxiety in the pit of my stomach grow. There was a table in the corner, where we'd stashed some of the supplies that had arrived. Drake leaned against it. This room was going to be turned into a get-ready room, and Dad was going to make the furniture.

Kane crossed his arms. "None of this sits right with me. I think they're telling the truth, but they got some fucked-up loyalties." Kane softened. "Sorry, Kory."

She gave a watery smile. "No, it's true. I'm sorry I'm a mess. It's just more awful than I imagined."

I pulled her close to me. "Nothing we can't survive, sweetheart. You're doing an amazing job."

"Damn straight," Drake said.

"Those assholes may be the Fraternity, but we're the fucking Fosters." Kane inclined his head toward Kory. "Don't feel guilty for having screwed-up parents. That's not your fault."

That brought another small smile from Kory. "Thank you."

He gave a wink. It was Kane's way of saying "We got this." I ran my free hand through my hair. "So, what are you thinking, Kane?" He wouldn't have brought us back to this room if he hadn't thought it was imperative.

Leaning against the windowsill, he crossed his arms. "You've got two options. Wait the asshole out. See what he's going to do. Or you bring him here on your terms. Set a date and a time. Invite him up. He might try to jump the gun, but if he's trying to get Kory peacefully, he might wait if it's not too long. It could buy us a few days. Personally, I'm a fan of option two. But I'll back you guys however you decide to play it."

That's how Kane was. He told it like he saw it, but he backed his family regardless.

"I like option two as well. Hayden?" Kory looked at me to confirm.

"I'd prefer to stay in control of the situation," I said.

Drake said, "When we go out there, we need to be in control of the game plan. Tell her parents what to do. If they don't have a plan, I think they'll fall apart."

"I agree."

Maybe that was why they were wishy-washy. They were used to being told how to think, act, and what to say. Independent thought wasn't a luxury the Fraternity granted to its people.

Drake cracked his neck. "I'll support whatever play you guys decide to make."

I thought for a second. "After her parents leave, Kory can call Landon and invite him up this Friday or Saturday. I don't know if we could push it much past five or six days. If he asks about me, she can act disinterested and more interested in seeing him. As long as she's not gushing, he shouldn't suspect anything. Landon needs Kory to cooperate to make the entire situation easier."

"Agreed," Kane said. "And during those five days we figure out our plan."

And hoped to hell it would work.

CHAPTER Twenty-Nine

Hayden

Kory's parents hadn't moved an inch since we left the room. Mariah's low growl obviously added to their mounting concerns. Kane waved his hand and Mariah stopped. After he took a seat, Kane stared at Kory's parents. "I'm glad you made the right choice. I hate messes."

Good ol' Kane.

Nervously, Kory's mother fumbled with her clutch. "We really need to go."

Enough is enough. "I'm tired of playing the games. Where does all this leave us? I think your daughter has a right to know." Even to my own ears, I sounded aggravated. I *was* aggravated.

Kory held my hand tighter, and we waited.

Kory's father took one step forward, and I gently pulled Kory behind me. "I'll ask again. Where does this leave us?"

"We want to help our daughter. We'll search for something that will allow Kory to be free. But she can't mention she knows about the Fraternity. Ever." Tate turned to Kory. "You can never mention it. If they find out, the Fraternity will claim you. Or worse yet, kill you."

I got the impression that wasn't an empty threat but the truth of their world. But I'd be damned if that ever came to pass. Kane leaned forward. "Are you going to double-cross your daughter?"

I hadn't seen any sign of that from them, but Kane must be looking for something.

Kory's parents shook their heads. Though they seemed hard on the outside, these two people were most likely broken on the inside. They might be beyond repair from the brainwashing they endured.

"How will we communicate? The Fraternity watches everything of ours," her father asked.

That was a good question. We would need to figure out something. Kory spoke up. "We could use the temporary phone I got over the summer."

After I loaned Kory my phone, she remembered the phone was hidden in the lining of her suitcase in case her parents looked. It was easier to keep letting her use the spare until we added another line to my account.

I nodded. "That might work."

"Let me get it." She hurried up the stairs.

Taking this as my moment, I stepped forward. Her parents needed to get their heads out of their asses. "I'd suggest you not hurt your daughter more by betraying her. If you do, I swear there won't be anywhere you can hide. Do you understand?"

Her father leaned forward. "If you don't think it hasn't killed my wife and me to see Kory suffer, you don't know us at all. But what we're doing now is for her. We're trying to save Kory. Everything we've done has been for her. It might not be what you're used to, but we've kept her best interests at heart. Just because it's different doesn't make it wrong."

Oh, hell. It was like arguing with a fence post. But at least he cared for Kory in some capacity. That would help keep them loyal to her. Her mother touched her father's arm as Kory came back down the stairs. I took a step back, and so did he.

"Here's the phone. I'll get it turned back on and text you when it's done."

Her mother took it. "Thank you. We'll try to do everything we can, Kory. For what it's worth, I am sorry we weren't able to be better parents and show you the love you deserved when you were a child."

Kory stiffened. "I won't say it's okay. But at least I have an explanation."

I was glad she hadn't excused it away. They had made the choice to abandon their daughter. Now they had to live with it.

"Can I hug you?" her mother asked.

Hesitantly, Kory took a step forward, and I readied myself in case they tried anything. It was an awkward hug, but I saw the emotion as her mother closed her eyes and savored the moment. Her father opened his arms, and Kory walked into them. When she came back to my side, there were tears running down her cheeks. It gutted me to see them.

Her father's phone chimed. "We really must go. What's the plan?"

Kory chewed her lip. "Can I ask one last question?"

"Yes, but I don't know if I can answer," he said.

"You mentioned my grandparents were part of it. But I don't remember them being cold to me."

Her father pinched the bridge of his nose. "You've chosen to stay out of this life. It's best if you don't know the details. But your grandparents refused to cut you off emotionally when the rest of us had. There was a price to be paid for the disobedience."

Kory gasped. "They were murdered? How can you be part of the Fraternity if they murder people?"

Our world is cruel at times. His words from earlier came back to me.

Her father shook his head. "Kory, you either want in our world or you don't. You can't have it both ways."

I squeezed Kory's hand, reminding her I was there for her. Her eyes brimmed with tears, and she tried to choke back the emotion. What a fucked-up situation. It was her choice to press or not. She took a step closer to me. "No, I don't want in. Hayden's going to tell you the plan."

They'd lost Kory. I saw the emotional detachment as it happened. "Kory's going to invite Landon up here this Saturday. Let's hope you find something that gets her out of this mess."

"We'll try."

They stepped toward the door hesitantly to see if anyone would stop them. They were free to go. We had what we needed for now. I went to follow them, asking Kory, "Can I speak with them for a moment alone?"

"Sure." Her left eyebrow lifted in question, but she stopped walking.

Out on the front porch, the colder weather had set in. I should have grabbed my jacket. I folded my arms over my chest and met their gazes. "One question. When all this is finished, where does this leave your relationship with Kory?"

They both looked down.

Their world is cruel at times. And they are still part of the Fraternity. They will always be part of the Fraternity.

"So, your true allegiance lies with them?"

How can we trust them? I couldn't tell if they would turn in their daughter to save their own skins.

Her father shook his head. "You have no right to judge me or my wife. We love our daughter, and make no mistake, we wish things could have been different, but they aren't. This is our life. And we've tried to make the best of it."

And yet they will walk away from Kory.

There was nothing else to say. I called to Kory, and she stepped outside. "Safe travels, Mother and Father. And thank you for seeing if there's anything that can end this."

Kory gave them each a quick hug, but she was more distant. They waved good-bye and walked toward Doug's waiting truck, the snow crunching beneath their feet. At some point, Kory would realize she'd never have a relationship with her parents. And I'd be there for her in whatever capacity she needed.

After they pulled away, Kory turned to me. "I heard it all."

Shit. "I'm sorry, sweetheart."

"I was curious myself. And now I know." She wiped a stray tear away. "I wish things could be different with them, but it would be nearly impossible. I never want to be involved in the Fraternity and they love their organization. My grandparents' car accident was most likely not an accident. It hurts knowing that they'll turn the other way. But it's probably for the best. I wouldn't want my kids near it. What if some future leader saw our kids and decided to claim them?"

I was grateful we were on the same page. No one would be claiming my child. "I agree. How are you doing with all this?"

She blew out a ragged breath. "I'm dealing. It'll be better once we have a plan and I have time to just process everything. Right now, I feel like I've got a knife in my chest."

I pulled her closer to me and hugged her hard. "We're going to get through this, sweetheart. And I'm going to be by your side the entire way."

"Thank you." The wind whipped around us, and Kory shivered. "Let's go inside. I have one more phone call to make. It's going to be rough because I hate him more than I've hated anyone in my life."

The feeling was mutual.

Inside, Kane was leaning on the windowsill. "Got the phone turned on. Also, Dad is going to follow them to the airport to make sure they leave."

"Good." Since I wasn't the owner of the airport itself, it wasn't necessary to contact me to land. If someone wanted to use a hangar or refuel, then they had to reach out.

Kory took a deep breath. "Here goes nothing." She dialed the number, her lips turned down in a frown. I hated that she was in this position. "Landon. Hey, it's Kory. Mother and Father just stopped by, and we got to reminiscing. Yeah, I told them where I was. I know. I don't know, I just felt the need to reach out to see them. I know it's crazy. Me? Meh. You know some day I just… I don't know. I'm in Skagway, Alaska. I thought I needed a change, but I miss home."

There was a long pause. I noticed Kory wasn't able to look at me while she spoke. It would be hard for me to have this conversation with another woman, playing a part. "Oh, that would be nice. How about Saturday? Sooner? I don't think I could. I'm so busy. Saturday works. Yeah. That sounds good. I look forward to it, too. See ya then."

She ended the call and shivered. "I hate him. I hate him. I hate him."

"He sounds like a sack of shit," Kane murmured.

Kory gave a small, tired chuckle. "He is. Let me call my parents and tell them." She dialed the number Kane handed to her. "Hi, Mother. Yes, it's working. I talked to Landon. He's going to come up on Friday. I mentioned you guys came to see me, and we got to reminiscing about old times. No, none of that was mentioned. No, none of that, either. Yes, only the overall and my location. Okay. Sounds good and be careful."

Hanging up, Kory looked exhausted. "Well, that's done."

It wasn't completely, but we were getting closer. Now we needed to come up with a game plan. There was a chance Landon would ignore her request the way her parents had. We hadn't discussed what we were going to do in the interim. I threw some ideas out, not knowing how my brothers felt about the situation. "I think we all need to get under one roof for the week. Strength in numbers."

"Agreed," my brothers echoed.

Kane added, "Dad asked if we could meet him at the house when we were done. I'm sure they have a lot of questions."

No doubt. I looked at Kory because I wanted her to be part of the decision-making. She looked down at her fingers. "They deserve to know. I want them to know."

I hated putting Kory in this position. But she was right; they had to know.

CHAPTER Thirty

Kory

I had never been more nervous in my life than I was at that moment as I watched everyone's faces. My spine was stiff as a board as I sat in the chair, facing the Foster family. Hayden held my hand, rubbing soothing circles on it, but it wasn't helping. Hearing him relay the story to his family made it seem a little surreal. These were my parents. So much of what I knew of my life had been untrue, and it hurt.

To hear my parents confirm that they would not leave the Fraternity cut deep. And the possibility that my grandparents had been murdered, no matter how much they'd been caught up in this mess, stung even worse. I knew I'd never have the relationship with them that I wanted, but at the same time, they were sacrificing for my happiness. It was a tangled web, and I really couldn't wrap my head around it. I couldn't even tell if they were telling the truth.

It helped having Kane and Drake already up to date on the

situation. They'd been there, and they hadn't said one word of criticism. If anything, they were beyond supportive. I was most afraid of what Amie would think. She was the cornerstone of this family and loved her boys.

To her, I was a stranger bringing unnecessary stress into their lives. And my world colliding with theirs could get someone hurt. From the way my parents described Landon, he sounded dangerous. And in a few days, he would be coming to Skagway. Who knew what that would bring? The family had barely had time to get used to the idea of Hayden having a girlfriend, let alone one with a crazy past.

I hate this.

If they wanted me out of their lives, I would understand. It would hurt more than I could imagine, but I would respect it. I worried that, at some point, Hayden would realize he'd had enough. I came with more strings than a puppet. And it was exhausting to keep those strings untangled.

Finally, the story came to an end. To my right, Kane watched his mother's face closely. Across from me, Drake studied Alexa. Her brows were drawn. I cleared my throat. This was getting to be too much. I needed them to know they had a way out if they wanted one. They had a choice not to be part of this craziness. "I'm so sorry this has happened. I had no idea, and I would never want to put you guys in danger. I—"

Amie stood. I felt the blood drain from my face as I waited to hear what she had to say.

"Oh honey, I can see you're worried. Don't be. We're going to figure our way through this because that's what family does. We don't choose our family. Lord knows, I wish I wasn't blood to some of my kinfolk, but it happens. And we make the best of it."

My eyes brimmed with tears. It was the best response I could have asked for. They accepted the good with the bad. This is what I imagined a family was like. It was what I dreamed about as a kid.

Amie walked over to me with the kindest smile on her face. "Don't you fret for one second about what we think. You and Hayden are a unit now. And I support my boy's choice. I always have and always will." And then she put her arms around me and hugged me tight.

"Thank you," I whispered.

It was all I could manage to get out. If I spoke any louder, I might cry. And once I started, I might not be able to stop. Truth be told, I was only hanging on by a thread.

Pulling back, Amie looked at me. "As far as I'm concerned, Landon is the asshole of all assholes."

Everyone gasped, and I pressed my lips together to keep from laughing. It wasn't like Amie to cuss. But after the stress of the day, hearing her pop off an A-bomb was too funny. She turned to her boys. "Take note, my dear sons, that's how you cuss properly. It has dramatic effect that way. You don't have to throw it out there willy-nilly all the time. If you're going to cuss, make it count."

The boys grinned at their mom. Kane said, "Good one, Mom."

She patted his head, and he rolled his eyes lovingly as she walked behind him. "Kane, I can tell you're rolling your eyes at me. I know all and see all."

Drake looked at Hayden and tsk-tsked. "Eye rolling is a girl thing."

"Hey, it is not." Alexa slapped Drake's arm, and he grinned.

Beside me, Hayden folded his arms. "It is kind of girlie. Maybe the princess title should be transferred."

"We have a deal for when I get the princess title, which isn't happening. Stop being di—dopes." Kane rocked back in his chair and gave his mom a satisfied smile. "I saved it, Mom. I'll use the D-word when it can be more dramatic."

Amie let out a sigh. "Lord, give me strength. How about we have some pie? I made some homemade apple pies this afternoon. I think we could use some while we discuss our options."

Everyone raised their hands. Apple pie sounded delicious. Now that I thought about it, I hadn't eaten a bite all day. Food might help settle me some.

Ike stood. "I'll help, darling."

She gave him the sweetest smile.

One day, I wanted to have what Ike and Amie had. Ike worshipped the ground Amie walked on. Someday, Hayden and I would have this… hopefully.

They left for the kitchen, and Alexa hummed something to herself. She definitely had something on her mind as she toyed with a piece of blond hair that had escaped from her messy bun. Drake watched her work it out. It was sweet how he gave her space when she needed it. Setting the wedding date was an example. They'd be married already if it had been his choice. Instead, Drake let Alexa come to him when she was ready to talk about it.

I had heard Alexa had a temper, but so far, I hadn't witnessed it. There had been stories about poor Hollis getting a book to the head because he'd been grumpy. And one about her chopping wood to work out some frustration. That one was hard to picture. I hadn't seen Hollis be anything but cheerful.

But apparently if you took away his Starbucks, that awakened the ugly bear inside.

Finally, she said, "So Landon wants to marry you?"

The thought made me sick to my stomach. "Yes, that's what my parents said. From the way he spoke on the phone, it seemed like he wanted to reconcile."

Hayden gritted his teeth. When I glanced his way, I saw the veins in his neck bulging. His hand tightened on my knee. If I were in his shoes, I would feel the same way. The thought of him with another woman nearly drove me mad. I placed my hand on top of his to soothe him.

Alexa held up her hands. "Just bear with me for a second. I have an idea that might solve—or at least delay—Landon wanting... forcing... the marriage thing."

"Go ahead. I would do anything to keep him away." My palms were sweating from the anxiety.

She scrunched her forehead. "What if you married Hayden? That would keep Landon from being able to marry you. Legally, you can't be married to two people. And Hayden would have to sign off on the annulment or divorce. Otherwise, it becomes a lengthy process."

Marriage.

To Hayden.

We're not ready yet.

I opened my mouth to speak, but nothing came out. That had been the farthest thing from my mind.

Marriage.

A wedding.

An instant headache formed.

Alexa held up her hands. "I'm sorry. I probably shouldn't have said that."

I glanced at Hayden, who was as pale as I felt.

Drake leaned forward and steepled his fingers. "There's some merit to the idea. It's not bad, and it solves one issue."

But marriage? That seemed so... drastic.

Amie came back into the room with the pie. Ike set down the plates and utensils. "What did I miss? You guys look like you're having a serious discussion."

"Hayden and Kory might get married," Kane quipped.

Hayden stared off into space without a word. We had to be a sight.

Amie paused for a second. "I was only gone for a couple of minutes." She didn't say anything else, just began to cut the pie.

How can she be so calm in a moment like this?

"A shit ton happened in those minutes." Kane held up his hands when she whipped her head around to glare at him. "That S-bomb was for dramatic effect."

Amie threw her napkin at Kane. "That does not give you an excuse to start cussing all the time, Kane Foster."

He shrugged. "It was worth a try."

I stood, and my chair made an awful noise against the floor. "Would you excuse us? Hayden and I need to talk for a second." My voice sounded unnaturally high and squeaky.

Taking my hand, Hayden led me to the office. Someone else could fill Amie in on all the particulars of us getting married. Hayden and I sat on the couch staring at each other, not saying a word. I wondered what he was thinking. Finally, I broke the ice. "Hayden, we don't have to do this."

"I know, but honestly, Kory, it makes sense." He sounded distant, and his eyes weren't completely focused.

He was right; some parts of it did. I swallowed hard. "But

we're not ready."

After blinking a few times, he turned his eyes to mine. "No, we're not. But if it keeps you safe, I'm all in. I don't want to lose you. I love you too damn much to lose you."

My throat tightened. "I can't lose you, either." I could feel the tears welling up in my eyes. "I just hate that I've put you in this position, Hayden. I just can't stand bringing all this drama into your life. I never wanted to cause all these problems."

Hayden held out his arms to me. "Come here, sweetheart."

I climbed onto his lap, and he stroked my hair. "I'm taking all this on with you willingly. Yes, I was a little shocked at the suggestion, but it makes sense. Take the emotions out of the equation and think about it rationally. Landon can't marry you if you're already married."

Rationally wasn't how I wanted to discuss my wedding. I wanted nothing but love. There had to be a way to make this work. I thought for a second before I spoke. "If we do this, I don't want it to be our official wedding. I want it to simply be a means to an end."

Hayden cupped the back of my neck and tilted my head to look into my eyes. "When we're ready, I'm going to give you the proposal of your dreams, sweetheart. And one day, we will be ready."

"Yes, we will."

Relief swept through me. He got it; he understood where I was coming from. In fact, Hayden wanted the same thing.

He leaned over and kissed my lips. We were going to be okay.

Knock.
Knock.

Knock.

Hayden pulled back and smiled. "You good?"

"Yeah, You?"

"Yeah. I will be."

I pecked him on the lips one more time before I called, "Come in."

Alexa poked her face in, her bottom lip firmly stuck between her teeth. "I'm so sorry if I caused an issue. I shouldn't have said anything. I wasn't thinking."

I walked over to her and opened the door. "No, you *should* have. It was a brilliant idea. I think it just took us off guard."

Hayden joined us. "We're taking your suggestion."

She winked. "So, we're planning a wedding."

Vehemently, we shook our heads, and Alexa tipped her head in confusion.

At the same moment, Drake walked around the corner. "Everything okay?"

"Yes. We decided we're going to use Alexa's idea and get married, but we're keeping it businesslike, almost clinical."

Alexa nodded. "I get it. Completely."

Drake shook his head. "I can't believe this asshole is going to beat me down the aisle."

We laughed, and Alexa rolled her eyes. It was just the right amount of levity needed to diffuse this immeasurably stressful situation.

If only there weren't other more serious issues to worry about lurking around the corner.

CHAPTER Thirty-One

Hayden

I was married.
To Kory.
I had a wife.

It had been three days since Alexa suggested it. And today in front of the preacher, we'd said our vows. It was more like a business transaction, which was what we both wanted.

But fuck, I'm married.

The idea still hadn't fully sunk in, especially considering the circumstances.

One day, I would make Kory my wife for real, the way we both wanted. But for now, marriage was a means to an end.

To help diffuse the stress of the day, Mom suggested having Hollis and Devney over for dinner. Not a celebration dinner, just friends getting together to shoot the breeze. At first, we'd been skeptical, but I believed it had been a good idea. Kory seemed to agree.

We still hadn't heard a word from her parents. I hoped to hell they came through for us because if they betrayed Kory, I would find a way to make them pay. Typically, I wasn't a vengeful person, but there were some lines that should never be crossed. Betraying your flesh and blood to a psycho was one of them.

The creak from the back door brought me out of my thoughts.

Hollis came out with Drake and Kane. He handed me a beer. My parents had space heaters and a firepit that allowed the back porch to still be used during the winter. "Here you go."

"Thanks, man. I needed one of these."

They sat in high-back Adirondack chairs that were arranged in a semicircle around a firepit. Kane shuddered. "We can never, ever let the girls win movie night. They're watching and crying while painting their toenails." He grimaced. "That's some fucked-up shit. Something about a girl named Shelby dying at the end of the movie. Hell, the movie just started. And before she even dies, they were boohooing about what was to come. I feel like I've entered an alternate reality."

I chuckled and took a swig of my beer. "They're watching *Steel Magnolias*. It's Kory's favorite."

Kane glared at me. "You should shut your mouth. The fact that you know the movie because I said a character's name makes me ashamed to call you my brother."

I quipped back, "Alexa told Kory that Drake watched *Pretty Woman* with her the other night. At least I'm not actually *watching* it. So be more ashamed of having Drake as your brother."

Drake shrugged and then smirked. "And I got rewarded

for it afterward."

Clinking my beer to his, I said, "Nice. And that's the way it's done."

"Exactly."

Kane looked up to the ceiling of the covered porch. "I've never been so disappointed in my older brothers. I need to remind myself to never look at them as role models." He turned to Hollis. "Have you been watching any of that shit with Devney?"

Holding his beer up, Hollis grinned. "Last night Devney and I watched *Deadpool*."

"Hell yeah. Finally, another man in my midst." Kane held out his fist for a bump. "Don't let her yank you around by the dick and talk you into watching something that'll make you a pussy. It's not very Alaskan."

Kane held out his beer bottle to Hollis and they clanked them together. Hollis toasted, "To Alaskan men."

Drake and I held out our bottles, but Kane shook his head. "No, you can't be part of this toast. You can toast to crying, princesses, and being a disappointment to the Foster name." Kane stood and shook his head. "I need to go carve something to get all this pansy stuff out of my head. Maybe I'll help Dad make some furniture. Anyone want to join me?"

"I will." Drake stood. "He's working on a new liquor cabinet for me. Maybe we could help him."

"Sounds good."

They crossed the lawn to Dad's shop. Hollis chuckled. "Man, your brother is one of a kind."

"Yeah, he is."

One of these days, when he finally found someone, I was going to give him so much hell.

The silence of the night was peaceful and calming. Hollis took a swig before asking, "How are you dealing with this?"

"I'm dealing. I hate that our hand was forced. But hopefully the way Kory and I did it, it won't be ruined when we do it next time."

Today we decided to tell Hollis and Devney about what we were facing, excluding the Fraternity stuff. It seemed the fewer people who knew about the organization the better. We'd told them everything else about Kory's controlling parents and the arranged marriage to Landon. No matter how we tried to describe them, they sounded like psychos.

"That makes sense. If you need anything, just know you can talk to me. I know I sometimes come off a bit... off-kilter, but I'm here."

"Thanks, man. I appreciate it. So how have things been with you and Devney?"

He let out a sigh. "After the auction, I refused to let Devney pay for the date. I paid the two grand. It kills me knowing how hard she has it and having the means to help, but she won't let me. She's independent, and I respect that. I explained that she saved me from what would have been a wretched date with whomever won, and she gave me an answer about where we stood." Hollis leaned his head back. "And things were great, fantastic even."

Were? That didn't sound promising. Hollis seemed to have more he wanted to say as he stared off into space, so for now, I stayed quiet.

"I feel something different for Devney. I've never felt it before in my life. We're not to the *I love yous* yet, but I think we're headed there. Well, that was until she dropped the bomb on me last night."

"What bomb?"

"Her mom wants her to move to Washington so they can get a place together. Since Devney lived with her dad as a kid, she feels obligated to help her mom now. I don't think her mom even knows about me, which adds another layer of confusion."

Women were confusing. Hell, I had been tied up over one for quite a while before I flew to get her.

"Is her mom pressuring her?"

"No. Yes. Kind of. I can't tell. It's like things get on track with us just to fall off the rails again. I can't win."

"Have you told her how you feel?"

Hollis took another swig of his beer and stared out into the night. It was like he had the weight of the world on his shoulders. "No, I don't want to add to her pressure."

Man, I knew right where he was emotionally, and it was a bumpy ride. "If she doesn't know how you feel, she can't make an informed decision."

"Yeah... I get it. It's a lot to think about."

And I understood. If Hollis put himself out there and she still chose to leave, it would hurt like a motherfucker.

CHAPTER Thirty-Two

Kory

We waved good-bye as Devney and Hollis drove away. Before they'd left, we loaded up Hollis's SUV with leftover food Amie insisted they take. I had noticed a lot of people sent extra food home with Hollis. Apparently, he could burn water if left to his own devices.

A day that had started out stressful and with me on edge had turned out to be pretty wonderful. When Amie initially suggested a get-together with friends, I hadn't really wanted to. As it turned out, it was exactly what we needed.

Hayden laced his fingers with mine, more relaxed than he'd been in days. I leaned into his side for warmth. The air was cold and crisp. As the SUV turned onto the road and the taillights disappeared, I realized how much my heart ached for Devney and Hollis. They were in such a rough spot right now. "Did Hollis mention Devney possibly moving?"

"Yeah, I think he's pretty torn up about it."

"So is Devney. I don't know what she's going to decide."

"Me either, sweetheart."

Devney had mentioned earlier that she wasn't sure how serious Hollis was about them. Devney hadn't wanted to talk about it with Alexa since she was best friends with Hollis. My only suggestion was to tell Hollis how she felt.

"Let's head inside. I'm worn out." Now that the day had come to the end, I was ready for bed.

Hayden led me inside the house. "Head on up to bed. I need to clean up our beer bottles from the back porch and say good night to Drake and Alexa."

"Okay, sounds good."

In the small sitting room to the right, Drake and Alexa were going over the suggestions I'd given for their wedding. During some of my free time this week, I'd begun a list of possibilities that seemed possible to pull off in a short amount of time, given the logistical issues of getting things to Skagway during the winter. Hopefully my suggestions would spark what they wanted.

"Night, guys," I called.

"Night," they answered in unison. I could get their notes in the morning. I figured it would be easier for them to discuss things on their own. Drake looked so ecstatic to finally be to this point. I doubted the type of greenery on the fireplace mattered to him. He wanted to be in the moment with Alexa. I admired Drake for how in tune he was with himself and not afraid to admit his feelings.

Hayden and I reached to the bottom of the stairs. "I'll be up in just a few minutes. You need anything, sweetheart?"

"No, I'm good. See you in a bit."

He gave me a quick peck on the lips, and I headed up the stairs. I needed a few minutes to myself to get my thoughts centered.

I wasn't sure it had sunk in yet.

It was still hard to believe I was married. I was a wife. Yet, at the same time, I felt like we weren't married. And I had insisted that Hayden sign a prenup. I brought nothing to the marriage, financially speaking. Hayden was well off. And it made our marriage feel less like a true marriage by having a contract. And I wasn't going to go by Mrs. Foster. I would still go by Kory Reynolds. No one but the family would know we were married.

If it kept Landon away from me, it would be worth it in the end. But I hated having to be forced into this. My parents hadn't responded to either my phone calls or text messages, which left me uneasy about what was going on with them.

Did they betray me?

There were times in my life where I thought I'd felt their love. But they would remain with the Fraternity. And that was something I would never subject my kids to. The price was too high. If they had been responsible for my grandparents' deaths... that was unforgivable. I just wasn't sure where I stood with them, but I knew in some way, I might never get closure.

I got ready for bed. Taking off my makeup and putting on my flannel pajamas brought me comfort. I folded back the blue down comforter—with the other two blankets on the bed, plus the heat Hayden generated, the comforter made it too warm.

I spun the propeller on the little plane on the nightstand. This reminded me of Hayden. The whole room did. I could picture him as a little boy, playing with his airplanes and models in this room. He'd wanted to be a pilot since he was three.

For as long as I could remember, I wanted to be a mom. I wanted to love my kids and be there for them in every way. *Maybe someday.* Kids were so far off. We still needed to have the wedding we actually wanted first. And before that, a proposal. There were a million steps before we got to kids.

Hayden came in and locked the door behind him.

"Is everyone headed to bed?"

"Mom and Dad are. Kane is off to who knows where. It looked like Drake and Alexa might be up for a while going over that folder you gave them. It's hard to believe their wedding will be here next month."

"It'll be here before we know it."

"Yeah… I'm going to take a shower."

"Okay."

We still hadn't discussed our wedding. After we said our vows, we got in the truck with his parents and came back here. The rest of the day had been filled with other people. Now I was worried Hayden regretted the decision.

The shower turned on, and I listened to him get in. This was ridiculous. If I was worried about something, I needed to ask him. *As soon as he's done.* Accosting him in the shower probably wasn't the most productive way to begin this discussion.

The water turned off, and shortly after, Hayden walked in with a towel wrapped around his waist. He pulled on some lounge pants with a great yawn. It had been a long day.

My cell phone rang beside the bed. It was one of my parents. I put it on speaker before I answered, "Hello?"

It was my mother. There was music in the background. "I can't talk long. We're at a party, and I snuck away to call you."

"What's going on?"

"We haven't been able to find a minute to communicate with you until now. Since we've gotten back, we've been staying with Landon's family. They're preparing for a wedding this weekend, Kory. Your wedding."

I felt a little dizzy, and I focused on her words. *My wedding. Me? Landon plans to marry me this weekend?* Hayden narrowed his eyes; he was beyond angry. We'd decided we wouldn't mention our wedding to my parents just in case they decided to tell Landon. I barely managed to choke out, "Is there anything else?"

"We're still looking. Your father is meeting with Eric right now. Kory, you need to know Landon plans to bring you back to Washington on Saturday. The wedding is scheduled for Sunday morning at dawn. One thing you should know, the Fraternity won't recognize a successor conceived out of wedlock. No exceptions."

My palms were clammy, and my mouth went dry. *Children? With Landon?* My stomach knotted. "Thanks, Mother."

"We'll be in touch if we find out more. Got to go. Bye, Kory. Your father and I love you."

"Love you, too."

It was weird hearing the words from them. But maybe they were trying to right the wrong choices they'd made when I was a child for the small amount of time we had left together. They told Hayden on the porch we would never really have a chance to have a relationship. It was a choice—a choice they left up to me.

I ended the call but stared at the phone. My breathing began to increase, and I felt an odd sort of pressure on my chest. "I won't marry him. I can't. There's no way... I would rather—"

I was nearly hysterical when Hayden touched my face. His touch instantly calmed me down. "Kory, he can't marry you because I'm your husband. This is why we did this today. If somehow he succeeded in taking you, which isn't possible, he can't legally marry you. And if he tried, you tell him you're married. After what your mother just said about illegitimate children, this is a good thing. We'll keep our marriage as the ultimate backup plan."

Playing with my fingers, I prepared to face whatever answer he gave. As long as it was the truth, we'd manage through it. "Do you regret today? Do you feel like I trapped you?"

Hayden looked a little confused. "No, not at all. Why?"

That was a good sign. But I still felt uneasy about the whole thing. "I don't know. We just haven't talked about today. And just all this craziness with my family. And the phone call. It's just a lot."

He came over to the bed, and the mattress dipped under his weight. "The only reason I haven't said anything is that I didn't want to take away from when we do get married. Kory, I don't want to ruin the dreams I know you have."

This man was amazing. More amazing than I deserved. "I just don't want to be a regret."

"You never could be." He thought for a second. "I really hated signing the prenup today. Loathed it. I need you to understand that when the time comes for us to do this for real, we're going to make sure it's void. A prenup is a deal breaker.

I'm not setting up our marriage for failure because I'm never letting you go."

I chewed on my lip. "But I have nothing to bring to the marriage."

"Material things don't matter. All I need is your love."

He leaned me back, and his mouth consumed mine. A fire was lit within me as Hayden lifted up my shirt, trailing heat in the wake of his touch. "We're going to get our happily ever after."

"I hope so."

"I know so."

CHAPTER Thirty-Three

Hayden

Kory snuggled closer to me, and I tightened my arms around her. It had been one hell of a week. Tomorrow, Landon would arrive in Skagway. His pilot had called to see about refueling while they made a "pit stop" in Skagway. Keeping my anger under control had been difficult, especially since I'd been on speakerphone. For all I knew, Landon had been listening in.

From the brief conversation with the pilot, Kory's mother's information had been correct. The pilot only planned to be on the ground for a couple of hours before taking off. On the off chance snow came, the pilot had asked if I had hangar space to rent.

Fucker.

I knew it wasn't the pilot's fault, but he *had* to know Landon was shady. No amount of money was worth your ethics. None. I took a deep breath, willing myself to chill out. So far,

I'd managed to stay pretty calm this week, although I knew Kory was a nervous wreck. If I allowed myself to get out of control and angry about Landon, it would only frazzle Kory.

I pulled her closer to me. The idea of being married to Kory sank in a little more each day. I liked—no, loved—knowing she was mine. All mine.

But first, we needed to get through this mess and then we could focus on our relationship.

Kory made a little noise in her sleep. "Love you, Hayden."

Déjà vu hit me like a smack in the head. This was what had happened right before Kory left Alaska and ran back to Washington. It had messed me up so badly that I'd disappeared for a few days. This time it was different. I held her closer, knowing I would spend the rest of my life making sure I earned her love. "Love you, too, sweetheart."

Her breathing shifted and grew more rhythmic, more relaxed. Kory really hadn't had any decent sleep all week. Tonight, she'd passed out from sheer exhaustion. We hadn't heard from her parents since the call about the wedding plans. I still had doubts about whether they were going to betray Kory.

I hoped to hell they didn't.

My private investigator hadn't turned up shit on Landon. I wasn't sure what we were going to do at this point. The plan was to confront Landon at the airport and hopefully send him on his merry way. But I doubted it was going to be that simple.

Kory's phone chimed, and she shot up out of bed. "Where's my phone?"

Please let it be them with some news. "It's on your nightstand."

She snatched up the phone and looked at the display. "Hayden, it's from my parents."

Finally.

She clicked the button, her brows knit in confusion. "It's just a link with a password."

"No message?"

She shook her head. "Should we check it out? Or do you think it's a trap?"

That seemed a little odd. "Let me get my laptop."

I grabbed my old one from my bag. If the link was a virus or something else, we could always trash the computer and nothing would be lost.

"Okay, type this in." Kory gave me the site address and password.

Since it was an older computer, it took a little bit longer for it to boot up. "What is it?" Kory asked.

"I don't know yet. This computer is pretty slow."

We stared at the screen, willing the blue circle to stop spinning. Then it went blank, and my heart sank. Finally, a file folder popped up.

Kory leaned over to peer at the screen. "Are you going to click on it?"

"Yeah."

Another window popped up with a list of all sorts of documents. I read one after another with Kory until what we were looking at made sense. My heart soared in victory, and I whispered, "Got you, motherfucker."

Kory looked at me, tears in her eyes. "They found our way out. They came through."

"Yes, they did, sweetheart. We need to make a new plan."

CHAPTER Thirty-Four

Kory

As we stood outside, the bitter cold numbed my face. Hayden wanted to make sure he heard the plane approaching in case the pilot chose not to make the proper calls. There was no air traffic control in the area to report him if he didn't.

Everything was eerily calm. So far, we hadn't heard or seen the plane. Waiting for the pilot's voice to come over Hayden's handheld device had me on edge. As each second passed, my nerves frayed a little more.

After the text message from my parents, we'd been up pretty late discussing different options. I was exhausted, and my head throbbed from the stress. The speaker handheld unit came to life. "Skagway traffic Cirrus November 180 Kilo Tango, ten miles south inbound to land runway two zero. Skagway."

That was the first of three calls they would make. This

was it. Hayden looked back at his brothers, who stood a few feet away. Their eyes were focused on the sky. Even Mariah tilted her head up, imitating Kane. "We've got about five minutes, give or take, before they land. That was the first of what should be three calls."

By the next call, we'd be able to hear the plane. The anticipation set in. We only had one chance to do this right. If we didn't play things correctly, I wasn't sure what the results would be. And it *really* wasn't something I wanted to find out. There weren't any good options.

After an in-depth discussion, we'd decided I should have a sit-down lunch with Landon at the Red Onion. If we confronted him with hostility, it might cause more problems.

Lunch at the Red Onion seemed safe. If anything happened, Drake would have his eyes on me while Kane and Hayden would be watching me from the office via the cameras. I refused to be alone with him. If I thought about all the times throughout the years that I'd gone to lunch with Landon, I'd be sick for sure. All I'd been was a pawn in the Fraternity's twisted games.

After last night's discussions, Hayden and I had come to the realization that this might not be over today. I wanted it done. Best case scenario: Landon decided it was best to move on without me in his life. There would be no mention of the Fraternity. That wasn't something we were prepared to tackle, nor did we want to.

"Skagway traffic Cirrus November 180 Kilo Tango, five mile final two zero. Skagway."

The headache pounded a little harder. That was the second of the three calls. The landing gear would be coming down soon.

I want this over. I want my life back.

"Sweetheart, we need to go inside."

That was when I heard the plane. Soon, it would come into view. It was time. I straightened my shoulders. *This is my life. No one else controls it.*

Hayden put his arm around my waist and guided me to follow his brothers into the office. "This is going to work, Kory."

"I hope so."

"If not, we'll improvise. One thing I know for sure is that you're worth all this, Kory. Never doubt it for a second."

"Those were the exact words I needed to hear." I'd tried to sweep away my fears, but they remained under the surface, chipping away at my security. Hayden had been nothing but supportive, and that helped keep the negative thoughts away.

We can do this. We'll figure it out. We're meant to be together.

I took off my gloves and flexed my fingers, appreciating the heat of the reception area. I turned my eyes up to the sky and waited for the plane to come into view. The time was drawing closer. Closer than I wanted.

"Skagway traffic Cirrus November 180 Kilo Tango, short final two zero. Skagway."

Finally, the plane came into view.

"Kory, you need to get in the office."

I heard the words but couldn't move—I just stared at the black dot growing larger in the sky. The man who wanted to control every aspect of my life was on that plane. Own me like I was a piece of property. Landon wanted to take away my freedom. I was a means to an end—produce as many heirs as possible. My skin crawled at the thought that he'd had my gynecologist monitoring my fertility.

Sick. Bastard.

"Kory, did you hear me?"

I nearly jumped out of my skin when Hayden touched my shoulder. "Wh-what did you say?"

Hayden turned me to face him, breaking my visual with the plane. He squeezed my shoulders. "Sweetheart, you need to get in the office. We don't want them to see you."

Part of me wanted to confront Landon right here and just get it over with. However, now that we had leverage, I had suggested we hear him out and find out what he wanted. *What if my parents are wrong?* It wasn't a foregone conclusion that they were telling the truth. This could all be a well-orchestrated game like my entire life had been.

Stiffly, I walked to the door of Hayden's office.

When I went to close the door, Hayden's foot appeared in the doorway to stop it. He stepped in and closed the door behind him. This wasn't part of the plan. In one swift movement, he grabbed the sides of my face and fiercely kissed me. I clung to him, pouring every ounce of myself into the kiss. When Hayden pulled away, he whispered, "I love you. Don't forget that."

"I won't. I never will. I love you so much, Hayden."

"I need to get back out there, but you've got this. You're strong, Kory. One of the strongest people I know."

"Thank you."

Hayden hurried from the room, leaving me alone. I was grateful he'd taken a moment to reassure me. He was amazing—always building me up. I felt like I could conquer the world with Hayden by my side.

I can do this.

One step at a time.

I took a seat in Hayden's black leather chair behind his huge oak desk. The furniture was exquisite. Ike had made most of it and incorporated a wooden propeller into the front of the desk. The coordinating pieces had aerial maps stamped onto them.

The monitors had been moved so I could see the office area better. Since the camera feeds were video only, Kane had rigged a speaker for me to listen in. One thing I'd noticed was Drake and Hayden had some kick-ass security. From what Hayden had told me, Kane had installed it. He wanted to be prepared if the shit ever hit the fan.

Well, his preparation had paid off.

I put one of the earbuds in and flipped the switch to turn on the volume. There was only a slight static. Hayden stood in front of the window and looked outside. "He'll be on the ground in less than a minute."

Hayden turned from the window, his fists clenched, and paced a few steps. Seeing the nerves taking hold of Hayden sent a new current of fear through me. He'd been my rock through this.

Drake stood next to him and put his hand on his brother's shoulder. "This will only work if you're relaxed. You gotta calm down. I get it. I would be this way, too. But you got to pull your shit together on the outside."

"You're right."

"Dickhead has landed," Kane said from the window. "Maybe we should have had some shirts made that said *Dickheads Not Welcome*."

It was hard not to chuckle. At the oddest times, Kane would say the funniest, off-the-wall things.

Hayden shook his head. "Why didn't we think of that?"

"Because you're not as smart as I am. Sorry, brothers, I got all the brains in the family."

Drake laughed. "Someone has always had the big head."

Kane hadn't shifted his attention from the plane. Hayden shook his head. "I hate this asshole."

"I'd be okay if you sucker punched him. Just sayin'," Kane said.

That made Hayden crack a smile, and he took his seat. Abruptly, Kane turned to the guys and said something I couldn't hear. *What's he saying?* I heard his next words. "Mariah, come."

He turned on his heel and stalked toward the office, Mariah tight to his left side. The door opened, and they filled the doorway. He gave that same fist signal to the dog, and she lay down and faced the closed door. It would be hard to tell she was alive were it not for the gentle breaths she took.

Kane narrowed his gaze on the screen. Something was up. "Can I have the extra earbud?"

"Sure." I took the one still sitting on the desk and handed it to him. He put it in and leaned a little closer to the monitor without saying anything else. "What's going on?"

"Change of plans. I'll explain later." This is what I imagined Kane would be like in the woods. Nothing mattered to him except the target he was after.

I heard Drake say through the speakers, "Here they come."

When the door opened, Drake casually walked over to the chair and picked up a magazine. A man wearing aviators came in first. He was tall and lean, and his angular face gave him a harsh look. *Have I seen him before?* There was something familiar about him.

The door opened again, and Landon walked in. He surveyed the room before taking off his sunglasses. On instinct, I tried to push back from the desk, but Kane was there to keep me from moving. He held up a finger to his mouth to remind me to be quiet.

I'm okay.

He's not going to get me.

I took a few deep, quiet breaths before focusing on the screen. There wasn't a dark hair out of place on Landon's head. He had it slicked back in his usual way. Landon was strong but lean; he wasn't broad and rugged like Hayden or his brothers. Just the sight of him rolled my stomach. I thought about different memories throughout my life, and so much made sense now. Right before college graduation, I'd told Landon about wanting to go away for the summer before I settled into my life. He'd been the one to tell my parents to let me. He'd been the one in control the entire time.

It was all a ploy to get what he wanted.

I hate him.

Landon offered his hand with an easy confidence. "Landon Masterson. My pilot, Jack, will be in to do the necessary paperwork and pay for the fuel."

"Sounds good. Anthony should be here in a few. He'll take care of the refuel for you."

"Thanks. If the plane needs to be moved, let Jack know. We shouldn't be here more than a few hours."

A few hours. Only a few hours and we'd be done.

Hayden stood. "Sounds good. Is there anything else you need?"

"Do you by chance have a courtesy vehicle? On the way

here, I spoke to the wife of a man named Doug who said he was the only taxi in town. Apparently, he's out with someone named Ol' Man Rooster, and they're hunting?"

The way Landon questioned the validity was almost funny. To someone from the city, having one taxi in town, not to mention someone with a name like Rooster, wasn't common.

"Sounds about right," Hayden said. "Sorry, though. I don't have a courtesy vehicle. Where are you headed?"

"The Red Onion. I've heard it's fantastic. We're making a pit stop on the way back from Anchorage. I needed to stretch my legs for a bit."

Anchorage? Liar. And I noticed he failed to mention anything about meeting an old friend.

Drake put aside the magazine he'd been reading. "I'm headed into town. I work at the Red Onion if you'd like a ride. I was here just shootin' the shit and catching up."

That was pretty smooth of Drake.

Landon looked at Drake and nodded. "I'll take you up on that. Thank you. My associate Ray is going to come, as well, if you don't mind."

"Not at all."

Ray. I searched my memory, trying to figure out where I'd seen him before. I was typically good at remembering faces even after meeting someone only once, but this one eluded me. *Where have I seen him?*

When I blinked again, they were gone. Hayden locked the front door. Kane just stared at the screen. "Can you get the office door for Hayden?"

I scooted back in my chair and walked over to the door. Mariah still lay stock-still. "You're a good girl. Thank you for guarding."

She cocked her head and stared at me while I opened the door.

Hayden pulled me to him, and I melted into him, needing the connection. "They're gone. Pilot is staying with the plane. Anthony should be here shortly to help refuel and keep an eye on things. Are we ready to go?"

It was time to move to the next part of the plan—meeting Landon at the Red Onion.

"There was a fourth." Kane's words stopped us in our tracks.

We whipped our heads around to look at him. "What?"

Kane rewound the footage and pointed to the plane. "Watch the back right corner of the screen. If he'd gotten out a few seconds before, we would have never seen it."

In the next few frames, something black rolled out of the plane and then took off. Kane switched cameras. A man ran between the two buildings and into the woods. "Gotcha, prick. Mariah, you and I are going to go hunt us an asshole."

Kane set his jaw with the harshness of steel.

Mariah stood at attention, waiting for Kane's command. "Change of plans. I'm going to track this guy while you go to the Red Onion."

CHAPTER Thirty-Five

Kory

It was hard to tell how far from town we were. To keep from being seen, I'd crawled onto the front floorboard of the truck. Since the pilot had stayed with the plane, we'd had to get into the vehicle without being noticed. If Landon knew I was there watching him, it would change the entire tone of our meeting. Hayden had pulled his truck into the garage that connected to the office. Kane, Mariah, and I had slipped in before Anthony arrived.

My goal was to convince Landon to move on. But he'd brought an additional person we weren't supposed to be aware of. That left me uneasy. Landon had contingency plans himself. That alone gave some validity to the information my parents had given me. I hoped they had been truthful. Even if we weren't able to have a relationship, deep down, I needed to know they loved me.

The image of the man in black running into the woods

circled through my mind. From the moment I saw him, ice ran through my veins.

From the back seat, Kane asked, "How far are we? From the tree line it looks like we're getting close."

To make sure no one saw him, Kane lay flat in the back seat. Mariah was on the floorboard.

"One, maybe two minutes."

There was some shifting in the back. "Don't roll to a complete stop. Just slow down enough for us to hop out. I'll have my phone on silent, but I'll check it frequently. Text, don't call. I won't pick up. Has anyone followed us?"

Hayden looked in the rearview mirror. "No, not a soul. Are you armed?"

The truck began to slow down.

"Does an elk shit in the woods?"

Hayden shook his head and chuckled. "Smart-ass. Okay get ready."

"Be careful," I called from the floorboard.

"That's my middle name. You put that bastard in his place."

I smiled. "That's the plan."

The door opened and closed, and then we were speeding up again. Hayden seemed to keep a keen eye on his surroundings as we drove. I hated not being able to see, but so far, things seemed okay.

"You've got this, sweetheart."

I hugged my knees closer to my chest as we got closer to town. "I know. I just wish it could be over with. And we knew the outcome."

"We will soon enough. Do you remember the sign if you think something is wrong?"

"Touch my forehead."

"And don't let him talk you into going anywhere else."

"I won't."

We'd gone over the plan a hundred times since we'd finalized it in the wee hours of the morning. Everyone was running on fumes. Ike and Amie were with Alexa at the clinic, which brought everyone we loved closer to town. "You can get up now. No one is following us."

I crawled up in the seat and settled in. "What if he refuses to listen? I know we talked about this last night, but, Hayden... he might never let up."

"Let's not go there until we have to. If Landon is as smart as your parents give him credit for, he'll distance himself. I'm sure he'll monitor things to make sure we hold up our end of the bargain, but he doesn't have to be here to do it."

I hated the fact that there was a chance he'd always be in our lives, lingering around the edges. Loose ends were never good. People like Landon hated loose ends. And we'd be a huge stain in his carefully crafted world. But like Hayden said, we had to focus on the hand we were dealt until we knew more about the game we were playing.

We reached my truck, and I expelled my breath in a rush. "Here we go."

I grabbed the door handle, but before I could get out, Hayden leaned over and grabbed my hand. "Be careful. You're the most important thing in my life."

"I will." I touched his cheek. "Thank you for saving me from a life I never wanted."

He put his forehead to mine. "Kory, you saved me, too."

Maybe we had saved each other. He gave me a quick kiss that I wanted to last longer. "I need to go."

"I know. I'll be right behind you."

When I opened the door, the cold air greeted me with a renewed fervor. From what the locals were saying, it was unseasonably cold so far this winter. Everyone expected record-setting snowfall. Thanksgiving was less than a week away, and I hoped this was all behind us by then. I was excited to have a holiday full of laughter and love. Growing up, Thanksgiving had been a formal affair with Landon's family. This year, I planned to get up early and cook with Amie all day.

I got in my truck and picked up my phone. Sure enough, I had a couple of missed calls and a text from Landon. We'd decided to leave my phone in the truck just in case Landon was tracking me.

I opened the texts.

Landon: *Landed. Call me when you get this. Looking forward to seeing you.*

My stomach turned a little more. *Here we go.* I pushed call on my phone and put the truck in drive. I couldn't look at Hayden, or I would lose focus. It was time to bring my A game and end this nonsense. It was up to me to seize my future.

Landon picked up on the first ring. "Hey there. I thought you might have stood me up again."

I laughed, hoping it sounded real. "No, not this time. When did you get here?"

"About a half an hour ago. I figured I'd walk around town to see what Skagway had to offer."

"Oh, I'm so sorry. I thought we were meeting closer to noon. I saw a friend and stopped to talk. Time got away from me."

A horn honked in the background. Landon was still outside. "No worries. Yeah, it seems like everyone knows everyone here. Welcome to Mayberry."

"Yeah, it's nice."

I wondered if Landon had asked about me. If so, he would have questions about Hayden.

Landon didn't say anything else. "How was your flight?"

"Smooth. We had a great tailwind from Anchorage."

"Anchorage?"

So, he was keeping with this story. *Why didn't he come straight here from Washington?*

"I had a little business to attend to up there. I'm considering expanding some operations. I thought maybe we could meet at a park, talk before we went to eat. There are some things I'd like to talk to you about in private, get your thoughts."

No way was I going to be with him alone. *Think.* My mind was getting more confused the closer I got to town. *Stay in control of the situation.* "Can we do that after lunch? I skipped breakfast, and I'm starving. The Red Onion has the best fries in town."

He paused for longer than necessary, probably thinking of a way around what I'd said. He had to know if he pushed too hard, I wouldn't show up. "Sure. I'll get a table. How long until you arrive?"

"About fifteen minutes."

"Perfect. I'm looking forward to catching up, Kory."

"Me, too."

We hung up, and I took a few measured breaths. My skin was crawling at the thought of sitting down to a meal with him. I decided to update Hayden. He answered on the first ring.

"How'd it go?"

I glanced in the rearview mirror. Hayden was about five car lengths behind me. "It went well, I think. He wanted to meet at a park first. But I convinced him to go to the Red Onion. I think my assertiveness startled him."

"Ass."

Before, I would have agreed to meet at the park first. So much about how everyone catered to Landon's family made sense now.

"He's out walking and mentioned everyone knowing everyone. I wonder if he knows about us."

"Doesn't matter."

I wanted to be as confident as Hayden sounded. We entered the city limits, but he stayed back a few car lengths. "Just remember, Drake and I will have eyes on you the entire time. If you get uncomfortable, get up and leave or give me the sign. Don't put yourself at risk."

"I won't. Promise."

CHAPTER Thirty-Six

Kory

Hayden followed me into town. It wasn't too busy, which was good. The fewer people who saw me with Landon, the better. I parked in front of the Red Onion and stared at the door. *This is it.* And there was no script. For the first time since leaving the hell of my old life, I wished I knew how this was going to go. If only it could be perfectly orchestrated right down to the responses I would receive.

But that wasn't life.

I saw Sylvia poke her head around the corner of the building. Damn it. The Twiner sisters had a knack for being in the right place at the worst possible time. I loved the ladies, but today was not the day to deal with them.

Hayden stayed in his truck and stared where Elvira came around the corner. When they made eye contact with me, I knew they had some questions.

Yeah, if I tried to avoid them, they might make things

worse by lurking around the Red Onion.

I got out of the truck and waited for Elvira. Where had Sylvia gone? There was no telling. "Kory, you're just the person we wanted to see." Elvira pulled out her pencil from her gray bun. "Do you, by chance, have a second for a few questions?"

"Of course. What's going on?"

She patted my shoulder. "Well, we saw there was a newbie in town. He asked if you were seeing anyone. Is there trouble on the horizon?"

Oh shit, Landon asked about me. For a second, I wasn't sure what to say, then recovered. "Oh, he's just a friend I met. We're meeting for lunch to catch up."

I gave her a placating smile, hoping she left the topic alone.

Sylvia ran up to us, nearly out of breath. "I told you not to leave me, Elvira. I had to get my notebook out of the car."

"Well, Kory was about to go inside. And you know how Drake has told us we can't harass his patrons." She tilted her head. "Did you want me to lose the story?"

Sylvia rolled her eyes and retrieved her pencil from the notebook around her neck. "Still… you should have waited." Then they turned their attention on me. Sylvia beat Elvira by asking the first question. "So, no problems between you and Hayden?"

I looked at Hayden, who got out of his truck and gave us a wink. "No, none. We're going to go have lunch with a friend."

They giggled, following my gaze. Sylvia said, "He sure is smitten. Okay, Elvira, let's head to the clinic. We need to let Hollis and Devney know they're going to be a success story in our new matchmaking business."

Oh, geez. Matchmaking? I wasn't getting into that now. Hayden must have heard because his shoulders shook with laughter.

"Good luck with Hollis and Devney. Do you have any other questions?"

Elvira finished jotting something down. "I think we're good. We're going to go get this newsletter out."

"Sounds good."

They scurried off, talking a mile a minute. *A matchmaking business? Heaven help the town of Skagway.*

I entered the Red Onion. A few patrons were scattered about, but other than that, it was fairly empty. Normally the smell of the food here was welcome, but right now my stomach was in knots.

The man I'd seen at the hangar earlier sat at the bar. He glanced my way, and I still wasn't able to place where I'd seen him. It was bothering me, and I searched my mind for people I knew who were associated with Landon. I couldn't remember a time I had been with him or his family when this man had been there.

Landon stood and interrupted my thoughts. His green eyes were calculating even as he gave me a soft smile. Until today, I hadn't noticed how ruthless he seemed. It was hard to keep a smile on my face, but somehow, I managed. My instincts screamed at me to not go to him. I had to force one foot in front of the other.

I loathed him. I loathed everything about him. I especially hated what he stood for.

As I got closer to him, the smell of his cologne made my stomach roll. It was smooth yet potent. "It's good to see you,

Kory." He gently touched my elbow and pressed his fingers into my skin.

It was a possessive touch that put me on edge. I paused, saying nothing but simply staring, and he released me. I managed a smile and put a little distance between us. "It's good to see you, too."

"You look beautiful. More beautiful than I remember."

I hadn't expected him to be that forward. "Oh... umm... thank you."

I took the seat across from where Landon stood and was surprised when he moved to sit next to me. This was beginning to make me a little uncomfortable, but I needed to press forward.

Drake approached the table. "Can I get you something to eat?"

Landon looked at his watch. "Yes, two burgers with fries. One medium rare and one medium well. Add extra ketchup on the medium well one. That'll be all, thank you."

What the hell? It was creepy that he knew how I took my burger. It was getting a little hot, and I sipped the ice water in front of me.

Drake stared at Landon. Hard. Then he said, "Order coming right up. It's good to see you, Kory. I don't think I know your friend."

I waved my hand through the air dismissively. "This is Landon. He's a friend from back home. He thought he'd drop by on his way back to Washington."

"Well, enjoy Skagway. I'll have the burgers out in a few."

It was unlike Landon to be so rude and ignore Drake. He checked his watch again; there was definitely something else on his mind.

"So, tell me about this place. What made you pick Skagway? Was it the guy you are seeing?" There was a slight bite to his tone.

Something was off, but I couldn't place it. My head began to throb as the headache came back with a vengeance. A fog settled into the corners of my consciousness, and my skin grew warmer. I felt like I was growing numb. I tried to respond, but whatever I'd wanted to say seemed less important than it had a few minutes ago. "I... umm... I..."

Words were hard to sort through as the fog rolled in faster. *What's going on?* I was supposed to do something if I felt uncomfortable. *Am I feeling uncomfortable?*

Landon leaned in closer to me. "Kory, I want you to take a drink."

Without another thought, I picked up my glass and took a drink.

"Good girl. I want you to tell me you're ready to go home to Washington."

Like a robot, I responded, "I'm ready to go home to Washington."

"Good girl." He nodded, leaning even closer. "I'm going to make you my queen. You'll want for nothing. I've wanted you for as long as I can remember."

I stared at him, trying to make sense of what he was saying. *Queen?* I knew I wanted to stay here, but I couldn't voice my thoughts. Or maybe I wanted to go.

He checked his watch again and then reached across the table. "When I tell you, we're going to get up. You're going to come with me. Understood? No questions."

"Understood." It felt like I had no control over anything, and I just had to listen to everything Landon said to me.

"Good girl. It's time for all the games to end. You belong by my side."

There were loud bangs all around. I tried to move, but Landon grabbed my arm. "Come, Kory."

I stood and followed him outside. Something was wrong with me. I wanted to scream out for someone to help me, but the words never came. My body refused to listen to me. The fog rolled in thicker, heavier, weighing me down. It brought the darkness. The woozy feeling was taking over.

Landon put his arm around me. "The dose I gave you might have been too strong. There's a medical bag on board. Stay with me a little longer, Kory."

The words meant nothing to me, and I fought to stay awake. My eyelids felt heavy. I wanted to fight, but I couldn't. My body wasn't my own anymore. As we cleared the door, I took big gulps of air, trying to fight off whatever was happening to me.

"Take her. She'll be out in the next five minutes. We need to get her to the plane for treatment. Do you have a car?"

Treatment?

"Yes, it's around the corner. I hot-wired one that was parked just outside of town."

"Good, let's go."

My legs left the ground, and I was in someone's arms. *Who's holding me?* Before I could turn my head to look, the alley door burst open. Hayden came out holding a gun. *Why is there a gun? What's happening?* Nothing was making sense. "You're not taking her."

"Yes, I am."

"Over my dead body," Hayden responded.

Landon pulled something out of his pocket. "That can be

arranged."

Hayden took a step closer.

"If you shoot me, this man will kill her." The grip on me tightened, and I moaned. He was hurting me.

We lurched back a couple of steps. A dog growled. Then a deep, raspy voice came out of nowhere. "Not if he has a knife to his throat, motherfucker."

Kane. That has to be Kane.

It took too much effort to look his way. Hayden cocked his gun. "Put. Her. Down."

My head became heavier, and it was getting harder to breathe. None of this made sense. I wanted to panic, but the world was closing in on me too fast. *What's happening? Who's holding me? Why is Hayden yelling?* I was too tired to fight anymore, and I let my eyelids close.

"Kory, are you okay? *Kory*? What did you to do her, asshole?"

Through the fog, I could make out the sounds of sirens. Pain shot through my head, and the darkness finally claimed me.

CHAPTER Thirty-Seven

Kory

Whoosh.
Whoosh.
Whoosh.

"When is she going to wake up?"

That was Hayden's voice. I wanted to run into the safety of his arms. But I couldn't move.

"Hollis, you have to give me some answers."

He sounded worried. More worried than I could remember ever hearing him. *What's wrong?* I wanted to answer him, but I couldn't find my voice.

Someone touched my wrist. "I don't know when, but it should be within the next few hours. It's difficult to predict, and I try not to give more than a general time frame. Every body reacts differently and needs whatever time it needs to heal. When her body is ready, she'll wake up."

"I can't lose her, Hollis."

So much anguish. I wanted to take it all away.

Lose me? Hayden, I'm fine. You're not going to lose me. But the blackness was calling. It wanted me back. I was so tired.

I tried to understand what was happening, but nothing came.

Hollis vowed, "I'm going to do everything in my power to make sure that doesn't happen."

Someone squeezed my hand. "I know you will." There was another squeeze. "Kory, come back to me, sweetheart. It's safe. Landon can't hurt you anymore."

Landon? Did he come already? Where is he?

The more I tried to make sense of it, the more tired I became. It was no use fighting—the darkness was calling. It wanted me, and I had no choice but to succumb.

Whoosh.
Whoosh.
Whoosh.

The whooshing sound was back. *What's that noise?* It kept waking me up. I was so tired.

"I would like to question Ms. Reynolds."

I wasn't able to place this new voice. *Who is it? Why do they want to question me?*

Someone let out an enormous sigh. "As I have told you—and you can plainly see for yourself, Special Agent Stenton—Ms. Reynolds is unconscious. Mr. Foster allowed you in for a few minutes so you could see for yourself. As soon as she wakes up, I'll let you know. However, I will have to clear her for questions first. I won't have you jeopardizing my patient's health."

"I'd like to speak with her before I leave. Here's my card." His voice was cold and detached. He wasn't someone I wanted to speak with.

Hollis's reply was short and sharp. "Thank you. I'll add it to the other two you've given us."

The door opened and closed. *Is he gone?* I wanted to ask but couldn't find my voice. Again, my mind grew tired.

Where's Hayden? Did he leave?

"That motherfucker doesn't care." *There he is.* Hayden sounded so angry. *Why's he angry?* I had so many questions. I tried to speak but nothing came out.

Maybe some more sleep.

Hollis said, "Hayden, you need to remain calm. I know you're pissed off right now, but it's not going to do Kory any good. Kory is going to need you when she wakes up. We don't know what all the ramifications are at this point."

Ramifications? I tried to hang on to listen to what they were saying. But it was getting harder. My mind tired so quickly.

"I know. It just pisses me off. He's more concerned about building his case."

"Most likely. But until I clear her, he won't come back in this room."

Unable to hold on any longer, I fell asleep again.

Whoosh.
Whoosh.

Whoosh.

That annoying noise woke me up again. This time, everything seemed a little clearer. My eyes fluttered open but immediately closed against the light. It was so bright.

Where am I?

Somehow, I had managed to make it through the sludge that had held me captive. I swallowed, and fire raced down my throat. I tried to speak, but my voice stayed locked away. Everything felt so heavy. It was like an elephant was sitting on me. I cracked my eyes open slowly to adjust to the light.

What happened?

That was the question that continued to bounce around in my head without an answer. *Where's Hayden?* I sensed him. He had to be close. I rolled my head to the side and saw him asleep in the chair, holding my hand. Even in rest, his face was drawn and tired. *What happened to him? Is he okay?* I didn't want to wake him. He needed sleep.

I tried to work out what was going on, but my brain felt weighted down.

Slowly, I moved my head to the left. Amie and Alexa sat in the chairs, fast asleep. It hit me that I was in the clinic. *But why?* I had no memory of getting sick or having an accident. The last thing I remembered was waiting for Landon to arrive in Skagway and hoping my parents had found something to get him out of my life.

The oxygen tube on my face itched. I moved my arm to scratch it, and Hayden jumped.

"Kory. Oh, sweetheart, you're awake. Alexa, get Hollis."

Suddenly, there was so much commotion. Hayden pressed his lips to my forehead. "Oh, thank you for giving her back to me. Thank you."

Amie came to my other side. "It's so good to have you back, Kory. We were worried."

"Th-th-thank y-you."

She patted my hand. "I'll be right outside if anyone needs me."

The door opened, and Hollis came in wearing his white lab coat and an easy smile. "Glad to see you awake. How are you feeling?"

I swallowed a couple of times before answering, "Confused."

"That's normal after what you've gone through. Let me get you checked over, then we'll explain everything. Can you be patient for just a few minutes before you get answers?"

Hollis understood what I was dealing with. I wanted answers but could wait. "Y-yes."

Hollis pulled out a penlight from his coat pocket and shone it into my eyes. It was so bright, and I wanted to close my eyes to get away from it. Next, he used a reflex hammer on the bottom of my foot, which tickled. Satisfied, he tucked the penlight back in his pocket and handed the reflex hammer to Alexa.

Taking a seat on the edge of my bed, he focused on me. "Your pupillary and reflex responses are normal, which is a good sign." Alexa handed him a printout from the machine I was hooked up to. Thankfully, she pressed a button to silence the sporadic beeping. "Your vitals have continued to be stable, as well."

That was good news. I felt Hayden squeeze my hand, and I weakly returned the gesture. The fire in my throat made itself known. "W-water?"

"Yes, Hayden can give you a sponge full of water. Gently

suck it. For now, let's start with two and see how that settles in your stomach, okay? After a few minutes, you can have another."

I nodded. Hayden gently pressed the blue sponge on a stick to my lips. "There you go, sweetheart." He took the sponge away for a moment and then offered it again. The cool water helped the sandpaper feeling in my throat. I was so tired, but I had so many questions.

My body still felt weighed down and my mind was a little cloudy. "What... happened?"

Hollis watched me closely but his face was relaxed. "What do you remember?"

I went over it all again. Images filtered through my mind. "Going to... bed. Waiting for... Landon... to come."

"That was the night before everything happened," Hayden interjected.

Night before everything happened?

I didn't have a chance to ask anything before Hollis continued. "That would make sense. You were given a drug called scopolamine, which is sometimes referred to as Devil's Breath. It was on a patch near your elbow and is easily absorbed through the skin. It's been questioned whether or not the drug can be used to render people helpless in reports received from Colombia and Paris. Until this point, there hasn't been anything verifiable. The drug makes the person compliant to begin with before they enter a coma-like state. It acts like Rohypnol but is more dangerous. Studies show it can cause memory problems for approximately twenty-four hours."

"Who... drugged... me?"

The realization of what happened became clearer, and I felt my heart beat a little faster in my chest. I'd been drugged.

Who would do this to me?

"Landon. He came to town," Hayden supplied.

He'd been here? When did he come? Why couldn't I remember? My chest ached, and I needed more air.

"Kory, listen to me. You have to remain calm, or I may need to sedate you. You are safe. Hayden is here. Landon is in custody. No one is going to hurt you. Breathe with me, okay?"

I followed Hollis, breathing in and out a few times, and began to calm some. "You have a slight concussion from when you hit your head after being dropped. But your vitals are strong. I expect you'll make a full recovery."

There were so many gaps. My memories were gone. But the last thing I wanted was to be sedated, so I took another deep breath. More answers might help. "What... happened with... Landon?"

"I'm going to let Hayden explain since he was there. But, Kory, remember to stay calm. We have all the time in the world to answer your questions."

I nodded. "Did he... touch me?"

The thought terrified me. *If he had... would Hayden still want me?*

Hayden squeezed my hand. "No, sweetheart. You were only out of my sight for less than a minute. No one touched you like that."

I let out a shaky breath and closed my eyes for a second. "Good. What... happened?"

"Landon arrived yesterday morning. A man named Ray Longston slipped out the back of the plane right after they landed. We dropped Kane off in the woods to track him, and you drove to meet Landon at the Red Onion. When you got there, things seemed to be going okay. Someone came into the

Red Onion with firecrackers. They caused a lot of chaos and slowed me down as I was trying to get to you. The drugs he gave you made you compliant. Ray dropped you when he tried to run from Kane, who had a knife to Ray's throat."

Oh gosh. I closed my eyes for a second to process. That was a lot. I worked through everything Hayden had said. "Where is Ray?"

"In custody. Turns out one of the guys traveling with Landon was an undercover agent. We don't have any other details."

I had absolutely no memory of any of this. Hayden continued to explain in detail what had happened that day. None of it jogged any memories. I remembered lying down with Hayden last night; the rest was a black hole. No images or recollections. Nothing. I yawned.

Hayden patted my leg. "Why don't you rest. When you wake up, we can talk about it some more, if you want. Like Hollis said, we have all the time in the world to talk."

"Okay." My eyes closed without warning. Maybe some sleep would bring back some of my memories. Or would the memories bring nightmares?

CHAPTER Thirty-Eight

Hayden

I balled my fists as I watched Kory sleep. If they hadn't dragged that asshole away, I probably would have killed him. Landon deserved everything he had coming. I hoped they locked his ass up and threw away the fucking key.

The first twenty-four hours after Kory had been drugged were scary. I thought I might lose her. Time had crawled during those first hours as we waited for her vitals to improve. Every stat had been too low. And if they'd declined any more, she might have needed life support. The idea terrified me.

But her body bounced back. Once the drug had worked through her system, Kory's heart rate strengthened, her oxygen levels improved, and her blood pressure stabilized. I touched her hand to reassure myself. *She's here. She's going to be okay.* Never in my life had I been so scared.

The door opened, and Kane popped his head in. He motioned for me to come out of the room. In the hall, Devney was behind the desk working on some paperwork. "Would you mind sitting with Kory?" I asked her. "She's been out for about an hour. I don't want her to wake up alone."

"I'd be happy to. Alexa and Hollis... or umm... I mean, Dr. Fritz are in with a patient. Will you guys let me know if anyone comes in?"

"Sure," I answered.

Kane led me over to the far corner of the room. "How's Kory?"

"Good. Or as good as can be expected. Thanks for being there, Kane."

He nodded. "You're welcome. I like Kory. She's part of the family."

I slapped his shoulder. "Means a lot."

"Enough with the sappy shit. I don't want the princess title." He smiled before getting serious. "Did Agent Stenton say anything to you?"

The name had me seeing red. He'd been by countless times. Once, he'd asked if he could give Kory a shot of something to force her to wake up. *Dipshit.* "About?"

"Me."

I thought back on our conversations. Not once had he mentioned Kane, but I knew Kane had explained when he was interviewed how he'd tracked Ray through the woods and into town. "No. What are you talking about?"

"Seems he wants me to help a fellow agent track someone."

"For what?"

He folded his arms over his chest. "They won't say, and I wouldn't agree to do it without details. They want to meet with me again this afternoon. What's your read on him?"

I scoffed. "He's an asshole."

"That's what I thought, too." Kane scowled for a second. "I'm not sure if I'm going to go through with the meeting."

"What about your buddy? Have you called him to get his take?"

A couple of years ago, Kane's friend Butch had moved to Skagway. He was ex-military intelligence. "Yeah, but I got no answer. Butch is off the grid for a while. Wanted to get away to clear his head. He rented out his cabin for a couple of months and asked me to help if something happens. He owes me big."

Normally Kane was somewhat of a hermit in the winter. After Christmas, he normally only came around once a week, if that, until spring.

"Where'd Butch go?"

"Hell if I know. But he could live anywhere and survive. He's one tough motherfucker."

It was probably why he and Kane got along so well. "State your terms and if Special Agent Stenton doesn't want to meet them, walk away."

Kane nodded. Knowing him, he would analyze the situation half a dozen ways until he decided what he wanted to do. "They seem like they're hiding something. Stenton had been almost desperate when he talked to me."

"What about?"

"No fuckin' clue. I guess we'll see." He slapped me on the shoulder. "Okay. Gotta run."

"Let me know if you need anything."

Kane waved as he stalked out the front door. Mariah had been waiting outside.

One of the exam room doors opened and Alexa came out

with Fred, the local builder. "Thanks, Dr. Fritz. I paid Devney already."

"Thanks, Fred. Take care."

"I'll try."

Fred greeted me, looking miserable. "Hey, Hayden. I'd shake your hand, but I got a nasty cold. Best be scootin' on home."

"Get to feeling better, Fred."

"Will do."

He left, and Hollis laid a clipboard on the desk. "Is everything okay with Kory?"

"Yeah, Kane just needed to talk. Devney is in with her."

All day, there seemed to be a bit of a strain between those two. At some point I'd have to check in with Hollis to see how things were. "I expect she'll make a full recovery. Just remember, Kory needs to remain as calm as possible."

"Do you think she'll get the memories back?"

He adjusted the stethoscope around his neck and thought for a second. "I don't know. There's not much data on this. I'll be submitting my findings, and I've sent queries out to some colleagues. But from the amount in her system, I doubt it. But sometimes that's a good thing. I've read studies on Rohypnol when the victim remembers, and it brings on an additional level of fear for them. They remember being helpless and at the command of someone else. It's food for thought. Maybe trying to remember shouldn't be the focus. The best thing to do for Kory is remain calm. She's going to be looking at other people for cues on how to react to what happened."

"Makes sense." With the issues of being controlled her entire life, it might be best if Kory had no recollection of what happened. The void of not knowing was sometimes better than the nightmare of reality.

It was time for me to get back to Kory. Being near her helped keep me calm. "I appreciate what you've done for us. I'll never forget it. I'm sorry if I got a little short."

"It's understandable. We were all on edge watching this play out. I'm going to keep her here for a couple of days just to observe because of the concussion. It's strictly precautionary. At this point, based on what I'm seeing, I don't have concerns."

"Sounds good. Mom was going to bring everyone dinner tonight if you guys don't have plans."

Hollis's eyes tightened as he ran his fingers through his hair. "I'll never pass up food. I'll check to see if Devney is staying."

The door opened, and Anita from the bakery walked through. Alexa came out of the empty exam room. "Hey, Anita. Let me get you into exam room two."

We said hello as she passed by. Hollis pushed off the wall. "Duty calls. We've definitely begun the cold and flu season. Let me know if you need anything."

"Will do."

Hollis disappeared back into the exam room. I walked back into Kory's room to find her sleeping. Devney was quietly reading a magazine but looked up when I walked in.

"Thanks so much."

"You're welcome. She's come to be such a good friend. Is there anything I can get you?"

I studied Devney closer; it looked like she'd been crying. "Are you okay?"

"Yes. It just... I have a big decision ahead of me, and I'm not sure what to do."

So things hadn't been resolved between her and Hollis. I laced my fingers behind my head. "My only piece of advice is if you can't imagine yourself with anyone but Hollis, don't throw it away. I used to think all that sh-stuff about love and soul mates was bullshit." I nodded to Kory. "Now, I know it's not. Don't make the same mistake as me."

Devney sniffled. "Thanks, Hayden. I needed to hear that." She stood. "I'll let you spend some time with Kory."

I hoped to hell I hadn't just fucked up my friend's relationship.

CHAPTER Thirty-Nine

Kory

"When is she going to wake up? I'd like to talk to her before I leave."

There was a very irritated someone talking near me. At least the beeping was gone. I took a second to remember what Hayden and Hollis had told me before I opened my eyes.

Hollis sounded tired. "I'm not sure. Ms. Reynolds has been through a terrible ordeal. Please show her some respect and wait in the lobby."

I opened my eyes. A man with aviators tipped back on his head stood just outside the door. *Who's he?* I called out, "Hayden?"

"Right here, sweetheart." Hayden's thumb rubbed soothing circles on my hand.

The stranger in the doorway looked toward me. "Am I cleared to ask her some questions, Dr. Fritz? The patient is clearly awake now."

Hollis grabbed the handle of the door. "You'll need to wait out here while I examine my patient."

The man looked none too pleased as Hollis closed the door in his face.

"What's going on?" My voice definitely sounded stronger. Hayden held up the straw to my lips, and I took a small sip.

Hollis checked the machines and then looked to me. "Special Agent Stenton is here. He wants to ask you some questions. He's been persistent. Are you feeling up to it?"

I wasn't sure what I would add since I had no memory of what happened, but I figured it was better to get this over with. "Sure."

"If at any time you get too tired, let me know, and I'll have him leave."

"Thanks, Hollis."

Hollis left the room and came back a moment later with the irritated, unfriendly stranger.

"Ms. Reynolds, I'm Special Agent Stenton."

There was something familiar about him. *Where have I seen him?* "Hello. It's nice to meet you."

"I wanted to ask you a few questions. Is that all right?" He paused and waited for me to answer.

I was still trying to place where I had seen the man before. "Yes." He took out a notepad. His face was angular and harsh. I cleared my throat. "Do I know you?"

Everyone looked at me, and I wondered what I'd said wrong. "Do you remember me from two days ago?"

Two days ago? Was he there? I shook my head. "No, I don't remember anything from that. But I remember seeing you... somewhere else." And then it came to me. "You always sat at the corner table at Roasted Beans. I used to see you there when I walked past in the mornings back in Washington."

When I knew things were going to be hectic with my parents on any given day, which was more often than not, I took an early morning walk to clear my head for the day. It helped keep me grounded. This man would be there almost every morning, reading his paper and sipping coffee. I remember wondering what he did.

"Yes, that was me."

I knew I recognized him. Normally I could place people fairly quickly. "Why are you here?"

"Most of it is classified, but I've spent years conducting an undercover investigation of Landon Masterson. He's become one of the largest drug traffickers in the Northwest. He was expanding distribution to Anchorage."

"What? He's a drug dealer?" That was news to me.

Special Agent Stenton squared his shoulders. "Yes, but I'm not allowed to comment any further on the subject, ma'am. But I want you to know that where Mr. Masterson is going, he won't be seeing the sun for the rest of his life."

That was a relief. I hoped I never saw him again.

"What can you tell me about Mr. Masterson, ma'am?"

I paused for a second as I tried to organize my thoughts. "Our families were friends. They'd hoped we would get married, but things fizzled out. Because of that, I don't have any communication with them anymore."

He made a few notes. "And what about Mr. Masterson's trip here. Do you know why he came to Alaska?"

It was strange how these memories were crystal clear, yet there was nothing from the moment he actually arrived. "To reconcile. But I had no plans to. I hoped we could be friends."

"Anything else you can remember?"

I wasn't going to go into anything about the Fraternity. My parents had warned us to never mention it to anyone else. "I have no memory of Landon arriving in town. I've been told what happened, but I don't remember any of it. I would never have suspected Landon of trafficking drugs or being capable of drugging me. I guess sometimes if people want to hide who they are, they find a way."

"That's true. I appreciate your time, Ms. Reynolds. If anything else comes up, I'll be in touch."

Stenton turned to the door, but I had one last question. "What if he gets out?" My voice broke on the last word.

He turned around. "You'll be the first to know. I promise you he'll never be able to hurt anyone again. But if he somehow escapes, I'll make sure you are notified. But I really wouldn't worry about that."

That was a relief. He left with Hollis following behind him. I turned to Hayden. "He was dealing drugs? Did you know this?"

"Yes, your parents gave us that information the night before he arrived. That's the leverage we were going to use against him."

They'd come through. My parents had put me first. Knowing they cared for me helped ease the ache I knew would come when they weren't able to be part of my life. "So it's really over?" I asked, afraid it might not be true.

"Yeah, it is, sweetheart."

My eyes filled with tears, and they began to slip down my cheeks. I was finally free to live my life.

CHAPTER Forty

Hayden

I pulled the omelet off the stove and added it to the tray. It felt so fucking good to be home. There had been some tough moments, but overall, things were progressing well. I couldn't imagine what it felt like to have no memory of a particular day. But Hollis's words stayed with me, and I hoped—for Kory's sake—they never returned. So far it had been four days since she woke up with no memory in sight.

Thanksgiving had been low key. Kory had been a little disappointed at not being able to go all out with my mother this year. But we always had next year.

So far, her parents hadn't reached out to us. But we knew they were safe. I'd asked my private investigator to check on them. They went to work like normal, went home, had dinner, and went to bed. It was crazy that they hadn't checked on their daughter. But then again, they'd also been questioned by the FBI, according to my contact. Hopefully, they'd stay away until it was safe to resume communication.

As for Landon, there had been nothing in the media. It was like the whole thing hadn't happened. Maybe where he was going, there was no trial process. Maybe he was a small piece of a bigger picture. Whatever it was, I hoped it stayed far away from us. The FBI had taken Landon's plane and disappeared. The *Twiner Tellings* newsletter ran rampant with conspiracies. From the latest newsletter, the story was that Kory's friend had fallen in love with her and fallen off the deep end. And the Twiner sisters had launched their new matchmaking services they talked about.

There hadn't been any sex since we'd gotten home. I wanted Kory. I wanted her bad. But I had to restrain myself, regardless of the fact that it had been too long. Hollis had advised that sex should wait for at least six to seven days. We were on day five since she woke. Hell, I hoped we could make it through the day, but it wasn't looking very likely.

So far, Kory hadn't experienced any other concussion-related symptoms. So maybe if we took it easy, we could have sex. Fuck. The last thing I wanted to do was hurt her. But she'd been trying to tempt me since we got home. And a man only has so much willpower.

I added a cup of orange juice to the tray I'd been preparing and headed upstairs. In our bedroom, Kory stretched and scooted up on the bed. She had a mischievous smile on her face.

"What are you smiling at?"

She was the picture of wide-eyed innocence. "I don't know what you mean."

I smirked. I was on to her game and clearly wanted to play. This woman was my life. I would do anything for her.

When I thought I may have lost her, it made everything clear. I wanted Kory to be my wife. I was no longer scared of that word. I just needed to find the right time and make sure she was ready.

She took a bite of her omelet. "Mmm, this is so good. You've been spoiling me."

"Anything for my girl."

The bruises on her body where that asshole, Ray, had dropped her had begun to fade. The thought of his hands on her still made me see red. "How are you feeling today?"

"Better. Maybe later we could take a walk around the pond. I could use some fresh air."

Kory would be cleared for normal activity tomorrow. This mess was almost behind us. It was going to be hard to let her out of my sight, but I knew at some point I would have to.

I sat on the edge of the bed. Kory's eyes roamed over my bare torso. "That sounds good to me. I'd like that." I nodded toward the window. "It looks like it snowed last night."

"Oh, maybe we can build a fire and watch a movie, too."

I smiled. "Anything you want. And I'll watch anything you want to watch, too. You just can't mention it to my brother."

Kory pretended to zip her mouth shut. "Consider it done."

My phone vibrated, and I checked the display. It was one of my buddies I'd met while flying. He'd been helping me set up the cabin for Kory right before her parents arrived. I hated canceling on the guy, but he understood.

Arthur: *Temperatures have been colder than normal. If you guys want to fly up here in a day or two for ice fishing, the cabin is yours.*

I'd mentioned some time ago about Hollis going ice fishing with me and my brothers.

"Who's that?" Kory asked.

"My buddy was offering his cabin for ice fishing in a day or two. I'm going to tell him no." He had a gorgeous place, but it wasn't the right time. His cabin was where I'd wanted to make love to Kory for the first time after she'd come to live in Skagway.

Perplexed, Kory asked, "Why?"

I cocked my head, surprised at her question. "You can't be serious."

"Because of me?"

"Yeah, Kory, I nearly lost you. I'm not flying anywhere and leaving you right now. I need to have you close. I get that we'll have to return to our normal lives sooner or later, but I'm not ready."

Her face softened, and she gave me one of those smiles that brought me to my knees. "Is this for the fishing trip Hollis has been talking about?"

"Yes."

She thought about that for a second. "Would it be out of the question to bring me, Alexa, and Devney? We could all go. The girls could stay together in the cabin while you guys are fishing. Win-win. I know Hollis has been looking forward to ice fishing. And he's done so much for us."

I considered her idea. *This might work. Maybe.* "Let me text the guys and see what they think."

Me: *Arthur texted me. It's been colder than normal. If we want the cabin we can go up there in two days. But if we go, I want to bring Kory. I don't want to leave her here alone. Let me know if you're in.*

Hollis: *Does a bear shit in the woods? Yes, yes it does. And in town. And everywhere here in Alaska. You know I'm in. And my new poles just arrived. I'll check with Devney.*

Drake: *I checked with Alexa. We're in.*

Ike: *Your mom and I have to help Jim Hathaway. But you guys go ahead and go. It'll be fun for everyone to get away. We'll catch you the next time.*

Kane: *Is Mom on here?*

Me: *No, just us guys.*

Kane: *I'm in as long as you guys don't act like pussies around your girls.*

Me: *No promises.*

Hollis: *I have an Alaskan certificate to prove I'm not a pussy.*

Drake: *You afraid it might be contagious, Kane?*

Kane: *Fuck off. I'll see you at the hangar.*

Me: *Once I check the weather, I'll let everyone know the departure time.*

Hollis: *Sounds good. Devney is in.*

Ike: *You guys have fun and don't get into too much trouble.*

With all that had happened, we hadn't heard any updates on what Devney had decided regarding her move. I hoped my words helped her make the right decision. She and Hollis seemed good for each other. If she left... I was afraid she'd be making a monumental mistake. Hollis was a gift to this town, so I hoped she decided to stay.

I opened up the text to my buddy.

Me: *Thanks, man. I'll take you up on it. There'll be seven of us total. The plan is two days from now.*

Arthur: *You guys can use the main house. I'll be out of town. That'll give people their own rooms.*

Me: *Perfect. I appreciate it. Let me know if I can ever give you a lift somewhere.*

Arthur: *I will.*

It felt good to have a plan to focus on. Hanging out here at the house was nice, but we needed something to move toward and think about besides the perpetual black cloud known as Landon. "Hollis, Devney, Drake, Alexa, and Kane are in. Dad and Mom are helping a friend and can't come."

"That's too bad, but I'm glad we're going somewhere. It'll be nice to focus on something else and have a mini vacation before the madness of the holidays."

I knew Kory also meant from the situation with Landon as well, but I didn't press. She'd done remarkably well.

She set her tray aside. "That was delicious."

"Do you need anything else?"

"I do."

She bit her lip, and I knew what was coming. "No way. No way. Hollis's orders."

"Come on. It's been so long." She reached for the hem of her shirt and pulled it over her head.

Fuck me.

Her tits were perfect. I leaned down and sucked one of her nipples into my mouth. "We have to be careful, Kory."

"We will be. I promise. Please, Hayden, I need you."

In two seconds, I had my pants off and was trailing my fingers up her legs. "You are so beautiful. And you're mine."

"Forever."

CHAPTER Forty-One

Hayden

We arrived in Fairbanks at the cabin two days later. When I had arranged to bring Kory up here initially, I'd planned to use the floatplane. Now with the lakes frozen over, I brought the King Air and landed it at the local airport instead. The guys there let us use the courtesy van, too. The friends I'd made through my years of flying really were something else. To drive up here it would take over thirteen hours in the summer. In the winter, it was near impossible.

The girls had decided to take naps. Kory was still not back to a hundred percent and tired a little more easily than normal, but she was getting stronger every day. The sex was out of this world. Nearly losing her made being together more special. This morning before leaving, she'd joined me in the shower for round two after having woken me up in the early morning hours for round one.

And no, I wasn't complaining.

Things were definitely getting back on track.

Kane was exploring the woods, probably setting up surveillance or tracking a moose or something. *Who knows what he does at times?* I'd asked him how the talk with Special Agent Stenton had gone, and he'd blown off the question with a shrug and called him some names. I couldn't read the situation completely, but it seemed like he wasn't getting involved. Something about city fuckers not knowing their asses from a hole in the ground.

Kane had said two words on the ride from the airport. *Cranky bastard.*

Drake was in the cabin's office, working on a few things for the city council. Hollis had been about to jump out of his skin with excitement to go fishing. He'd nearly hooked himself messing with his fishing poles.

So I decided to take Hollis fishing for a little bit. I looked around the fishing hut at all his stuff. Shit, he had more paraphernalia than any person I'd ever known. Normally all I brought was a pole and bait. But the extra chair was more comfy than the buckets we typically sat on. Maybe there was something to Hollis's thinking. Kane was going to have a field day when he joined us. This was the opposite of minimalism.

It hadn't taken long to get the hole in the ice cleared for us to fish. Arthur had everything already in the hut. We'd baited our hooks, and now it was time to wait. Sometimes it took a while. Hollis watched the hole his fishing line disappeared into with an intensity that was almost comical. He adjusted his so-called Paul Bunyan hat. "How long do you wait before they bite?"

"Just depends."

He kept staring at the line. "I bought premium bait. It's guaranteed to work."

Of course it is. I wondered if the website had swampland to sell people, as well. In the next second, Hollis's reel started to move.

"Yes! True Alaskan here!"

He grabbed it and reeled it in. Man, the fish was giving him a fight. Finally, he pulled out a large-ass rainbow trout. It had to be one of the biggest ones I'd seen in a long time.

"What the fuck?" I said.

He kept fighting with the fish, unsure what to do with it as it flopped around. "What?"

"That is one large fish." I leaned over to show him how to hold it while taking the hook out. "Just like that."

Hollis studied my movements. "So you grab him behind the pelvic fins and keep your hands away from the operculum."

"What language are you speaking?"

Shrugging, Hollis said, "Fish anatomy. I studied it before we came. I figure it would help me pick up the proper technique quicker."

I sometimes had no words for this guy. "Do you want to keep him?"

"Nah, I'll catch more."

"Hollis, this is a huge fish."

"Yeah, I know. But I'll catch more. It's fine."

It almost hurt to let such a beautiful fish go, but it wasn't my catch. Hollis grinned. "It's all in being prepared."

I took a sip of my coffee. "Beginner's luck."

"We'll see."

Hollis rebaited his pole and lowered it down again. Not

four minutes later, he pulled out another trout as big as the last one. He smirked. "Beginner's luck?"

"What kind of bait is that?" I needed some of that shit.

"A true fisherman never shares his secrets."

"That's not a motto I've heard."

"I might have made it up, but it should be one."

We laughed, and an idea hit me. "So, you know Kane is going to give you shit about all your..."

"Accessories?" Hollis offered.

"Yes, accessories. What if we put your bait in my canister when we all come back to fish? We'll challenge my brothers to some sort of bet."

Hollis nodded, a wide grin on his face. "I'm in. And I know the perfect thing for when we win." He leaned back with a smug look. "Let's just remember the moment when the New Yorker taught the native Alaskan a little about fishing."

"Touché, my friend. Touché."

Later that day, we all sat around the hole. Hollis and I were in the comfy folding chairs, and Kane and Drake sat on buckets. Drake shook his head. "Man, I can't believe you guys didn't get me one of those chairs."

"I've got one on the way for you. We'll have it for next time," Hollis said.

Drake held out his fist. "Thanks, man."

Kane closed his eyes in obvious distress about his brothers embracing the finer things in life. I nearly spit out my coffee when Hollis asked, "Are you sure you don't want one, Kane. My treat."

Kane shook his head. "No. Anyone I camp with would piss on my blankets if I brought that."

We all laughed, but Kane continued to scowl. He and Drake were losing our fishing bet... big time. Hollis and I kept reeling in the fish while Kane and Drake cursed like no one's business.

"What the hell, man? Are you cheating?" Drake asked when I reeled in my next fish.

I chuckled. "Sore loser much? I have a pole and bait, same as you guys."

Kane narrowed his eyes. "Something seems fishy."

"I don't know how it would seem fishy since you've only caught one each," Hollis whispered.

Grinning, Kane nodded. "Good one." Then deadpanned, "Not."

Hollis reeled in another one and said, "I'm tired of counting, we're so far ahead. I think I'm going to sit here and drink my coffee until you admit defeat."

We set our poles down. My brothers cursed again.

I smirked. "I hope you guys are ready to pay up."

When we'd initially made the bet, my brothers were so smug they never thought we'd win, especially with the novice fisherman who spoke about the lateral lines and peduncles of the fish or whatever the fuck he spouted. Hollis grabbed his backpack, where the punishment awaited.

"My life fucking sucks right now." Kane leaned back. "Are you seriously going to make us wear those ridiculous hats?"

Hollis pulled out two of the Paul Bunyan hats he'd ordered for us; both were black with black fur. It could have been worse. I'd seen him debating about blue ones with red fur at one point.

I gestured to the hat. "Maybe it'll help you get back into your Alaskan mindset. Something must be wrong with your chi since you only reeled in one fish."

Kane shot me the bird. Drake took the hat and put it on. He looked like a doofus, and I nearly fell over laughing.

Drake patted his head. "Man, this is warm."

"Told you." Hollis replied. "Here's yours, Kane."

Kane begrudgingly took the hat. "I'm about to lose my manhood. So help me... if I start spouting shit about love and whatever else the fuck you guys say, I'm going to lose it."

I raised my eyebrow. "You're not doing very well with that dramatic-effect cussing Mom taught you."

Kane's scowl only deepened, and I got two birds this time. We laughed. Poor Kane. He wasn't used to losing, especially when it came to hunting or fishing.

Hollis quipped, "You never know, Kane. Maybe you'll reach a level of enlightenment you never knew existed."

He closed his eyes and shook his head. "I seriously doubt it."

When Kane put on the Paul Bunyan hat, I swore I nearly died. Hollis took his off. "There's a great feature to the hats. If it's not quite chilly enough, you can tie up the earflaps on top of your head like this."

Kane's eyes widened in horror while Drake nodded. "That is a nice feature."

"What is *wrong* with you?" Kane playfully punched Drake. "You're acting like you like this hat. You look like a penis wearing it."

I nearly rolled out of my chair I was laughing so hard.

"You're an ass," Kane spat at me.

"And you look like a princess," I replied.

Drake put his arm around Kane. "A penis and a princess. Now that's a combination."

Kane threw his head back and whispered, "Kill. Me. Now. Please. There's no way Paul Bunyan would have traded his beanie for this ridiculous piece of shit."

We all laughed. Life was good.

CHAPTER Forty-Two

Kory

What a nice escape from reality. We'd been at the cabin for two days; I'd needed it more than I realized. At this point, I'd given up on regaining my memories. Part of me wanted to remember, while the other part was afraid of what those memories would bring. If it was meant to be, it would happen.

Tomorrow we were returning to our lives back in Skagway. I loved it up here and hoped we could come back again in the spring, but I was ready to go home. Earlier today, Hayden and I had taken some time to ourselves to go exploring. He'd shown me the smaller cabin down the way. It was where he'd planned to take me before my parents showed up. It was beautiful. He promised me we'd fly the floatplane here at some point for a weekend escape.

At times I wanted to pinch myself to wake up from this dream I now called my life.

The guys had decided to do some night ice fishing since they most likely wouldn't be able to go in the morning. Drake and Kane were pissed at how much Hollis and Hayden were catching. And the hats they had to wear when they were outside were hysterical. Hayden had confided in me that he was using Hollis's secret bait. I wondered what he had bought, but Hollis was remaining tight-lipped on his little secret.

I was glad those two had become good friends. Hayden had friends all over the place, but Hollis was his closest guy friend. Someone he could talk to about anything. It made me happy for him.

Kane was fiercely competitive, and not understanding why he wasn't able to catch the same amount of fish as *Hollis* was eating him up.

I stretched and set my book aside. Alexa had gone up to soak in the bath while Devney and I read on the couch. It seemed like she was done reading, too. "How are things with Hollis?"

She leaned her head back on the couch. "I feel like I'm losing him. I've tried to talk to him a few times about this, but he only tells me he wants me to be happy."

"And what would make you happy?"

"I love Hollis. He's not like anyone I've ever met. What he's done for my mother. For me. I..." Her eyes grew teary. "I'm not sure he feels the same way about me."

I touched her hand. "I think he does, but I think he's afraid to sway your decision. Hollis doesn't want to be something you'd regret."

She sniffled, wiping her eyes. "Maybe, I don't know. I'm going to have to decide soon. I know what I want, but I'm afraid to take the leap. And I think he's hurt that I haven't told my mom about him yet."

"Why haven't you?"

She shrugged with a sigh. "With her being so sick, it just hasn't come up. The focus has been on her treatments and what's going on with her health. I feel guilty sharing that I'm happy."

That made sense. "The only real advice I can give you is to follow your heart." That was one thing that had never led me astray in the years I was alone. It had kept me strong, fighting for independence and a way out.

Alexa opened the bathroom door upstairs and called down to us, "Anyone need anything while I'm up here? I'm almost done."

"Nah, we're good."

Devney grabbed my hand. "Please don't say anything. I don't want Alexa to feel like she has to get involved. Hollis is her best friend."

"Anything we say, I'll always keep in confidence."

"Same here."

A few minutes later, Alexa came down the stairs holding two DVDs. "Are we feeling *Pretty Woman* or *While You Were Sleeping*?"

Devney and I said at the same time, "*While You Were Sleeping*."

"Excellent. I'll pop the popcorn." Alexa tossed the DVD to me.

Devney got up. "I'll make the drinks."

"I'll get the firewood."

I loved the comradery that came with having girlfriends.

I stepped out onto the porch, pulling my coat tighter around me. The porch creaked, and I nearly jumped. In the shadows, a man sat, smoking a cigarette. The red tip burned on his inhale. "Run, and it won't be good."

I froze and nearly screamed. "Who are you?"

"Eric."

Landon's father. I glanced around to see if anyone was with him. *Stay calm.* I wanted to scream for Hayden, but I remembered his warning. "What are you doing here?"

"Trying to figure out what happened to my son. The last I heard, he was heading up here to visit you."

My heart beat double time in my chest. There was something dangerous in the way Eric spoke. He'd always scared me, but right now he was exposing his true nature in a way I hadn't seen before. I cleared my throat. "I'm told he came."

"You weren't here?" He shifted and inhaled his cigarette again.

No memories had come back, and for that, I was glad. "No, I was there, but I don't remember it. I have no memory of the day he came."

"What the fuck happened?" he snapped.

I jumped at the irritation in his voice. A shiver trailed down my spine. "I... uh... I only know what people told me."

"Which is..."

I quickly relayed what I'd been told. "Landon flew in. We met for lunch at the Red Onion to catch up. Landon put a patch laced with drugs on me. The doctor said it was something called Devil's Breath. Landon planned to kidnap me. Why, we aren't sure. The FBI was there. When they questioned me in the hospital, I learned Landon was involved in drug trafficking. There was something about expanding into Anchorage. They said it was classified and wouldn't give details."

"Where did they take him?"

"I don't know. They wouldn't say."

Another moment passed, and I saw the end of the cigarette light up again. "Have you talked to your parents?"

"Not since they came to visit two week ago. After they left, I reached out to Landon because I missed my friend. I was in a rough spot. When I woke up at the medical clinic, the last thing I could remember was going to bed thinking Landon was coming the next day. I've tried to remember, but nothing comes."

He swore under his breath. "Who was with him?"

"They said his name was Ray Longston, but I don't remember him. There was a pilot, but I haven't heard what happened to him. And Landon. That's all I've been told. I don't remember anything. I swear I don't, or I would tell you." I asked without thinking, "Is it true about the drugs?"

"I'm not here to answer your questions. Are you involved with someone?"

Why are we switching topics? If Eric thought he was going to take me back to Washington, he had another think coming. I wouldn't go without a fight. "Yes, his name is Hayden."

Since our wedding was a secret, I omitted the fact we were technically married.

There was another long pause, and my insides shook from the nerves. "Answer this carefully. Have you ever heard of the Fraternity?"

Oh shit. I was glad it was dark so he couldn't see my eyes. I thought for a second. "The what?"

He sighed. "The Fraternity. Think hard. If you lie, it won't be good."

The threat sent a chill down my spine. If I answered too quickly, it would be obvious I was lying. It had to be timed well. "I don't think so. Why? What is the Fraternity?"

I hoped my voice sounded convincing because inside I was shaking like a leaf.

"Nothing. If your memory comes back, I suggest you pretend it never did. Do you understand?"

What does that mean? Is Eric giving me a pass? "Y-yes."

He stood. "My son's made quite a mess out of things. I don't need the added stress of dealing with you. Consider yourself lucky."

"Mr. Masterson, I don't know what you're talking about, but I wouldn't want to cause your family or mine any issues. You've been part of the family for quite some time. And though things didn't work out with Landon and me, I still consider you family."

"You're either a very good liar or you mean that. It doesn't matter; keep it that way, and we won't have issues. You've made your decision to stay away from your family. Don't contact them again."

"Yes, sir. It won't be hard. They've never wanted anything to do with me."

I heard voices just past the cabin. The boys were coming back. "I must go. Just know, I could be watching at any moment. I suggest you not fuck up this gift."

And like that, Eric Masterson disappeared into the night.

My hands shook, and I leaned against the pillar for strength. He would be watching me. If I said something too soon it might cause problems. I would have to find a way to tell Hayden. Find a safe place where I could tell him everything.

For now, I would have to put on a brave face and pretend nothing happened.

Will I ever be free of the Fraternity?

CHAPTER Forty-Three

Hayden

As we touched down back in Skagway, Kory chewed on her lip as she looked out the window. I wasn't sure what was going on in her head, but she'd been withdrawn since last night. Shortly after I got back from ice fishing, she'd told me she was tired and going to bed. To give her space I took a shower first. I'd planned to ask her what was wrong after giving her some time to work it out, but she'd been asleep when I'd come to bed. Then this morning, there hadn't been a time for us to be alone. By the time I got up, Kory was in the kitchen, cooking breakfast for everyone.

Maybe she had remembered something. Or maybe she was truly tired. I wasn't sure.

After getting the plane hangered, we said good-bye to everyone. The walk to the truck was strained. This wasn't my imagination. When we got home, we'd be discussing what was wrong. I cranked the truck, and Kory laid a piece of paper on my lap. It was her handwriting. I went to pick it up, but she gently placed her hand on my leg, keeping the note there.

What was going on?

I read it from my lap.

> Be discreet. Don't say a word, but we need to go to a place we can talk. Not home. Someplace private that can't be watched. A place no one would expect for us to go. Eric, Landon's father, visited me while you were ice fishing. He said he was watching me.

What. The. Hell?

My eyes searched hers, and she looked back at me, imploring. *Be discreet. Did they bug my truck?* I drove out of town. Even locked away somewhere, Landon was still causing issues. "Are you too tired to do something? I had a thought."

She gave me a smile, and I saw relief that I had taken her seriously. "No, I'm not too tired. The last few days have been nice. I feel rested."

"Good. I'm going to take you to a favorite place of mine. It has beautiful sunsets."

This place wasn't on our property, and I had only been there once. There was no way they knew this wasn't a favorite place of mine. About thirty minutes later, we pulled up to the side of the road. I put on my Paul Bunyan hat. "This thing is actually really warm. But man, making my brothers wear one for shits and giggles was the highlight of the trip."

She giggled. "Kane looks so miserable. It's like someone stole his Christmas presents."

"I know. It's going to be great seeing him wear it all winter long."

We got out of the truck, and I took Kory's hand as we walked through the field listening to the snow crunch beneath our feet.

"Where are we?" she asked.

"It's just a random field that has a pretty view. Not on our property, so it should be clear." I stopped and nonchalantly checked my surroundings. There wasn't a soul in sight. And if there was, there was no way they could hear us if we kept our voices low. To the passerby, it would look like we were admiring the sunset.

"What happened, Kory?"

She relayed the story to me, and I saw red. The asshole had threatened her. Actually threatened her. And he said he was giving her a gift. Who the hell were these people, thinking they could play games with someone's life? When she finished, I asked, "Anything else?"

"No. It's a blessing I don't have my memory back. If I did, I'm not sure what Eric would have done. But I think in light of what happened to Landon, he doesn't want any more attention brought on him or those associated with him."

"Agreed. What about your parents?"

She tucked some hair behind her ear and leaned into me a little more. "I was warned not to contact them. It hurts. I wonder if they're okay. They came through for me in the end, and that's hard to walk away from. They do love me."

"Yes, they do." It broke my heart to hear her like this. "You know the private investigator we hired?"

"Yeah."

"If you want, from time to time we could have him check on your parents to make sure they're okay."

She took a moment to respond. "I'd like that. Thank you."

We needed to change the subject. I knew something that would make her laugh. "Let's go stop by Kane's. We'll tell him what's going on, and he'll spread the word for us nonchalantly."

She looked up at me with a smirk. "You just want to see him in the Paul Bunyan hat."

"Maybe. But you can bet your ass I'm going to have him come outside to meet us."

Kory's laughter filled the air. Through all the bad, we'd find our way. Somehow, some way... we'd make it.

CHAPTER Forty-Four

Kory

Three days before Christmas

The air smelled of evergreens. It was like a winter wonderland, inside and out. Twinkle lights and heavy greenery filled the room. Over the past few days, the house had been transformed for Drake and Alexa's wedding. Amie and Devney had been instrumental in helping make this a dream come true for the bride and groom.

Alexa had chosen to walk down the aisle to a beautiful orchestra edition of *Silent Night*. When she and Ike appeared at the bottom of the staircase, I looked at Drake. The way his eyes lit up when he saw Alexa touched me deeply. I wanted Hayden to look at me like that someday.

Ike walked toward the fireplace with Alexa on his arm. He was so proud. The preacher asked, "Who gives this woman away?"

With his shoulders back, Ike looked a picture of Alexa's

dad, Lloyd, before he turned to the preacher. He took a deep breath and said, "Lloyd has given me the honor of giving away his daughter to my son, Drake. Because of Lloyd, my son was able to find his soul mate. Thank you, Lloyd, for giving my family such a wonderful gift. We will love her forever and always as she officially becomes part of the Foster family today."

There wasn't a dry eye in the room. I handed Devney a tissue. There were few moments in life that could be described as perfect, and this was one of them. Alexa leaned up, her eyes shining, and kissed Ike on the cheek.

Drake took a step forward. "I've been waiting for this moment my entire life, Lex."

Drake took Alexa's hands, and they stood in front of the mantle. A low fire crackled. The greenery filled the air with a fragrant smell. The frosted red berries accented the mantle perfectly. Green topiaries stood on either side, wrapped in twinkle lights. Against the rich, dark colors, Alexa's simple gown of satin overlaid with gold organza was stunning.

As the wedding progressed, love filled the room. Pure love. It was exquisite. Hayden grabbed my hand and squeezed it. Over the last few weeks, we'd gotten even closer as we found our way together. I was ready for the next step but wouldn't mention it to him.

In the days since Eric paid me a visit, no one had brought up Landon, my parents, Eric, or the Fraternity. It was as if they'd never existed. Maybe someday, Mother and Father would be able to reach out to me again. I continued to pay the bill for the phone I'd given them, hoping at some point they could.

But if staying away from me gave me freedom, I understood why they had to do it. But it hurt. Somehow, they'd managed to right their wrongs by helping me escape the grasp of the Fraternity.

If Eric was watching me or listening, it didn't matter. He would find nothing.

Kane had researched Landon. It was like he, too, had never existed. There were no news articles, no public hearings, no indictments. Maybe Special Agent Stenton had thrown away the key just as he'd stated.

As the days had passed, Hayden and I had grown a little more comfortable being away from each other as the realities of life took over. It was nice that Hayden's job slowed down during the heavy snow months since he wasn't able to fly as frequently. He'd been helping me do some of the setups for the various parties. Business was thriving, and I couldn't be more proud.

I truly felt like Skagway was my home. At the Christmas Jubilee two days ago, I had known almost everyone there. *Yes, this is home.*

The preacher announced, "I now pronounce you husband and wife."

Drake gently held Alexa's face. "You're it for me, Lex. I will always put you first."

The grin on Alexa's face was breathtaking, and her voice broke when she said, "I love you, Drake Foster."

"I love you, Mrs. Foster."

The family applauded as Drake pressed his mouth to Alexa's and held up his fist in victory. After their tumultuous road, they deserved this happy ending.

When it was my turn to embrace the happy couple, I held Alexa close. "Congrats. Thank you for letting me be part of your day."

Alexa brought me close. "You've been such an amazing friend. Thank you."

Friend. I had found the best of friends through this mess. That was one of the many blessings I'd received since coming to Alaska.

The reception was small since it was only family. Drake and Alexa wanted us to eat and mingle. After dinner, the bride and groom cut the cake. Drake cocked his eyebrow while Alexa held out her piece with a mischievous grin on her face.

"You know you want to, Lex."

She giggled and smeared it across his mouth. In the next second, Drake dipped her and pressed his lips to hers, effectively covering her face with icing.

As the reception went on, Drake appeared to grow restless. He leaned into Alexa, and she gave him a playful slap on the chest. It wasn't hard to imagine where his mind was going. After the reception, they'd chosen to go back home to the cabin Drake built for Alexa. When we found out, Amie and I put a plan in motion to have their bedroom decorated with rose petals. We also had champagne on ice and food waiting for them. Hopefully it made their wedding night special.

The tapping of a knife against a glass brought the focus to the fireplace where Drake stood with Alexa. "I'd like to give one final toast before I take my wife away." A delicate blush crept up Alexa's cheeks. He'd finally talked her into leaving. "This toast is to the man who raised the most amazing woman I know. Before Lloyd passed, he told me to take care of his Alexa." Drake turned to his wife. "I will always take care of you. To the man who gave his blessing. He was one of a kind. To Lloyd."

"To Lloyd."

Once again, there wasn't a dry eye in the room.

Alexa sniffled. "Thank you to everyone for being part of our day." She looked at Drake. "Thank you for loving me unconditionally."

"Always, baby. Never doubt it."

After Drake and Alexa left, we were able to get the place cleaned up fairly quickly. Since it was so close to Christmas, I was going to use the same decorations through New Year's. I stood by the fire, watching the flames. Tonight's festivities had me wishing for a proposal from Hayden more than anything. *Give him time.* I would be happy waiting, but I wanted to start my life with him. There was no one else. And there never would be.

Technically we were still married, but neither of us acknowledged the fact. To everyone we were still dating.

Strong arms wrapped around my waist, and I leaned back into a familiar chest. "What are you thinking about, sweetheart?"

"What a perfect day it was. I loved being part of their moment. It reminded me of a fairy tale. It was beautiful."

He rested his chin on my shoulder. "What would you say if we left Skagway for our first Christmas? I want to take you somewhere special."

For a second, I wanted to jump at the chance, but I remembered all his family was here. "What about your mom? Wouldn't she be sad without you here? I don't want to upset the family balance."

He kissed my neck. "She's fine with it. I mentioned wanting to spend it with you and she was happy for us. Thrilled actually."

"Where are we going?"

"I want to surprise you. It's one of my gifts to you."

I straightened and turned toward Hayden, my eyes wide. "One? Hayden you don't have to get me anything."

He nuzzled my neck again and my thoughts were running amuck. "I want our first Christmas to be special. I know how disappointed you were about Thanksgiving."

It was true. I hated that I hadn't been physically able to help Amie cook dinner. It had been nice, but there'd been a layer of worry that overshadowed the event. I'd spent a large part of the day wondering what would happen with the Landon situation.

His tongue tasted me, and I moaned. "I would love to go somewhere for our first Christmas. But, Hayden, I would be perfectly happy staying here."

"I know." He let go and grabbed my hand. "Come."

His deep, commanding voice sent shivers through me. I would follow Hayden Foster anywhere.

CHAPTER Forty-Five

Kory

I couldn't contain my excitement. Hayden was flying us to a surprise destination. Well, it was a surprise to me, at least. Flying on Christmas Eve had been a bit hectic. At one point, Hayden had been stressed when the weather threatened to change before we could get out of Skagway. Luckily it held off.

My knee bounced uncontrollably as I sat in one of the passenger seats and waited to land. Hayden had asked that I put on noise-canceling headphones for this last part of the flight. *Where in the world are we going?* It had been a long day with a refuel stop in Rapid City, South Dakota. A pilot friend of Hayden's had joined us in South Dakota for the last leg of the flight so Hayden could get some rest.

He was going to fly back commercially once we landed. None of it made a lot of sense right now, but I tried not to worry about it.

Where in the world are we going?

I was nearly coming out of my chair in anticipation. *Someone pinch me.* A year ago, if someone had told me this would be my life, I never would have believed them. Hayden had told me to pack for six days. The only constraint we had was that I had to be back the day before New Year's for the quilting circle party.

Drake and Alexa weren't coming back until the fourth or fifth of January. Their honeymoon destination was a secret because Drake wanted it to be a complete surprise to Alexa. I couldn't wait to hear where they'd been.

I was a little disappointed I hadn't gotten to see Ike and Amie before we left. The plan had been to stop by their house for a mini Christmas celebration, but Amie had a cold and needed to postpone things. Next year, I was going to make sure we were home so we could celebrate as a family.

I felt the plane descend ever so slightly. *Maybe we're getting ready to land.* Moments into our last leg, Hayden had insisted I put on a blindfold with my noise canceling headset. I grabbed onto the armrest as I felt the plane descend a little more. Being in the air but not being able to see the ground was a little disorienting.

The wheels touched down and the plane came to a stop. Hayden was most likely doing his postflight checklist. I tried to wait patiently. His cologne filled the air around me, and I knew he was close by. The headset was gently lifted off one of my ears. "I'm going to guide you to the car. Keep your headphones and blindfold on."

"Where are we?"

"It's a surprise."

He kissed my cheek and replaced the headset over my ear.

I was dying to know where we were. We deplaned, and Hayden helped me into a vehicle. It had to be some sort of SUV or truck because I had to step up to get in.

As the minutes passed by, the anticipation grew; no one had ever done something like this for me before. We took one last turn and slowed to a stop. *Are we here?* I waited for us to start moving again in case we were at a stoplight or stop sign, but there was no further movement.

I jumped when I felt Hayden's hand on mine. The headset was lifted off my ears. I reached for the blindfold, but he stopped me. "Not yet. I'm going to lead you there. I want you to leave the blindfold on."

"Okay. How long until I see?"

"Less than five minutes."

I giggled, giddy as a school girl. Hayden helped me out of the car. The first thing I noticed was the quiet. *Where are we?*

Hayden gently led me across concrete, which turned to soft ground and then back to concrete. We stopped, and Hayden put his hands on my shoulders and turned me. I strained to hear. *Was that a car that passed by? Are we close to a street?* I had no idea where we might be. My only clue had been the pit stop in South Dakota. The total flight time had been around ten hours.

Hayden squeezed my hands three times and then let go. I stood still for a second. "Hayden?"

"I'm right here. Just a second." A few seconds later, he said, "Take off the blindfold, sweetheart."

I pulled it off as quickly as I could. I stood in front of a red brick house with huge columns. A million Christmas lights decorated the yard. It looked so familiar.

I gasped. "Is this?"

But there was no answer.

Where's Hayden?

I twirled and found him behind me on bended knee. My hand went to my mouth, and my heart nearly jumped out of my chest. This was our moment. *Ours*. He was making my dreams come true.

"Kory, you are the one for me, for better or worse. I swear to be by your side for the rest of my life. I promise to cherish you and support you in all things. Will you do me the greatest honor of becoming my wife?"

I sobbed, "Yes! I want that more than anything."

It was happening. Hayden wanted this with me. He wanted a life together. This wasn't a decision being forced upon us. My heart was about to burst with joy.

Hayden stood and slipped the ring on my finger. It was a beautiful teardrop solitaire. My hands shook as I admired it. "It's beautiful."

Hayden picked me up and twirled me, shouting, "She said yes!"

The front door opened, and the entire family came out onto the front porch, cheering and clapping. I gasped. "How did they get here?"

"I flew them to Vancouver yesterday so they could catch a plane. They came early to set up."

"Oh, Hayden." I squeezed him tighter. "This house looks just like the one in *Steel Magnolias*. It's perfect." One night when Hayden and I were lying in bed, I told him how much I loved the house in the movie. For him to propose in front of a similar house was so thoughtful. I kissed him hard.

When he pulled back, he gave me a breathtaking grin. "Sweetheart, this is the house where the movie was filmed."

I gasped again. "What? This is *the* house?"

I rushed toward the front porch, where the entire Foster family stood with Hollis and Devney, but Hayden pulled me back to him. Before I could speak, he said, "I have another question to ask you."

There was nothing that could top this moment. "What is that?"

"Will you marry me tomorrow? Here."

I paused, wanting to make sure I heard the words correctly. Hayden's eyes searched mine.

"Are you serious?"

"Yes."

I jumped into his arms. "Yes! Yes! A million times yes!"

Hayden kissed me, and I heard his father say, "Sounds like we're having a Christmas wedding."

None of the details mattered.

I was going to be Mrs. Hayden Foster to the world now. And even though we were technically married, this felt like our real one. My Christmas gift from Hayden was to become his wife. I loved this man with everything I had.

CHAPTER Forty-Six

Hayden

It was nearly midnight, and I had to hurry. Once the clock struck twelve, I wouldn't be able to see her until morning. It had been the only thing Kory requested. The first time she wanted to see me on our wedding day was when she walked through the doors and onto the terrace to become my wife.

But there was one thing left to do. I checked the clock—twenty minutes to spare. I made sure the piece of paper and book of matches were in my pocket before I climbed the stairs. We'd been setting up for the wedding on the first floor. I wanted it to be a surprise for Kory, and she agreed.

This week, I was going to actually man up and watch *Steel Magnolias* with Kory here in this house. The last time we tried, I fell asleep. When I showed her the DVD, I swore her eyes lit up. I would do everything in my power to continue to put that same look on her face.

I quietly opened the door. Kory shot up in bed. "Everything okay?"

"Can't sleep?"

She turned on the lamp. "No, I'm too excited. You aren't supposed to be in here."

"I've got nineteen minutes. I promise I'll be gone before midnight."

She leaned over to look at the clock. "Eighteen minutes."

We smiled like loons at each other. I chuckled. "I know." I grabbed the metal trash can from the corner of the room. "Before we wake up tomorrow, there's something important I need to do."

Kory cocked her head in the most adorable way. "What's that?"

I pulled the prenup out of my pocket and put it in the trash can. "Tomorrow, when we get married, there are no prenups. This is about you and me. I don't care about who has more money. We're in this together. No contracts besides the vows we're going to take."

Kory's eyes welled up with tears. She had never said anything about the prenup, but it felt like a damn weight on my chest since we signed it. When I saw the first tear slide down her cheek, I wondered if I'd made a mistake. "Oh fuck, Kory, what did I say? I don't want you upset the night before we get married."

She threw her arms around me. "I'm not upset. I'm so incredibly happy. You have no idea."

I pulled back. "You ready to do this adventure together?"

"More than ever."

I struck the match and threw it in the garbage can. The paper lit, and it disintegrated in seconds until there was nothing left to burn. When the last of the embers went out, I whispered, "To new beginnings."

"To new beginnings."

CHAPTER Forty-Seven

Kory

The house was in chaos the following morning as we got ready for the wedding. I'd stayed in Shelby's room last night. As it turned out, the owners used the home where *Steel Magnolias* had been filmed as a bed and breakfast. Each of the bedrooms was labeled with a different character from the movie. I'd stayed in Shelby's room, and Hayden in Jackson's. For fun, we'd put Kane in Ouiser's since he reminded us of the grumpy old lady. Needless to say, he was not impressed. Drake and Alexa had taken the third floor, which felt more like a honeymoon suite.

I couldn't believe it.

One by one, Hayden was making all of my dreams come true. This morning, I'd had a bath in the famous pink bathroom. We would have the house to ourselves for nearly an entire week after his family flew back to Alaska. I couldn't believe Hayden had rented out the house. We were going to spend our honeymoon in Natchitoches, Louisiana, in this amazing house.

After the wedding, Drake and Alexa were leaving to officially start their honeymoon. It blew my mind how the entire family had rearranged their schedules at the beginning of December to be part of our big day.

We were to be married on the back terrace. I'd always wanted a love like Shelby had with Jackson. And I'd found it.

Amie walked in with a garment bag draped over her arm. "Are you ready to see it?"

"Yes."

She placed the bag on the bed. Hayden had asked for the wedding to be a surprise, and that's what I wanted, too. Amie, Alexa, and Devney were in charge of all the arrangements. There was nothing I'd want to change. I never imagined I wouldn't want to be involved in the details, but when the time came last night for me to decide, I only wanted to focus on enjoying every second.

Amie unzipped the bag, and the dress spilled out. I touched the soft fabric, blown away by its beauty. "We had Alexa try on the dress to make sure it would fit since you guys are the same size. I hope that's okay. She made notes of which dresses you liked as you talked. I hope you like this one."

I held up the dress, mesmerized. It shimmered in the light. The white fabric was fitted up top and then flowed out from the waistline. As I had helped Alexa, this dress had been my favorite. I bit my lip, and Amie touched my arm. "Oh no, is everything okay?"

I turned to her and threw my arms around her neck. "Thank you. Thank you. Thank you so much. It's breathtaking."

She held me close. "You're breathtaking."

We were both sniffling as she pulled back. "Let's get you ready. You have a very anxious soon-to-be husband."

Before we got dressed, I took Amie's hand. "Thank you for welcoming me into your family. I will spend every day of my life loving your son."

"I know. You are such a blessing to all of us. I couldn't ask for a better wife for Hayden. You were made for each other."

I hugged her to me again. "Thank you."

"Let me go check on things."

"Sounds good."

Having her there helped ease the ache of not having my own mother. I stared out the window and sighed. It was hard not having Mother here even after all they'd done. Over the last few weeks, I had come to terms with everything and truly forgiven them. I refused to let the anger fester within me anymore. In the end, I had been blessed in immeasurable ways. But I remained hopeful that someday we'd be able to see each other again.

Someday...

I glanced at the ashes left in the garbage can and smiled. *New beginnings.* Hayden and I would always be partners in everything.

The door opened, and I peered over my shoulder to see who it was. Devney came in, looking white as a ghost. "Hey, you okay?"

She shook her head. "I'm not sure."

"What's wrong?" *Maybe I should call for Hollis.*

I went to get up, and Devney grabbed me. "I think I messed up."

"What happened?"

She gulped. "I'm pregnant." She began to cry. "I'm so sorry I'm doing this on your wedding day. I just had to talk to someone."

I heard footsteps approaching on the stairs that led to the second floor. Alexa called out to let someone downstairs know she was checking on me. Devney tightened her grip on my arm. "Please don't tell Hollis."

I took a deep breath. "It's not my place to tell. But Hollis will be the best person to work through this with. He understands that a pregnancy is a chance anyone takes. He probably knows the statistics."

Devney gave a small smile. "Probably." She sighed. "I told him last night I wasn't moving to Washington. He was so sweet and told me he loved me. And now I'm going to mess everything up. He's going to think I stayed because I knew I was pregnant."

"Devney, it's going to be fine. Just talk to Hollis. He'll believe you."

She wiped away the tears. "What if he thinks I've trapped him? We're not ready for a baby. We barely made it through our first crisis."

The footsteps grew louder, and panic raced across her face. "Don't tell anyone. Please, Kory. Don't say a word."

"I won't. You guys are going to figure this out."

"I hope so because I want this baby. And if I have to be a single mother, I will be." She searched her purse. "I need my fake glasses so no one knows I've been crying."

She put them on, and we both laughed. We needed to defuse the situation before Alexa came in and sensed something was wrong. "They definitely had me fooled."

"Good to know."

The door opened, and Amie stepped in with Alexa behind her. Alexa looked at Devney, who was still a little tearstained. The glasses weren't able to hide everything. "Are you okay?" she asked.

"Weddings make me an emotional mess."

That was a good recovery. Amie looked at me. "Are you ready?"

"Yes. I've never been more ready in my entire life."

The girls helped me down the stairs. Though Ike had offered to walk me down the aisle, I had chosen to walk by myself. It had been a hard choice, but in the end, I was the one choosing to be with Hayden and giving myself to him. It was symbolic of the road we'd traveled.

At the bottom of the stairs, I took a deep breath. Amie gave me one last hug. "Welcome to the family."

"Thank you. It's an honor. Truly."

The girls left the room, and I took a moment for myself. *This is it.* The soft sounds of an orchestra played. That was my cue. With each step, I smiled bigger until I got to the double glass doors. Drake and Kane opened them, and I stopped to savor the look on Hayden's face as he saw me for the first time.

His eyes lit up, and his smile was contagious. It was that same look I'd longed for at Drake and Alexa's wedding. My Prince Charming was gazing at me with nothing but love and adoration.

CHAPTER Forty-Eight

Hayden

I barely heard a word of what the preacher said as I looked into Kory's eyes. She was stunning and soon to be mine. *Forever.*

"You may now kiss the bride."

Without waiting another second, I took her mouth to claim it. Possessiveness coursed through me.

Kory was mine to protect.

Mine to cherish.

Mine to love.

I loved her with my entire being. I never dreamed that settling down with someone would bring me such peace, but I wanted this. I wanted it all with Kory—a house full of children and laughter. Family cheered around us and I pulled back ever so slightly. Happiness shone in her eyes, which made me feel like the king of the world.

"I love you more than life itself," I murmured against her lips.

"You have completed my life in a way I never imagined. Forever and always," she whispered back.

"Forever and always."

It was early as fuck the next morning as I made my way to the door. I had kept my wife up until all hours of the night making love to her. *Wife.* It was the best sound in the world. I opened the door and there was a mail carrier. "Kory or Hayden Foster?"

"Yeah, I'm Hayden Foster."

"This is for you." The man handed me an envelope, turned, and walked away.

I shut the door to find Kory standing in the hallway, wearing my dress shirt from yesterday. "Who was that?"

"He brought us a letter."

On the outside were our names. "Who's it from?"

We sat on the couch, and I opened the letter and began to read.

> Kory and Hayden,
>
> We heard of your wedding. This was the first chance we had to send any communication undetected. The order to not contact us has been given, and we want you to follow that. Please don't send us any communication. We still have the phone. If it ever becomes safe again, we will reach out.
>
> We wanted you to know we do love our daughter and know you will have a happy life together. We're relieved you're able to be free of this life you never wanted. It's the one thing we can give you.
>
> Be happy.
> Live your life.
> And know that despite everything we did, we do love you.
>
>   Your mother and father

Holy shit. I let the contents of the letter settle in before I said anything. Kory kept staring at it, reading it again.

She wrapped her arms around my waist. "They love me."

"Yes." It still was all sorts of fucked up, but I wasn't going to restate something Kory already knew. Cautiously, I proceeded. "How do you feel?"

She thought for a second. "I know this is going to sound

strange, but it's closure. I know they love me. And this is their gift to me."

"That is a great way to look at it."

Kory's strength would never cease to amaze me.

After getting out of the house for a little bit, we strolled through the streets of Natchitoches. If I had my choice, we'd stay in the bedroom the entire time. However, Kory wanted to see the town. Since reading the letter from her parents, Kory seemed lighter. I respected her parents for giving her the closure she needed. I never would agree with their methods or what they did to Kory. However, we had to let the past be in the past if we were going to move forward in our future.

Kory came out of the next shop carrying a small shopping bag. When I'd tried to go in the store with her, she asked me to stay on the sidewalk. "What's in the bag?"

"You'll see."

I laughed. "Should we head home now?"

She leaned up on her tiptoes to give me a kiss. "As long as you promise to make love to me."

I picked her up, cradling her in my arms as I strode back to the house. "That's a promise I can keep right this instant."

Kory's laughter made my heart so full.

We canceled the dinner I'd arranged and instead, we made spaghetti together. I loved every fucking minute of it. To think that once upon a time, I'd been so scared of committing. Now,

I couldn't imagine not having Kory in my life.

I hit play on the remote, and the beginning of *Steel Magnolias* began to play. Kory snuggled closer to me. "I never want this feeling to go away," she murmured.

"It won't. I'm going to spend every day making sure it never does."

She looked up at me with love shining in her eyes. "Thank you for giving me my happy ending. Do you remember that it was what you told me to toast to that first night?"

I held up my beer to Kory's wine glass. "And now I want to toast to our happily ever after."

"To our happily ever after. I love you, Hayden Foster."

"And I love you, Kory Foster." I leaned down to taste her lips.

Kory would forever be my world.

I had been wrecked by Kory in the best possible way.

Epilogue

CHANGED by YOU

Kane

The night was cold as hell as I parked my truck in front of the cabin my friend, Butch, had rented out. He'd asked if I could help the tenant if there were any problems while he was away, and he'd given my information to the tenant. Of course, there would be problems with some stupid city slicker renting it out. Butch owed me big.

I'd gotten twenty text messages stating the heater was out. *Twenty* damn text messages. *Who sends that many?* I had just as many voicemails but hadn't listened to one. I got the picture from one. No need for twenty.

Shit.

And it was some guy named Teske. *What kind of name is that?* I bet this guy wore some shiny-ass loafers with his business suit. It was the middle of January. Normally, this was my time to be away from all these jokers and recharge for the hunting season. Instead, I was here, dealing with a heating issue. Teske probably couldn't find the pilot to save his life.

I slammed my truck door shut before I clomped up the stairs. It was cold. Worse than cold. Skagway was having one of the coldest winters in history. We were getting so much damn snow no one could keep up with it.

I had too much shit to do.

The FBI was on my ass to find someone they believed could be a serial killer. There had been murders all throughout Alaska. The last one had been in Juneau, which was too fucking close for comfort. In exchange for my help, I'd bartered with the FBI to agree to leave Kory and Hayden alone regarding all the shit that happened. No more questions. No more irritation. Nothing.

So far, they'd been true to their word.

But they wanted me to pull a rabbit out of my ass and make whoever this was appear out of thin air.

News flash—rabbits weren't in people's asses. At least not in mine.

I needed a fresh crime scene to track. The ones I'd been to were too tainted. In some cases, it had been four months since the murder. Juneau was four weeks ago. By the time they brought me on board, the crime scene had been ruined. The pictures they took were shit. The whole case was a disaster. And they had no idea who was behind it.

He'd gotten the nickname Lumberjack Killer among the agents. *What the fuck ever.*

I pounded on the door. In the next second, it shot open. "Oh, thank goodness you're here! I was about to become a Popsicle."

For a second, I was frozen. I hadn't been expecting a woman to answer the door. Butch said there was only one occupant, and I'd assumed it was a man. She had on so much fur, it was hard to see much else. It was like what Hollis considered a Paul Bunyan hat on steroids.

"I'm looking for Teske," I said.

"Who?"

"Teske. That's what the text said."

She laughed. "No, that was supposed to say Teale. But my hands were so cold, my fingers probably slipped. And I can't see much. I'm freezing."

I stepped inside and was disappointed to find it was just as cold as outside. That wasn't good. "Why didn't you start a fire?"

The poor girl was shivering. "Umm... I couldn't find the remote."

"Remote?"

"Uhh... yeah. At home I push a button and *voilà...* let there be fire. There wasn't a remote or button to push."

Well, shit.

I wanted to laugh, but I kept a straight face. *A remote? Is she serious?* Even Hollis would be able to figure out the fireplace needed wood and matches.

"Let me check out the heater."

"Okay."

I walked to the back of the house and found it in a closet.

Double shit.

This thing was old as dirt. It looked like a rusted tin bucket. What the hell? Butch should know better. I screwed around with it for a few minutes, but the damn thing was completely shot. We needed to come up with a plan B.

I walked into the room where Teale had another blanket wrapped around her. There was a hell of a lot of luggage at the door. Maybe she hadn't had time to unpack. I wasn't going to concern myself with it. "Well, the heater is shot. Let me see if I can find some space heaters. We can get a fire going. You should be good to go until I can get the parts to fix it."

"Okay... sure."

I went to search the different closets, and I heard the front door open and close. When I walked back into the living room, Teale was gone. I looked out the window and saw her heaving one of her suitcases into the bed of my truck.

No. No. No. This isn't going to happen.

I opened the door. "What are you doing?"

She folded her arms over her chest. The damn fur obscured her face. "I'm going anywhere but here. I'll freeze to death. You do not want my death on your conscience. I'll come back to haunt you. I can be very scary."

For the second time today, I wanted to laugh, but I refused. That never happened. She wasn't coming with me. No way. "No, we'll start a fire and get you a space heater."

She opened the passenger door. "Hey, puppy. Don't bite me. I just don't want to freeze to death." Mariah looked toward me, and I shook my head.

"Teale, be reasonable."

"Nope. I'm going with you."

This was getting us nowhere. I would get her back in the house and show her how warm I could make it. Calmly, I walked toward the truck. Right as I got there, the door locks engaged.

Motherfucker. She yelled through the window, "I need you to get the rest of my luggage first. Then I'll let you in the truck."

"Teale, get out of my truck." I was tired of playing the games.

"Nope. Sorry. Luggage first. I'm coming with you."

"Teale, I will get the house warm again."

She cocked her head to the side and smiled at me. "Will you please get my luggage, Mr. Foster? Then you can take me into town. The one thing I do know is that I'm not staying in this house a second longer."

This woman was going to be the death of me. *Fine.* I'd take her to the hotel and be done with this shit. Hopefully the roads were clearer today.

I pulled out my phone and texted Dad. He was the closest to where we were.

Me: *Heard anything about the roads?*

Dad: *If you were thinking about coming into town, I wouldn't. They're still bad.*

Me: *Thanks.*

Dad: *Everything okay?*

Me: *Yep. Just had a few errands to run.*

If my brothers got wind of this… well, it wouldn't be good. I tried again. "Teale, let's talk."

She shook her head and pointed to the house. This woman was so damn stubborn. I grabbed all fifty million suitcases and threw them into the back of my truck. *Who the hell packs this much?* The locks disengaged, and I climbed in.

Teale pulled back her fur hat and looked back at me with the most beautiful eyes I'd ever seen.

Fuck me.

I was in over my head.

Lumberjack

I see her.

I want her.

I will make her mine.

Foster is no match for me. I'm going to fuck up his shit so bad, he won't know what hit him.

By the time I'm finished with him, he'll have lost everything. Including her.

Changed by You will be Coming February of 2019.

Check out www.authorkristinmayer.com for updates.

Other Books by Kristin Mayer

Available Now

The Trust Series
Trust Me
Love Me
Promise Me
Full-length novels in the TRUST series are also available in audio from Tantor Media.

The Effect Series
Ripple Effect
Domino Effect

The Twisted Fate Series
White Lies
Black Truth

Timeless Love Series
Untouched Perfection
Flawless Perfection
Tempting Perfection

An Exposed Heart Novel
Intoxicated by You
Wrecked for You
Changed by You

Full-length novels in the Exposed Hearts Series are also available in audio from Audible.

Stand Alone Novels
Innocence
Bane
Whispered Promises
Finding Forever (co-written with Kelly Elliott)

Coming Soon
Changed by You – An Exposed Heart Novel

Made in the USA
Middletown, DE
15 September 2018